DESPERADO LUCKY, KRAUSS

OWNER

Copyright © 2020 by Owner

All rights reserved.

No part of this book may be reproduced in any form or by any electronic or mechanical means, including information storage and retrieval systems, without written permission from the author, except for the use of brief quotations in a book review.

No part of this book may be reproduced in any form or by any electronic or mechanical means, without the written permission from the author, except for the use of brief quotations in a book review. This book is not intended for anyone under the age of eighteen(18) due to sexual content and language. This is a work of fiction. Names, characters, places, brands, media, and incidents are the product of the author's imagination or are used fictitiously. Any resemblance to actual persons living or dead, business establishments, events, or locales, is entirely coincidental.

 Created with Vellum

ACKNOWLEDGMENTS

I wish to thank my line editor, Erin, for her unwavering dedication to this project. Also, I want to thank my friends, especially R.L. Sloan for her support and encouragement, and Thomas Cole for keeping our spirits up and the enthusiasm for this project

CHAPTER 1

Staring at the empty horizon was not helping. Sahara hung on to the wheel with the last of her strength. If she let go, there was no telling where the *Lucky Desperado II* would end up. Everything she'd gone through the last ten days would be for nothing. She tried to find the sun, she had to keep heading west toward land. She'd made it into the Gulf of Mexico. If she got lucky, someone would find her before time ran out and she sank into the abyss along with the cursed, pirate treasure in the *Desperado's* hold.

Her eyes were drier than the Gobi Desert and refused to focus on the dot that might be a ship on the horizon. She fired off her last flare, closed her eyes and prayed. *Calling all Nereids, if you Sea Goddesses aren't too busy, I need a little help here. Maybe Eurybia can send a nice wind to blow me toward shore? That would be good.* She'd take what she could get and be grateful. She put her head down on her arm and leaned on the wheel, her last-ditch effort at holding a close to steady course.

Captain Boris Rustov stared through his high-powered binoculars and grumbled to his first mate. "Ivan, change course."

"Da, Captain. What direction? Where are we going?"

Boris pointed to a spot on the horizon.

He looked in the direction Boris pointed and followed his orders immediately. The *Connie* came around jostling the rest of the crew.

Niko shouted, "What happened?"

"Emergency flare. Something is wrong with that sailboat."

Boris lowered the binoculars and looked past Ivan to his brother Niko. "Boat is wandering footloose, sails hanging, not secured. Not right."

Boris had spent too many years at sea to not recognize a boat in trouble. American, Russian, it didn't matter. At sea, lives were at stake and he was an American now.

He growled, "Full throttle."

Forty minutes later, the *Connie* drew up alongside the battered sailboat. Boris drew in a deep breath and let it out slowly. "This is bad."

Niko stepped up beside him. "Too much damage. Looks like bullet holes and the sails are ripped."

"We will check for survivors. Tell Ivan, radio Coast Guard." Boris picked up a grappling line and threw it, catching the *Lucky Desperado II*. He yelled to his crew, "Secure lines."

His tugboat crewmen were masters at their craft and rushed to help the troubled boat. He took in the severed anchor line. Something was very wrong. Likely somebody had cut it loose to either lighten the boat or make a fast getaway. Either way it was a desperate measure.

As soon as the sailboat was secured, he went aboard. He assessed the damages along the way to the stern and found a woman clinging to the wheel. It was definitely a woman, her slender body and long, light brown hair blowing gently on the sea breeze gave her away. Her white tank top and loose, light-blue cotton pants hid the rest of her from his prying eyes. At her side was a Ruger Hawkeye rifle with a high-powered scope. There was a story to this catastrophe and he was curious.

Observe and assess had been his job in Russian Intelligence and he'd been very good at sizing up a situation. He couldn't see her face but that didn't matter at the moment. He moved the rifle out of her reach and placed two fingers on her neck to check for a pulse. He jerked his hand back when her head came up.

Her eyes flickered opened and she rasped, "You don't look like pirates." She let go of the wheel and crumpled.

Instinctively, Boris caught her before she hit the weathered wooden deck. The front of her shirt was streaked with dried blood and the bandana tied around her forehead was marked with red-brown stains.

She peered into his eyes. "Are you a Captain?"

"*Da*. Yes."

"My boat…" her eyes fluttered shut.

Boris cradled her to his chest as he marched toward the boat's cabin. He had a survivor and it was a miracle, judging by the state of her boat.

He looked at Niko. "Is Coast Guard coming?"

"No, we radioed. They have very bad emergency, not coming for a long time."

Boris kept moving toward the cabin with Niko following. "Get the door open."

"What we do with her?"

"Keep her alive." He stepped into the cabin and stopped dead in his tracks.

"Put my sister down."

A scraggly-haired kid pointed a nine-millimeter semi-automatic pistol at him with shaking hands. It was frighteningly obvious the kid had no idea how to handle a gun. Now was not the time to scare the crap out of him.

"*Da*. Okay. Do not shoot."

The woman in his arms stammered, "What?"

"What do I do, Sis?"

"Let 'em help." She coughed and gasped for air. She opened her eyes long enough to look up at Boris and mutter, "My boat's taking on water, we're sinking." Her eyes closed and her head rolled limply to the side.

"*Nyet*, no." He needed to put her down and get a good look at her injuries. He pushed his way past the young man that had finally lowered the wood-gripped pistol. After placing the injured woman on the first bunk, he glared at her brother. "She needs water."

Niko asked, "What happened?"

"We don't have any drinking water." The kid waved the gun around. "We ran out of bottles and the pump's not working. I think they shot it. I spend the summers with her in the Bahamas but I never learned to sail. I tried to help but I don't know what to do besides unfurl the sails and work the manual bilge pump."

"*Nyet.*" Boris and Niko said simultaneously as they shied away.

Niko barked, "Put the gun down."

The kid stopped talking long enough to catch his breath and swipe his tongue over his cracked lips.

"Oh, yeah, sorry." He put the pistol on the scarred dining table. "Is Sahara going to be okay?"

Boris glanced at Niko. "Go get some water and have the crew take down the sails. We will tow this boat in." Then he turned his attention to her brother and asked, "What is your name?"

"Mason Dixon, but I go by Mason."

Niko stalked out leaving Boris to deal with Mason.

"We will get water in her and she will be fine." He rearranged Sahara, hoping to make her comfortable on the shabby bunk. He quickly glanced over his shoulder and asked, "Are you okay?"

"I'm thirsty. Sahara told me to stay inside out of the sun so I wouldn't get dehydrated as fast, but I could use some water."

"Niko will bring enough for you."

Mason sat at the table, his eyes fixed on Boris and his sister. "Sahara tried to teach me to use her pistol but I don't like guns. I guess I should have paid better attention."

"You tell me what happened." Boris used his command voice.

"Sahara said they were probably poachers wanting the coordinates of the sunken ship she found." He shrugged. "She said we needed to get to U.S. waters. Then we sailed into a storm yesterday morning. It tore up everything."

Boris nodded, letting the kid know he'd heard while he kept his eyes on Sahara. She was breathing, that was his first priority. He'd look at her head wound once she was conscious enough to drink some water.

Niko came back with a first aid kit and a canvas bag full of bottled water. He dropped it on the counter while looking over his shoulder at Boris.

"What did you find out?"

"She found a sunken ship." Boris glanced at Niko. "Give me the water."

Niko handed a water bottle to Boris and pushed a bottle across the counter to Mason. "How old are you?"

"Sixteen." Mason twisted the cap off and drank half before taking a breath.

Boris grinned remembering how naïve he'd been at that age.

"You tell us everything," Niko demanded and jammed his hands on his hips, looking every bit the man in charge.

With a barely noticeable tilt of his head Boris signaled for him to continue. Niko commanded his crew and everyone around him with ingrained, military authority. Defying him was risky behavior.

"We'd just gotten up and were getting ready to leave. I was looking over the side at the fish swimming next to us when I heard Sahara yell at me to cut loose the anchor and get inside." Mason drew in a deep breath. "Then the shooting started." He stared at his sister. "She put a bunch of holes at their water line. She said it would slow them down. She's really badass with her rifle. She never misses."

Boris grumbled, "Tell Alexei keep watch, every man with a rifle, be ready if trouble comes." He nodded toward Mason. "Take him on *Connie and s*end Fedor to work the pump."

Niko looked over at the kid. "Come. You ride with crew on our tugboat."

Mason shook his head. "I'm not going without Sahara."

"Safer for you with us. Not good to move her and we must go." Niko nodded toward the door. "Now."

Boris nodded at the kid and grumbled, "You go. I stay with Sashara." He shook his head and muttered, "sister". Her name had come out all wrong.

Niko took Mason by the arm and steered him out of the cabin.

Boris watched them go. They'd be underway in a couple of minutes. Niko would get things handled. His brother had adapted well to life at sea. He'd been a Russian Army sniper and occasional interrogator. Niko was good at handling the rough jobs. Nobody was getting on board either vessel as long as Niko was breathing.

In the meantime, Sahara needed water. Her lips were dry and chapped. She had the signs of moderate dehydration. He took another bottle out of the bag and twisted off the cap. Getting it in her without choking her was his immediate problem. She had to wake up enough to swallow.

He pulled a shop towel out of his back pocket and poured water onto it. He let it soak in before wiping it over her face. Then he dribbled some on the filthy, red bandana. It needed to come loose so he could get it off without ripping out her hair. He'd take a look at the wound once he got water in her. First things first.

"Come on, *Kroshka*, little one, open eyes." He didn't even try to say her name again. He'd have to practice to get it right. Now was not the time for that.

The second her eyelids fluttered, he put his arm under her shoulders and sat her up. Holding the bottle to her lips he murmured, "Drink, *Kroshka,*" and tipped it up until drops trickled down her chin.

She sputtered and coughed and finally swallowed. It was a start.

After several swallows, she asked, "Who are you?"

"Boris." He studied her. So little and so tough.

"I'm Sahara."

"*Da*, Mason tells me."

"Is he okay? Where is he?" Her voice sounded a little stronger. She struggled to get up. It was not happening. He had ahold of her.

"He is on my boat. Very safe. All good." He tightened his grip a fraction to keep her secure. "Here is water. Good for you."

When she relaxed, he loosened his hold while still keeping her protected. The last thing she needed was to bang her head on the edge of the bunk.

"You drink." He held the bottle to her lips again.

It had been a long, long time since he'd had held a woman in his arms. This little one fit against him well. Perfect in fact.

He'd avoided new relationships for the last few years, not ready to risk getting hurt again. Maybe he'd waited long enough. There was something different about this small bundle of trouble.

Lately there were times he believed he'd be alone forever. Still, he hadn't given up all hope that someday he'd come across someone he'd want to come home to. He wasn't young and foolish anymore but he wasn't old and senile either. He was his own man. Not yet forty but it was closing in on him fast.

He gazed at Sahara. Under the blood caked bandana was some kind of head injury. Fortunately, it wasn't bad enough to keep her from waking up easily. Sunbaked and exhausted, she'd hung on to life. He admired her determination.

Fighting the sea for days in an antique sailboat with ripped-to-hell sails would wear down the toughest seaman. She was stronger than she looked. A faint grin tugged at the corners of his mouth.

He understood all too well what a person would do to get their family to safety. He'd sacrificed everything and swallowed his pride to call his distant cousin for help in bringing his family to America. He had to live with that.

Now, instead of a fine catch of fish the tides had brought him a woman. Was it fate? Had the stars aligned in his favor? Or would Sahara wake up, thank him nicely and walk away? Only time would tell.

She stirred in his arms. "Water."

"Da, *Kroshka*. Here, I have it." He held a fresh bottle to her lips. "I've got you. It's all good. Boat needs fixing. We will ask Misha."

He focused on the storage units. The First Aid kit would have medicines and bandages but he also needed cleaning supplies. If he happened to find some clues that might explain why someone would want coordinates to a derelict, sunken ship, even better.

CHAPTER 2

Sahara came around slowly, moving her hands over her bunk. One hand brushed over the soft material of her favorite, threadbare blanket. The other hand detected rougher material over semi-firm something? It moved. She opened her eyes. Holy shit!

It all started coming back. He was real. And he was extra-large. Thick, wavy, black hair, moustache, beard, and solid like a tank.

"What happened? Where are we?"

"We find your boat."

"Um, right. I kind of remember that. Did I make it to the Gulf of Mexico?"

"Yes, almost to Texas."

Okay, this guy didn't talk much. It was fractured English with a strong foreign accent, eastern European from the sound of it. He was straight and to the point. She could deal with it. God, she had the headache from hell. She rubbed her forehead and instantly wished she hadn't. "Ouch." She groaned.

"You rest. We get to Galveston in two hours, maybe three."

"I'm thirsty." She needed water. She needed her boat repaired. She needed to get Mason someplace safe and go back for the rest of her salvage. She needed to stop her sister from making the worst mistake of her life, and for that she needed the money the treasure would bring. She'd deal with the curse later.

She needed this man's help. It was obvious she'd been shot at, shot up, and almost sunk. She needed a believable excuse but she didn't have one. She'd have to wait and see if he would ask questions she didn't want to answer. Worse than that, he could turn her over to the Coast Guard. She didn't need that complication. It wasn't in their jurisdiction, but that wouldn't stop them from snooping in her business and poking around on her boat. Her headache was getting worse.

He rolled away from her and retrieved two bottles of water from a canvas bag. He took up a lot of space in her cabin. He had wide, muscular shoulders. The kind that carried the weight of the world. She was well-acquainted with that condition.

She'd been lucky that her worthless brother, North, had only nicked her head. Any closer and she'd be dead. Any closer and it was a good bet he'd have killed Mason too. She didn't need that on her conscience. God, she really was in bad shape. She'd be dead right along with her conscience.

Boris covered the distance between the table and her bunk in five steps. She caught a glimpse of his left upper arm. He had a snarling wolf tattoo with red eyes and blood dripping from the canines. She was too weak to shudder but it looked evil. Being half-dead meant the other half that was still alive registered the big man walking toward her. He stood at the edge of the bunk, twisted off the cap and handed it to her.

The struggle to sit up sapped her strength. Her hand shook as she reached out and took the bottle from him.

"Thanks," she said quietly.

She was so dehydrated. She wasn't feeling like herself. She needed fluid and lots of it. Her mouth was drier than the desert she was named after.

She asked the burning question on her mind. "How bad is my boat?"

"I looked. Fedor is using manual pumps to keep water draining. Maybe it can be fixed."

"We're still afloat. It can't be too bad." She guzzled down some more water and tried to smile. "I love my *Lucky Desperado*. We've been through a lot together. It's my home."

"When we get to Galveston, Misha will look. Maybe it is okay. He is very good with boats. Builds fine boats back home."

She didn't like the sound of that. There were a lot of "maybes" in there. This was her boat, all thirty-two feet of it. She'd go have a closer look now that she wasn't holding the wheel to keep them on course. She stuck her legs over the edge of her bunk and stood. Not the best idea she'd ever had. She took one dizzy step and pitched forward, landing in Boris's arms.

Good thing the guy had great reflexes and quick reaction times. And he was strong: he handled her like she was a feather-weight.

She grabbed his shoulders and did her best to get her feet under her but they didn't want to cooperate. She'd have accused Mason of tying her shoelaces together only she was wearing slip-on deck shoes. Between the two of them, she was able to stand up by holding on to him with a death grip. "Okay. I've got it."

"*Nyet*. Sit."

"I need to check my boat." She let go of his shoulders.

"Later. Now you rest. I look at your head." He guided her backward toward the bunk.

"My head is fine." But it wasn't, either the Gulf of Mexico was extremely choppy or she was on tilt. She reached out to catch her balance and failed. Her butt landed ungracefully on the edge of the bunk. She speared Boris with a glance. His glacial blue eyes narrowed with worry. Not good.

"Not fine." He pulled the bandana up and off in one swift motion.

"Ow!" she screeched. "What the hell is wrong with you?" She grabbed her forehead above the left eye and glared at him with her right. "That hurt."

"*Da*. Need to clean wound. Put ointment on so it does not get infected. Less scarring."

"It needs stitches."

"Too late for stitches. Put ointment. All good."

"What corner of hell did you crawl out of?" She kept her hand plastered over her wound. He was not getting near it. He'd probably heat up the oversized knife hanging on his belt and try to cauterize it. Not happening. *Barbarian.*

"Russia."

She blinked. "Well, that explains a lot."

Her arm sagged. Her strength was gone. She let it drop but kept her good eye on Boris. If he took one step toward her, she'd slap her hand back up there.

He was staring at her and she stared right back. "What?"

"Looks bad." He pointed at a spot over her left eye.

"Yeah, well, it feels worse." She winced. "I have some antiseptic wash in the head. If you can help me get there and if it didn't get broken during the storm, maybe I can clean myself up."

Boris turned away and then back holding out the bottle of antiseptic. "I have it."

"Did you go snooping?" Her voice came out accusatory even though that was not the best course to take. This guy had likely saved her and Mason from a sorry end. But still, he had no right to look through her things. This was her home after all.

"D*a*, I find." He grinned.

"What? What did you find?" Oh, lord, have, mercy. This was her boat. She lived on it. It had everything a girl might need. Guns, tequila, tampons, vibrating dildo, a couple smuggler's compartments. No, and hell no, this couldn't be happening. Some big Russian Cossack had found her private drawer under her bunk. She could tell by the stupid grin on his face.

"This is so not my week."

"What?" He shrugged his shoulders. "All good." He kept grinning at her.

Staring at the scarred toes of her deck shoes, Sahara muttered, "I need a drink."

Now that the worst was over, she took in her thin, used-to-be-sky-blue, cotton, summer pants hanging limply around her legs. What a sight she must be. One minute she'd been getting ready to weigh anchor and set sail. The next she'd been firing back and cutting loose to catch the wind and haul ass. She was a disgusting mess. And if having a salvage-poaching brother after her wasn't bad enough she'd run straight into a tropical storm that had torn up the *Desperado*. Thank whatever lucky star and sea goddess that had brought her grumpy Captain Boris.

Boris held out a bottle of tequila. "I fix cut on head. Then you have drink."

She looked up at him with her right eye and half of her left that was barely open. "How about I have a drink first and then you can fix my head?"

She needed more than a shot of tequila. Half a bottle was probably more in line with what she had in mind. She hurt and she wanted it all to stop.

Boris poured her a Russian-sized shot of golden pain killer. Then he downed one himself and waited for it to take effect. He watched her left eyelid close and the right eyelid droop.

She was too small to be out sailing with no crew and her younger brother barely able to help her. The kid was better than nothing but it wasn't adding up. There was more to this than they went diving on an old wreck.

There were modern-day pirates still sailing the seas but this old boat wasn't worth much, so they'd been after something else. Maybe whatever was in the hidden compartments he'd found.

Even shot up and barely standing, she wasn't afraid to call him out for rummaging through her boat and digging in the cabin's compartments looking for supplies. This little one wasn't afraid of him.

He wanted to help and he wanted to know more about her. It was second nature, his habit from years of intelligence work. He'd been all about gathering information when he'd been in the Russian Army. He'd been the best but he'd left while he still could, before he got in too deep to get out alive.

She was doing her best to glare at him and losing the battle. The tequila on her empty stomach was working and in a few more minutes she'd be asleep. He grinned. He liked strong women, strong enough to take him on. She was looking better and better.

"Okay. I fix wound now."

"Yeah, sure. Whatever you say." She planted her hands firmly on her thighs and took a deep, steadying breath. "I'm ready. Go for it."

He picked up the shop towel and soaked a corner with the antiseptic. Dabbing as gently as he could he cleaned and cleaned. Head wounds were notorious for bleeding profusely and this one was no exception. She'd been lucky. Some skin along the edge of her forehead was gone and a good inch of scalp was missing along with a little underlying muscle tissue. She'd have a scar but she could cover it with her hair.

He dabbed some more. "Okay, not bad."

Not compared to some of the gunshot wounds he'd seen in the past. But for a lady, this one wasn't good. It didn't stop him from thinking she had the softest brown eyes he'd ever seen. A man could spend hours looking into those eyes.

"Thanks. Can I have another drink?"

"When I am done."

"Okay." She sounded sleepy. That was good. She needed to rest and get her strength back.

He finished up and grabbed the tequila. Sahara had scooted further into the bunk, leaving him a ledge on the outer edge.

He sat and held out the bottle to her. "Ladies first."

"Thanks." She tipped the bottle up and took a long swallow. Handing it back, she choked out, "I really needed that."

"I put ointment on when we dock. I have on *Connie*." Boris lifted the bottle to his lips and drank.

"*Connie's* your boat?" Sahara rolled toward him.

"Yes, good strong tugboat." He put his hand on her shoulder and pulled her closer till her head was resting on his thigh using him for a pillow.

"That's nice," she whispered against his leg.

"I am Captain."

Sahara yawned and patted his stomach. "Yeah, me too."

Her hand slipped lower as she drifted off to sleep.

Boris could do the gentlemanly thing and move her hand but when was the last time a pretty woman had been anywhere near his personal equipment? He could let it rest there for a little while. It wasn't hurting anything. He put his hand over hers and adjusted her hold. *Da, perfect*.

He raised the bottle and took several more gulps. His mind drifted off as he closed his eyes. They'd get to Galveston soon. She'd get her boat fixed and go home, wherever that was. Or if it couldn't be repaired, she'd salvage it or sell it for scrap and go home. He frowned, either way he'd never see her again.

The *Desperado* was pretty beat up but if Misha could fix it, getting all the parts would take time. He could work with that. Her sailboat was definitely an antique. It had been upgraded and refitted but finding parts could be difficult. She'd need a place to stay while she waited. The corners of his mouth turned up thinking about that.

Then there was her brother. Shit. What to do with him? Niko could keep Mason busy. The kid could work on his brother's tug. Okay, this might work out fine after all.

She was still asleep when Boris heard a change in the growl coming from the *Connie's* engine. It was too soon to be nearing the Port of Galveston. He glanced down at Sahara. She looked good laying peacefully tucked up tight against him. He looked out the nearest port. It was still early in the afternoon. He really didn't want her to see the actual condition of her sailboat, not yet. Fixing it was a big "maybe" and closer to "maybe not," if you asked him. No captain wants to hear their boat isn't fit for service.

He slid slowly and carefully out from under her and walked silently onto the deck. Niko was waiting for him when he arrived at the farthest forward point on the bow.

Niko raised his voice below a shout on a hand signal from Boris. "What we do with her boat?"

It was riding low even with Fedor working the pump, a good indication that there was significant damage below the water line. "Misha's boat yard. Pull hard. Radio Annie if you need more help."

"Okay. Boy wants to know how is sister."

"Sleeping. Good for now."

Boris looked over at the *Connie*. She'd carried him a long way. They were good together. He wasn't planning on giving her up. He was getting way ahead of himself. But it was a sign: he was finally ready to try again. Still, that didn't mean the woman in the cabin would be interested in trying him on for size and fit.

She was going to need time to recover. He would start by helping her with that. He'd keep her close and get to know her. She might not like the idea but, to his way of thinking, it was finders-keepers. Yeah, it was a fine day to go out fishing. He sauntered back to the cabin. There was a change in the air. His life would never be the same. He could feel it. Score one for the Russian captain.

CHAPTER 3

The setting sun cast long shadows over the boatyard. Sahara took one look at Misha and muttered to Boris, "Are you sure he's a master ship builder?"

Boris grinned. "Yes. Best in Russia. Now, best in America."

The man was massive with shaggy, sable-brown hair, matching scraggly beard, and sweaty from head to toe. His worn jeans and grimy black t-shirt were nothing to brag about but they fit him well. He had to be at least six foot four with muscles like a gorilla. She was staring at a living breathing Sasquatch. *From Russia With Love.*

She wasn't all that sure they were even in Galveston. She might have sailed in the wrong direction and ended up in some uncharted Russian territory by mistake. The storm could have pushed her way, way far north. Not likely, but there were too many Russians for this to be Texas.

"Okay, if you say so." She looked at the big man straight on and asked, "Can you fix my *Desperado*?"

"Put in dry dock. Take long time but I fix." He nodded at her. "Fine antique boat. Don't make like that now."

"How long? I need to get back to my salvage site before those scavengers find it." She was not going to argue about the *Desperado's* antique status. What did he know anyway?

"One month, maybe two. Needs work. Very old boat."

His fingers firmly gripped his hips, his knuckles white. Apparently, she'd irritated him. Sahara tried not to wince. His hands were huge. He could strangle a good-sized man with one hand. She hoped to hell he never got a hold on her.

She inched closer to her captain. She'd found Boris and that made him hers, for now.

"Okay. You fix the *Desperado* and I'll figure out a way to get my salvage." She hefted her backpack onto her shoulder and gripped her duffle in the other hand. She turned to Boris. "Can you drop me at the nearest motel?"

"*Nyet*. Not safe. You stay with me. Nobody will find you with me." Boris took the duffle away from her. "Give me backpack."

"No. It's mine." She turned her shoulder away from him.

"Looks heavy. You give." He held out his hand.

"No."

"Stubborn *Kroshka*." He looked at Misha. "American."

Misha's lip curled up on one side. "*Da*, I like."

Boris grinned. "Come, we go home."

"Um. I'm not sure that's a good idea." She looked from one man to the other. "My brother needs a place to stay, too."

The second her attention turned to Misha, Boris relieved her of the backpack and hiked it up on his shoulder.

She snipped, "Hey, that's mine," as she scrambled to grab it back. He turned away, putting it out of her reach.

"No problem. Mason stays with Niko. Keep busy. All good."

She huffed, "Fine. Was that Niko with Mason when we docked?" There was no winning with this guy. She'd have to bide her time and see how things worked out.

She should have asked about her brother sooner but she needed her boat fixed. She'd seen Mason walking, well half-running, alongside a younger and slightly taller version of Boris when they'd docked. By deductive reasoning, she'd figured he was Niko and Mason looked like he was okay.

"Yes. Niko will teach him to work on tugboat." Boris walked toward the door.

"What? Wait. Mason doesn't know anything about tugboats. Hell, he's never worked a day in his life. He's only sixteen. He could get hurt." Sahara trailed after Boris. "You don't understand. He was out there with me to keep an eye out for those scavengers and warn me if he saw anything headed in our direction."

Boris kept walking.

"He gets seasick and takes pills that keep him from throwing up but they make him sleepy. He can't work on a boat."

She was breathing hard and barely keeping up with Boris when he stopped next to a large, dark green SUV.

He dropped her backpack and duffle on the back seat. After closing the door, he turned to face her.

She crowded him but she didn't step back. This guy was way too calm and too in charge. She was her own boss. A clash was coming but he'd saved them and she owed him some respect, at least for a few more minutes.

He wore the same poker face he'd had since they docked. "Come. We go." He took hold of her upper arm and walked her around to the passenger side where he opened the door and helped her climb in. "Fasten seat belt."

He shut her door, doing his best to hide a smirk.

She glared at him through the windshield as he walked to the driver's side. What the hell had just happened?

Before he could put the SUV in gear, Sahara found her voice. "Hold it. I don't know you. I can't go home with some man I've never met before. You should take me to a motel. I can take care of myself."

Uh-oh, she'd just poked the bear if the bulging muscle in his jaw was any indicator. He turned those fierce, blue eyes of his on her and stared, hard. They were so striking it was all she could do not to lean forward and stare into them.

"I am Captain Boris Rustov. Now, you know me. We go home. Motel is not safe." He pointed at her head. "Someone tried to kill you. Not smart to use credit card. Too easy to find. I take care of you."

Sahara pulled her phone out of her back pocket. "I'm calling my sister." Barcelona Starze definitely had a reputation and several, international martial arts trophies. That was enough to scare anyone that knew Lona.

Well, maybe not. The battery was dead. This was so not her day. She shoved it back in her pocket and glanced at Boris to see if he'd noticed. Sure he had. His smirk was a dead giveaway. Men, so exasperating. But this one had saved her, Mason, and the *Lucky Desperado II* from a watery grave. She'd try to tolerate his overbearing, annoying self a little longer, maybe. There was that word again. She was not a "maybe" kind of girl. He was infiltrating her speech, well, more like her thought patterns. *Ugh, men!*

She'd try a different approach. "I'm hungry. And I'm too tired to cook. If you stop at a drive-thru I'll buy dinner." Like with the last twenty dollars she had in her backpack.

"*Nyet*. I cook. You take shower, wash hair." He grinned without looking her way. "Then I fix cut on your head. Put ointment on. Less scarring. Okay."

She was sunbaked, exhausted, and nasty-smelling. Her hair was a tangled rat's nest coated with sweat, grim and blood. She wanted food, a shower and a bed. He had all three. It was a winning hand. She'd take what he offered tonight and they could fight about it tomorrow.

"Let me get this right. You're going to cook dinner?" She stared at Boris in disbelief.

"I fix good food so you eat, get strong." He kept looking straight ahead and smiling.

"Men don't cook." North didn't cook anything, ever. That was for her and Lona to do along with the shopping, laundry and housekeeping. Nope, this was not making sense.

"I take class with daughter. Natasha is very good cook. Married to good man, Ivan."

Yeah. Okay, now it was falling into place. He had a daughter and took cooking classes. How dangerous could he be?

"You have a daughter old enough to be married? Wow. You must have had her when you were really young." This guy was still too ripped to be an old man. Okay, so he was out of his twenties, probably in his late thirties. He might be pushing forty, maybe. There was that word again. But the faded, sleeveless, chambray shirt didn't leave much to the imagination and his well-worn jeans were just as form fitting. She couldn't miss the overall appeal.

"I married most beautiful girl in Kiev when I was seventeen. Natasha came when I was eighteen."

Sahara sat back and studied him. She preferred mature guys. They were more likely to be steady and settled down. She was not. According to her last semi-serious boyfriend, she was still running wild and living on the edge. Edge of what? She wasn't sure. Edge of the world? Edge of the map? Edge of extinction? She had responsibilities to her sister and younger brother. Every day was a challenge. She had to be ready to protect them from North. He was getting worse. There was no telling what he'd do next.

"Is your wife at home?"

Boris lost his smile. Sahara was pretty sure she'd stepped over a line. Maybe he'd stop the car and put her out. Oh, well.

His eyes were glued on the road. "I am alone. My wife was killed in Russia. I bring family to America. After Captain Jake died, his widow, Connie was with me. Good, strong woman. Died in car accident. Very bad."

"Oh, I'm sorry. Sometimes I ask too many questions. I didn't mean to pry. I was trying to get to know you before we get to your house. I guess I'm trying to figure out why you're being so nice."

"Is good to help other sailors. We will protect you and Mason while Misha fixes boat."

She wasn't sure what to make of that. "Thank you, for helping us."

She sat back and took a good long look at him. He was a decent man from what she'd seen so far. He had no trouble admitting he'd fallen in love young. He wasn't ashamed of who he was. And he still wore passion on his sleeve. She'd heard it in his voice from the minute he'd spoken to her on board the *Desperado*. What would it be like to have a man like that? Too bad she didn't have time to stick around and find out.

She had the rest of the cursed treasure of *El Anochecer* to salvage. She'd sleep on it and come up with a plan. She was low on cash and he was right about using her credit or bank cards. Selling the jewels she'd already taken aboard would bring questions. That was an easy trail for the wrong people to follow: people North liked to hang out with. She was not losing her salvage, *El Anochecer's* treasure was hers. She had the biggest pieces tucked away on the *Lucky Desperado II*. Her duffle had the most valuable small pieces. But what she cared the most about was in her backpack. She wasn't letting it out of her sight. The rest was still in the remains of the rotting hulk of *El Anochecer's* hold. All together it would be more than enough to keep them comfortable. Nothing extravagant but they'd be okay if they were careful. And if North didn't steal it, like he'd stolen everything else. He was out of prison and he needed money.

∼

A few short hours later, Boris put the last dish in the rack to dry. Dinner was over and the house was quiet. Sahara had asked to help but she was dead on her feet. He'd applied the antibiotic ointment to her forehead and sent her off to bed in Natasha's old room. She'd be asleep and oblivious to the world by now. He'd check on her later. In the meantime, he had questions he wanted answered. He picked up his phone and called Niko.

His brother didn't waste any time answering. "*Da*, what you find out?"

"Driver's license address is for Neptune Beach in Florida." Boris leaned back in his chair. "She has two brothers and one sister, parent's died in plane crash."

Niko grunted, acknowledging he'd heard. "Mason says his sister takes care of him since he was baby. Other sister is Barcelona and she teaches martial arts. He won't talk about their older brother. Only tells me he is a bad man and Sahara works to protect them from him. This is not right."

"We will get to know them while Misha fixes her boat."

"Mason will work with me. He wants to go but says he gets seasick. I told him. Okay, I can fix." Niko chuckled. "I will make him old-time sailor breakfast. He will be okay."

"Good. I take Sashara with me. She can rest. When she feels better she can learn how we work tugboat. Big change from sailboat." Boris grunted. "She is in for surprise in morning."

"You be careful." Niko grumbled, "Mason tells me his sister wins many trophies with her rifle."

"Good. I like." Boris smiled to himself. He'd taken a look at her Ruger when he'd put it away in the closet on the *Desperado*. "Her rifle is very expensive, very fine quality. Only an expert marksman would own that."

"But her boat is very old. Not safe."

Boris let that hang for a second. "Everything is very old on that boat. Blanket old, clothes old, and her deck shoes are worn out. She has nothing new."

"Mason's clothes are good, new shoes. Sahara spends money on him. She complains he is growing too fast." Niko chuckled. "She is good sister but something is wrong with older brother that won't take care of his family. I will look into him. He must be very bad guy to make them hide from him."

"How do you say her name so good?"

"Lulu helps me practice. She says you do not like any woman here, so maybe you like this Sahara. Maybe she becomes part of our family."

"Maybe." He was definitely thinking about it as a lazy grin spread across his face. He definitely liked the way her body had rested against his on the way in.

"*Nyet*. No." Flew out of Niko's mouth without hesitation. "Not good Russian woman. Too young for you, old man. Wear you out."

Boris grunted into the phone. "Lulu is too good for you. Too smart. Too pretty. Not Russian. You wear her out."

"I am lucky man."

Boris could picture his brother grinning from ear to ear. Knowing Niko was happy was the important part.

"I find *Desperado*. Maybe that is lucky for me." He chuckled.

Natasha was happily married. Niko was overjoyed with being a husband and a new father. Boris was ready to be sleeping double in his queen-sized bed. His *Kroshka* would be a perfect fit.

Niko snorted in response. "It should not be hard to find their older brother with name like North Dakota Starze. Parents must have been thinking crazy to name children after those places."

Boris grumbled, "Sashara tells me, they are named for place where their mother got pregnant. Father was some kind of treasure hunter so they went many places."

"You need put her back in the Gulf and find a good woman your age, maybe a little older if she's pretty." Niko muttered, "Ouch!"

"What happened?"

"Lulu pinched me. Very evil woman sometimes." Niko gave a short laugh. "But I like."

"I like, too. You lucky she only pinches you."

Boris disconnected the call and walked quietly past Sahara's room to his. He liked having her in his house. It was the first step to something new for him. He stripped down and got in the shower. He needed to get cleaned up and pay attention to his newly awakened condition. *Da*, it was still in working order. He only needed to be patient and pray his *Kroshka* took a liking to him.

CHAPTER 4

*D*ark and early the next morning, Sahara launched out of her pillow-nest when Boris's fist pounded on the guest bedroom door.

She bolted upright muttering, "What? What's happening?" She scanned the room, flopped down and pulled the covers up to her ears. "Monster. Who the hell gets up at…" she peeked at the clock, "five-damn-thirty in the morning? I've landed in Hell. I'm sure of it."

Rolling to her side she poked her toes out from under the covers and wiggled them, testing the temperature. Okay, it was a nice ambient degree of warm.

She clearly heard him shout, "Coffee ready. Come eat."

"Go away. I'm sleeping," she huffed sleepily as she closed her eyes. Maybe that would be good enough to appease the Tsar of Galveston. It might be a nightmare. If she waited a few minutes, she might wake up on the *Desperado* rocking gently in a nice peaceful cove somewhere far, far away from the Gulf of Mexico.

She had barely snuggled down deep into soft comforter when she was unceremoniously airborne, lifted out of bed and carried down the hall. "Wait. What? Oh my God, put me down."

"You eat breakfast. We have long day. Work on my boat."

She glared at a very smug looking Boris through sleepy eyes. "I'm not working. I can't dive in the Gulf. My boat's in dry dock."

He had no idea how worn out she was. She'd spent days hauling salvage up from the sea floor and loading it onto the *Desperado*.

Her butt handed on the cold kitchen chair. The only thing covering her was one of his old t-shirts she'd borrowed to sleep in. Thank goodness the flimsy thing hung to her knees.

He slid a paper across the table to her. "You sign. You work for Tuggers now. I will take you with me. Keep you safe."

"I'm a diver. I don't know anything about your tugboat. I can't work for you."

He grinned. "Okay. I teach you."

"This isn't Russia. American girls don't work on tugboats."

That ought to slow him down. What did he know about American girls anyway?

"Annie is best tugboat captain on the Gulf. I teach her when little girl. You work good, no problem."

"Tugboat Annie is a myth, an old movie. There's no such person." He was lying just to get his way. Men were good at that. She ran her fingers through her hair hoping to get it out of her face.

"Captain Annie is real. We work for Tuggers. You see. Now, eat and get dressed. We go. Not safe for you to stay here alone."

Sahara looked down at her plate. Who did he think he was feeding? She couldn't and wouldn't eat all that. Scrambled eggs, bacon, and some kind of sausage with hash browns. She'd weigh four-hundred pounds if she ate his so-called breakfast. She'd bob like a cork in the water if she ate like that. They didn't make enough weights to slip on her dive belt. It was enough food for an army. Or navy. Whatever. Make it stop. Let her wake up. It had to be the curse of *El Anochecer* come to haunt her. Did *El Anochecer* have a curse? The treasure did but that didn't mean the ship did. She'd have to check on that.

Boris inhaled his breakfast, put his empty plate in the sink, and disappeared down the hall. She sipped her coffee and almost gagged. Good lord, it was strong enough to take the enamel off her teeth. She got up and watered it down. Great, she had the kitchen to herself.

Which way was out? It was too early for anyone to be up. Nobody would notice her running half-naked down the street. Right?

∽

It was hard to tell for sure, but if she had to guess she'd say he took delight in torturing her. The Cold War was supposed to be over but her Russian seemed to be overjoyed with watching her run from one end of the *Connie* to the other like a crazy woman. She was not now and never had been a deck hand on a tugboat, fishing boat, or any other kind of commercial boat.

She'd spent the morning resting in the cabin till she'd gotten bored and gone out on deck to watch the crew until lunch time. Then, he and the crew ate enough beef to feed a platoon. A few minutes after she'd finished the dishes, he'd decided it was time for her to start learning how to work a tugboat. Never mind her argument that it would never happen.

Yeah, well, it did happen. He was very persuasive and bossy when he got his commanding officer thing going. She'd considered jumping overboard a couple times but they weren't in sight of land where she could swim to shore and escape.

Late evening rolled around and she flung a rope toward the dock, trying to hit him with it. And failed. He grabbed ahold and tied it off securing *Connie* to the dock.

All afternoon, she'd been plotting, waiting to be back on terra firma. They'd go home. He'd eat dinner and take a shower. She'd make her getaway as soon as he fell asleep or maybe while he was in the shower. She'd wait for the opportune moment to make her dash for freedom. She could come back for Mason later. Working a tugboat was not for her. This was one of those, every man and woman for themselves situations. She was getting out.

Boris called out, "Come. We go to Riptide and you meet Annie."

"What? No. I'm tired and sweaty. It's not a good time to meet anyone." Her sports bra was damp and stuck to her boobs, while her desert camo, cargo pants and beige tank top were sweaty and drooping everywhere. This couldn't be happening, not now. Come on. Really?

She desperately wanted him to go home and go to sleep, or fall unconscious in his recliner or on the couch. Anything that would let her escape. She was working for her keep like back in the really old days. Indentured servitude or something. She could give him the slip, catch a bus, take a flight, rent a boat and be back in the Bahamas in a couple days laying claim to her salvage site.

"No problem. Everyone works all day. We have cold beer and talk. You will like Annie. She is smart like you."

"I'm not all that smart. If I was, I wouldn't be here. I'd be resting under a palm tree with a cold drink in my hand. Something fruity, full of rum with a cute little paper umbrella sticking out of it."

"You will like the Riptide." He smiled and took her by the hand, leading the way along the dock.

"Can they put my drink in a glass with ice?" Her lip twitched. He really was dancing on her last nerve and it was fighting back. She needed something ice cold with lots of alcohol to numb it and the rest of her aching body.

"No problem. They have good, cold mugs and ice. We will get this for you."

She did her best to keep up with his long strides but failed. "You have to slow down. I can't run all the way to your tavern."

He slowed. "Sorry. Forgot you are so small."

Her face puckered up and she snapped, "That's it. I'm not small. You're big. Huge in fact. Huger than huge. So, slow down or go without me."

"We go. For you, I walk slow." He tugged on her hand.

"Not till you learn to speak to me politely. I'm not your dog. You don't get to command me to 'come and go'." She pulled her hand free from his grip and glared.

He gave one curt nod. "Sorry. You come with me, please. I want you to meet Annie."

"That's better." She turned back in the direction they'd been headed in before she had her melt-down. She didn't pull away when he slipped his big, rough hand around hers, again. The man had warm hands. They were hard and callused from his work but also strong and secure.

That was nice. There definitely were some things about Boris she liked.

He opened the door for her and ushered her inside with his hand resting on the small of her back. The place was older than dirt. The dim light was a blessing after spending the day out on the water in the blazing sun and the air conditioner was on super cold. The cool air relieved her sunbaked arms. She stayed close to Boris. He knew these people and she didn't. She didn't want any trouble.

She followed him to a long table and sat down next to him. Yeah, okay so her leg was bumping against his now and then. Big deal. She didn't like bars. She didn't like mean drunks and there was always one somewhere in the crowd. She knew the type, another version of North.

Boris ordered his beer and her wine cooler with a mug of ice. He remembered. God bless his bossy heart. He'd actually listened to her.

He nodded at the men and women sitting at the table. "Captain Tyler, Captain Lindsey, this is Captain Starze."

Captain Lindsey acknowledge with a quick nod. She said, "Good to meet you, Captain Starze. We can use another captain around here. Are you working with Boris for now?"

"Um, call me Sahara. I'm barely a captain, only light weight craft. Captain Rustov is teaching me how a tugboat operates. It'll keep me busy till my sailboat is repaired. If I get enough hours maybe I can move up in weight class, someday." She couldn't fool these people. They were way above her in rank. "My *Lucky Desperado* took some storm damage coming back from the Bahamas." That's all she was saying for the time being. They absolutely didn't need the details. The less said about *El Anochecer* the better.

"Well, welcome to the family." Captain Lindsey lifted her mug in salute.

Everyone nodded. She was not used to this. She was even more not used to Niko walking in and no Mason. She asked, "Where's my brother?"

Niko grinned. "I sent him home to help Lulu. She has our baby to take care of. He is good help."

"What? No. My brother doesn't know anything about babies. He's the youngest in our family." She started to get up and was stopped by

Boris. His hand came down gently on her shoulder and pulled her back onto the bench next to him.

"All okay. Lulu is good mother, takes good care of both." Boris grinned and poured her wine cooler into the mug full of ice.

His action didn't go unnoticed, if the looks he was getting from the other people at the table were a clue. Well, he could explain it if he wanted to or not. And judging from the frown he flashed at everyone who dared to stare, he was not going to be explaining anything to any of them.

She turned her attention to Niko. "Mason's probably seasick and going to hurl from one end of the house to the other. That's not helping anybody."

Niko sat across from Boris. "Mason did good for first day. Not seasick. He worked hard and did not complain. He makes good tugboat crew. We like him."

She didn't have an answer for that right off the top of her head except to say, "Oh, good. Maybe you can keep him." She managed a half-assed smile and her upper lip twitched. She was losing her grip. Giving her brother away to strangers wasn't happening.

He raised one eyebrow. "Okay." Then he raised his hand and signaled the bartender for another round.

Before it could hit the table, a young woman dressed in working seaman garb and wearing a Greek sailors cap, flew through the door and ran straight as an arrow to Boris. She stopped behind him and flung her arms around his shoulders and said, "Help me. Santos is right behind me and he found out I bought my own Harley."

"No problem. You sit here." He patted the bench on his free side. "I fix. I watched you learn. You are very good rider, very safe."

She climbed over the bench and sat down. "Thanks, Captain."

He smiled and bumped her with his shoulder. "All good. This is Sashara. Captain of *Desperado*."

"Just Sahara." She waved at Annie.

Annie's face lit up with a huge smile. She was beautiful. Sahara had to hand it to the lady. She had it all pulled together. Her own boat, her own Harley, and she was her own boss. Boris had taught her to take care of herself. Was there anything the man couldn't do?

Annie said, "All right. Great to meet you. I heard Captain Boris had a house guest."

"Yeah, he's letting me stay till Misha fixes my boat."

Annie nodded. "Wonderful. Misha's the best."

Before anyone had time to say another word, the front door banged open. A tall, dark, and scowling man stomped into the bar: a biker, judging by the well-worn, rugged leather jacket. He had to be Annie's Santos.

When he planted himself directly across the table from Annie and glared at her, Sahara was pretty sure World War Three was about to break out. How exactly was she going to wiggle her way under the table and out of harm's way? Maybe while they were massacring each other she could crawl out the back door. Surely this place had one. Wasn't that like a law or something?

"Annie, you're not riding that Deluxe. Take it back."

Sahara watched Annie screw up her face into something definitely along the line of stubborn defiance before blurting out, "No. It's mine and I'm keeping it."

He jammed his hands on his hips. "You could get killed."

"So could you."

"It's not the same thing. I've been riding all my life." He ran a hand over his mouth.

"I took the rider's safety course and passed." She didn't back down.

Yep, he was losing the battle. Captain Annie was a ball-buster. The rumors were true. Sahara smiled from ear to ear for the first time in a long time. Yeah, this was great. *Go girl, you tell him.*

"Annie." This time when he looked at her, his heart was in his eyes. "I need you with me."

Sahara studied him. She'd never seen a man turn to mush so easily. He was definitely in love with his woman. Wow.

"You got it. I'm riding with you from now on, but on my own bike."

Boris nodded. "All good."

Santos looked from one to the other and muttered, "You're killing me. You know that, right?"

"That old guilt-trip thing won't work on me, sweetheart." Annie laughed. "But I'll make it up to you when we get home."

Boris smiled. "See, everyone happy." He shifted his weight and looked directly at Sahara. "Annie is captain of very strong tugboat."

Annie leaned forward and looked past Boris. "*Mi Vato Santos* is mine." She looked across that table at the man staring at her and smiled. "I never go to sea without him."

"The *Lucky Desperado* is my sailboat. I'm a conch diver in the Bahamas. Sometimes I find other stuff that I can sell. Old pieces of boats or things that fell overboard. People love things recovered from the bottom of the ocean." She didn't want word getting around there was a treasure hunter in town. That came with lots of questions she didn't want to answer.

So far, so good. They seemed like nice people. She looked from Annie to Boris. There was more to their story. It would take a lot of rum and time to get to the bottom of that. She didn't have either at the moment.

The evening wore on and it was apparent she wasn't going to get away from Boris anytime soon. By the time they'd made it home and he'd fed her dinner, it was too late to do anything but get ready for bed. She'd have to try again when an opportunity presented itself.

Boris called out, "Let me know when you are ready. I will look at wound and put ointment.

"I'm okay. I can do it." She looked for the tube she'd left lying on the bathroom counter. She was so tired she'd forgotten all about her nasty gash.

Before she had time to twist the cap off, Boris was standing next to her with his hand out.

"Okay, here." She held it out to him. "I can take care of myself. You don't have to do this."

He took the ointment in one hand while brushing her hair back with the other. "I check. Make sure it does not get infected."

For a man with big hands, he had a gentle touch. It was not supposed to be like this. She didn't need him to be kind, and gentle, and thoughtful. All the men she'd ever known were takers. Boris was a giver. She had no clue how to deal with that. He was a complication she didn't need.

He finished smoothing the ointment on her sore forehead. "Good night, *Kroshka*."

"Good night." She mumbled, "See you in the morning."

He looked like he'd wanted to say something else but walked away.

Sahara walked to her room, stared at the door, and contemplated how to barricade the damn thing. She was so not getting up at five-thirty. He could huff and puff and blow the house down but she was sleeping till a decent hour. She needed to recover her strength. She was going back for her salvage. It wasn't an option.

She waited till she was sure he'd gone to bed before moving the furniture. She tried pushing the dresser without any success, so the bed was now a doorstop. That would keep him out. She took in the view of her handiwork and smiled smugly. Two could play at being the boss. Chalk up a win for her.

She crawled into bed and called her sister.

There was no telling what part of the world Barcelona Starze was partying in, but she always had her phone with her. She was so glitterati it wasn't even funny. And she was soon to be so broke if they didn't get the rest of *El Anochecer's* salvage retrieved and sold. But there was no point in ruining Lona's fun any sooner than necessary.

So, snuggling in under the soft, baby-blue, fluffy comforter, she waited for the phone to ring.

Her sister's voice chirped over the airwaves. "Hey girl, how's Nassau?"

"It was fine. I was in luck. But I ran into some bad weather on the way home. Can you help me out? I need you to pick up some special parts for me."

Bad weather was their code for trouble. And the parts she needed picked up were in the hidden smuggler's compartment dedicated to Lona on the *Lucky Desperado II*. Her sister's share of the initial haul was safe for the time being.

"Sure. No problem. Text me the details."

"Okay. Will do." Sahara could hear the music and laughter in the background. "How are you doing?"

"I'm good. It's beautiful here on the Amalfi coast. You should see it. We could rent a sailboat and go exploring."

"Sounds like a good idea as soon as we get this job in the bank. Try to take it easy on the credit cards. The account is getting a little low and the *Desperado* needs repairs."

"Sure, Sis, not a problem. I've got everything I need for the summer."

"Great. I'll see you soon." Sahara disconnected the call.

Misha was going to have company. Hopefully, he wouldn't notice.

Sahara rolled over and closed her eyes, confident Lona would handle it.

∽

Boris went to his room and closed the door. He'd made every effort to gently spread the antibiotic ointment over her healing wound. He liked taking care of his *Kroshka*. And he did think of her as his. That was dangerous. He was only beginning to know her and he was letting his imagination run away with his common sense. A smart man would slow down and take it easy.

The problem was he liked it when she touched him, when she leaned into him. He wanted the closeness of having her near him. He had zero intention of pushing her away. Luring her closer was his primary focus. And he was way out of practice.

Niko had married Lulu to her parent's horror and everyone else's surprise. He'd talk to Niko in the morning. If his younger brother could catch himself a fine bride, Boris could too. Of course, Lulu hadn't been able to sail away. He'd have a talk with Misha. The *Lucky Desperado II,* wasn't going anywhere for the foreseeable near future. He'd make sure of it.

Getting his *Kroshka* to open up and talk to him was the next thing on his list.

CHAPTER 5

It was still dark outside the next morning when Boris pounded on the guest bedroom door and shouted, "Open door now!" He grabbed the door knob and twisted. It turned. It wasn't locked but it wasn't opening either. "Get up. We go to work. Crew waiting."

"You go anyplace you want. I'm going back to sleep," was the groggy sounding, mumbled answer he got.

"*Nyet*. Get up. We eat breakfast. You come with me." He jiggled the door knob for no other reason than he could.

"You go to work. Enjoy your breakfast."

He stomped down the hall and called Niko. "She blocked door so it does not open. I cannot leave her here alone. Too dangerous. What do we do?"

Niko howled with laughter, damn near deafening Boris. He finally choked out, "You have met your match brother. Good. I like this one. I will tell Lulu. She will like her, too."

"Not funny," Boris growled into phone.

"Do not worry. We go to work. I will send Lulu over so they go shopping for baby. That takes all day. All good, you see."

"Fine." Boris disconnected the call, shook his head and mumbled. "I fix tonight."

Sahara's eyes drifted open a couple hours later with the sun filtering through the blinds in her room. She stretched lazily and got out of bed to a quiet house. Thank God.

She could make a run for it. Right after she raided the kitchen for some breakfast. She could use a cup of watered-down coffee and some toast.

After she moved the bed back to its usual spot, she wandered down the hall taking her time enjoying having the house all to herself.

She'd lived on her boat so long she'd forgotten how good it was to have solid ground under her feet. Boris kept his house clean and neat. Everything in its place. She was the disturbance in his world. Well, not much longer and he could have his orderly life back.

She pulled up short when she stepped into the kitchen. He had to be kidding. Really? He'd left her a covered plate of scrambled eggs and bacon next to the microwave. What was it about this guy? She shook her head and popped the plate in to warm.

No time to worry about it. She had to eat, get dressed and get the hell out of Dodge, Galveston, wherever. This was her chance to get gone while the getting was good. He was right about going to a motel being too dangerous. She'd catch a bus to the airport, and change planes in Miami. She'd touch down in Nassau by nightfall.

It didn't take long to wolf down breakfast and get dressed in her khaki cargo pants and tank top. She opened the front door with her backpack on her shoulder only to find a beautiful, dark haired, young woman coming up the walkway. Ugh, her timing was terrible. She had to be Niko's wife, Lulu. This had to be a curse of some kind. Or a conspiracy. Knowing Boris, conspiracy was more likely.

Lulu called out, "Hi! You must be Sahara. Niko asked me to take you shopping with me today. He said you needed to get some girl things."

"What? No. I'm fine." What in the hell was she talking about?

"Well, maybe you can help me. I can't try on clothes and watch Niki at the same time." She snuggled the bundle in her arms closer.

"I'm afraid I don't fit in my pre-baby clothes yet and I want to look nice."

Sahara looked her up and down. "You're beautiful."

"I still need clothes that fit right. So, how about it? Will you help me?"

Shit, shit, shit! What could she say that wouldn't hurt the girl's feelings? "Actually, I was just leaving. I need to catch the bus to the airport."

Lulu's smile disappeared. "You're running away. That's mean, after all that Boris has done for you." She walked closer and stopped directly in front of Sahara. "He likes you. Why would you do this to him?"

Because my brother and sister's futures depend on me getting El Anochecer's salvage. "I'm not running away. I'm getting back to taking care of my business and giving him his privacy."

"Your business got your boat practically shot out from under you. If Boris wanted privacy, he'd have dropped you off on motel row." Lulu shifted the baby. "Put your stuff back in your room and let's go."

Crap. She couldn't exactly run over a new mom holding a baby and pretend it was all right. Especially since Mason was staying in her home. "Do you have a laptop or tablet or something? I need to check if there's a curse on my boat." She couldn't exactly tell her about *El Anochecer*. This nightmare kept getting worse and worse. There had to be an explanation.

"Sure. The latest in smart-phones is in the car."

"Great. Let's go." She dropped her backpack and shut the front door.

It had been years since Sahara had gone out for a girl's day of shopping. Lona either wore work-out clothes, tiny excuses for beach clothes, or sparkling party clothes. Mason needed school clothes. That left Sahara on her own. She needed good scuba equipment and sturdy canvas sails to get her where she was going.

Her clothes didn't matter as long as they covered the essentials. She was definitely style-challenged. Lulu, on the other hand, was a fashionista extraordinaire. Lona would love her. Apparently, what Lulu had going on worked because her husband adored her from the talk she'd heard at the Riptide.

The man was totally devoted and Annie's husband seemed to have caught the same condition. She'd never seen anything like it and she had no clue what to make of it. Everything about Boris was new to her. One minute he was grumpy bossy and the next he was taking care of her like she was something special. She'd never been special to anyone, ever.

Lulu held up a sleep set consisting of shorts and a matching frilly top. "Do you like this one? It would be perfect for you."

"It's pretty but I don't need anything like that." Sahara glanced at the black and white, girly outfit. The lace ruffle around the legs was eye catching. Yep, that would make a man look twice.

Sahara rocked the baby gently, hoping he'd stay asleep. Little Niki was precious and brought her back to the days when Mason had literally arrived on the doorstep. Of course, he'd had blonde hair while Niki's was black like his mom and dad's. Babies were awesome.

"Sure, you do. You can't go around the house in old t-shirts. Boris is definitely a man and men like their women to look pretty."

"I'm pretty sure Boris doesn't care what I wear. He's a kind man, that's all. I'd look silly wearing polka dots and lace."

Lulu giggled and dropped the sleep set in the shopping basket. "He's Niko's brother. Don't kid yourself. You wear that and you'll have his attention." She grabbed another set in red for herself. "He's been alone a long time."

She picked up a different style in hot-pink. "He gave me and Annie away at our wedding. We had a double wedding." She looked pointedly at Sahara. "It would be good if he finally found someone for himself. I'm going to wear mine tonight. I'll let you know if it works."

"On you, a gunny sack would work." Sahara didn't know where that had come from but now that it was out in the open there was no denying the truth. Lulu was beautiful and funny and considerate. She snuggled Niki a little closer for a second. "He's perfect. You're so lucky."

She'd snuggled Mason close and asked her dad if she could keep him. How naïve had she been in those days? But she'd do it all again given the chance.

"Do you want kids?" Lulu wandered to the next rack and looked at athletic wear.

"Who me? Oh lord, wouldn't that be a wreck. Not with the way I live on the *Desperado*. It wouldn't be safe and there'd be no one to watch them when I'm diving. It would never work, so I don't waste time thinking about it."

"What do you dive for?" She shuffled through the sets in her size and looked over at Sahara.

"Stuff on the ocean floor. Conch mostly when I'm in the Bahamas, and other shells when I'm in the Caribbean. I have got about six years until Mason gets out of college. Somebody's gotta pay the tuition." She looked at Niki. "Right kid? That's the way that works."

"Mason could apply for scholarships." Lulu sauntered off toward the baby section of the store.

"He'll have to go to junior college first to get his average up. He gets bored in class and his mind wanders so when test taking time comes along, he hasn't got the answers." She followed Lulu a couple aisles over. "Mason is smart. Don't get me wrong. But if he's not interested in what's going on, he tunes it out. He likes building things and I'm hoping I can get him in to a university with a good structural engineering or architecture program. He might like that."

Lulu reached for boy's onesies. "Have you talked to him about what he wants?"

"I've tried but he gets fidgety, says he's going to become a hermit, and walks off."

Lulu broke out in a fit of giggles. "A hermit! I don't think there's any such thing anymore. Mason is so funny. He keeps me laughing."

After they finished shopping, they stopped for lunch and then groceries. Sahara desperately needed coffee fit for human consumption, sugar and creamer.

After Lulu dropped her off at the curb, she stood on the sidewalk contemplating how she was gonna handle Boris. He was bound to be mad and she hated confrontations. It always escalated into horrible fights.

At sea, there was no one to fight with and the dead couldn't yell at her. There was a certain peace out there under the waves. Well, unless she came across a pissed off creature from the deep.

Her options were limited. Her boat was in dry dock. She'd missed the flight to Florida that would have connected to Nassau and Lulu had driven off to go fix dinner and seduce her husband. There was nothing to do but suck it up and go inside.

The front door was unlocked so she didn't have to ring the bell and stand there like a door-to-door salesperson. She closed it quietly and glanced down. Yes, her backpack was right where she'd left it. Well, he might as well get it through his head that she was not staying any longer than it took to fix the *Desperado*.

She pushed on to the kitchen and put her grocery bag on the counter. "Here, I got some coffee. It's not as strong as yours."

"Good. I can fix for you on Sundays."

What? It was for everyday but telling Mr. Stuck-in-his-ways that wouldn't help. He'd do it his way, period, end of subject. "Well, there's sugar and creamer for the rest of the week."

"Okay. I fix for you."

Oh my god. It was a compromise. He did know how to meet somewhere closer to the middle.

"Thanks. Appreciate it. I'm going to go put my stuff away." She was still holding the shopping bag that Lulu had forced on her.

She would improve her look or Lulu would improve it for her. Great. The seagulls would love it.

"*Da*. Dinner is ready soon." The edges of his lips turned up in a half-assed grin.

She grabbed her backpack from the entryway and walked to the guest room. It didn't look right. Wait… The door was missing. He had to be kidding!

She yelled, "Dammit!", loud enough to wake the dead.

∼

Earlier that afternoon, Boris had taken the bedroom doors off their hinges and carried them out to the garage. He'd hear it if she tried to put hers back. Then he fixed dinner and waited for her to come home.

If he lived to be a hundred, he'd always remember his ears ringing from her shriek of disbelief. He was sure the neighbors heard her, too.

She stomped back to the kitchen, yelling her way down the hall. "Are you insane? Who the hell takes the doors off their hinges? Lulu lied to me. You're not a good man, you're nuts. I'm living with a crazy man."

He'd grinned at her and put their plates on the table. "Dinner is ready."

This was the most fun he'd had in years. He couldn't wait to see what she'd come up with next to challenge him.

He loved a good challenge.

CHAPTER 6

Boris listened to Niko laugh loudly on the other end of the phone and grumbled, "Shut up. Not so funny."

"Yes, it is. Lulu got her to buy some pretty clothes for sleeping and you make her too mad to look at you. She won't wear them now."

"Damn. Bad luck for me," Boris grumbled at his end. "Have to wait long time."

Niko quit laughing. "Long time for what?"

As if he couldn't guess. His younger brother could be a pain-in-the-ass sometimes, more like most of the time. "Not your business. I fix."

"Like you fix the door? Better not to fix." He chuckled quietly. "Lulu tells me Sahara dives for money to send Mason to university. Takes five, maybe six years to graduate. You have to wait long time for Sahara. Not good for an old man to wait so long. Balls could shrivel up."

Boris answered, "Not good for a man to take money from sister. We will give Mason a job. He can earn money and start taking care of himself. We help him learn how to become a man."

Niko lowered his voice and suggested, "You forget her and find woman that lives here."

"I have to sleep with woman, not you. I choose, not you." Boris disconnected the call.

He had things to say to Sahara. He walked to her room and stopped in the doorway to watch her. She sat cross-legged on her bed looking at a very old, extremely ragged book. The yellowed pages looked like they could crack and fall to pieces from the slightest touch. Reading intently, she didn't look up but kept writing in a spiral notebook.

"What are you reading?" He asked quietly. They'd made it through dinner without her throwing her plate at him. But it had been close. She'd had that look in her eyes. It had been hard to keep from laughing.

"None of your business." She glared at him.

He took one step inside the room. "I am sorry you are angry." There. He'd said all the words right.

She put her pen down. "Well, I'm sorry, too. Maybe." She looked directly at him. "You can't order me around. I'm not some little kid."

He took another step, shortening the distance between them. "I want to keep you safe. I can't do that with locked doors, or when I work and you stay here."

After all the years he'd been in America, he should be better at speaking English. For that, he'd need practice and his crew all spoke Russian. His fists clenched and unclenched. She might see it and think he was angry when in fact he was frustrated. He relaxed his hands. "I am captain and I live alone for a long time. Sorry, I am not used to explaining to anyone."

She kept her eyes fixed on his. "Okay, I understand. I'll get up early, but I won't like it. That's the best I can do."

He nodded toward the old book sitting on the bed. "What is that book?"

She grabbed her notes and laid them over the book, hiding the pages. "It's mine. Nothing for you to worry about, so go away."

He wouldn't get it away from her without a fight and that would only destroy it. He took a step back. "I am going to watch TV. I will make breakfast in the morning."

"Yeah, good. I'll see you at breakfast."

She kept the pages covered as he walked away.

He grinned. No problem. He'd look at it later, when she was asleep. For now, he was satisfied that she was speaking to him.

Sahara watched him go. Thank goodness he hadn't tried to wrestle Princess Alessia's diary away from her. The thing was in danger of falling apart as it was. She uncovered it carefully.

Alessia's last words were in it. Sahara was good at deciphering most of the romance languages but old Italian was not easy. She was going one word at a time to be sure she got it right and it was taking forever.

In truth, it was a miracle the thing existed at all. Back then women were not usually educated to read and write. Princess Alessia was able to describe what happened during her life in her own words. At the age of fifteen, her father promised her in marriage to Count Augustin de Balboa in Spain. She didn't like him and she invented every excuse she could come up with to delay the wedding. At the age of sixteen, she met Salvatore, a handsome merchant seaman that turned out to be one of the most notorious corsairs of the time. He was feared and hated by everyone but her. On her seventeenth birthday, she ran away with him. She was dead before she turned eighteen.

Sahara brushed a tear away and kept taking notes. A love story gone so wrong. It wasn't fair. No damn wonder Alessia had cursed her father and Balboa's family.

Salvatore had no family. He'd grown up an orphan, alone, starving on the streets, and mistreated. He'd survived the only way he could. Eventually, he'd gone to sea and become a very bad man. Alessia had found the tiny bit of good still hidden deep inside of him and fallen in love with that. What a disaster!

Sahara looked out the open doorway into the hall. Boris was a survivor. He could have been anything back in Russia. He wasn't a soft man. There was an underlying ruthlessness that she hadn't gotten a handle on yet. Lulu told her he'd been in the Army. It made sense considering the way he talked and the attitude. Hell, there were times he acted like he was still in the Army.

She, on the other hand, didn't do any kind of discipline worth a darn. If he wanted to play hardball, she had a solid-wood, baseball bat in the closet on the *Desperado*. She'd been her own boss from the time her parents died.

North had always been spoiled by their folks. He'd hidden being a bully well enough while they were alive, but he hadn't fooled her. She'd seen it up close too many times. And it was a good bet he hadn't gotten any better in prison. She had to watch her back, and Lona's and Mason's.

Boris might not realize it, but she did need his protection. It might not hurt if she was a little nicer to him. She appreciated his wicked sense of humor. Once she'd calmed down and gotten over the audacity of it, taking the doors off the hinges was genius and something she would have done. It made her giggle silently to herself.

She closed Alessia's diary, put it under her pillow and walked out to the living room.

She found him relaxed in his recliner watching TV. The living room was small but arranged so both the couch and recliner could have a view of the screen. "I thought I'd come watch with you. There'll be news later."

"Here, you can choose." He held the remote control out to her.

"Oh, no. It's fine. I don't really watch TV. There's no reception on the *Desperado*." She couldn't afford the expensive equipment other people had and besides she liked her books. Reading was quiet. She could hear the waves lapping against the hull and any approaching engines in case someone did try to sneak up on the *Lucky Desperado*.

She made herself comfortable on the couch, sitting cross-legged. Her mother had accused her of watching too many movies with people sitting like hippies on the ground. That wasn't exactly true. Back then she watched westerns and everybody sat around the campfires like that. It looked like it would be great to live out under the stars.

That was until it happened. She hated everything about camping. She looked at Boris. He'd been in the Army. He was probably good at it. "Do you like camping?"

Oh, shit. From the look she was getting she'd poked the bear again. She had to quit doing that.

He clicked off the TV.

She offered, "I'm sorry. Go back to your show. I'll keep quiet."

"*Nyet*. You want to talk. We can talk." He turned his full attention on her.

"No. It's okay. Watch your show." She gave him the best apologetic smile she could come up with. "I'm sorry."

He didn't turn the TV on. "I do not like camping."

"Oh, good. Me neither." She tried to think of something to say that wouldn't sound stupid. "I tried taking Mason to Yellowstone Park but it was a disaster. Lona went with us. She's better at that kind of stuff."

"What happened? Why your parents did not go? Very dangerous to let children go alone."

"Uh, well, that's complicated."

"I have time to listen. You can tell me."

She didn't like talking about the old days but she'd started this conversation. Damn. When would she learn to keep her mouth shut? There was no alternative but to answer him.

"Our folks had been dead a couple years by then. There wasn't anyone but me and Lona to take him. Our older brother, North, hates anything outdoors. He only learned to sail enough so he could hang around the people at the yacht club."

Boris voiced the obvious. "Mason is much younger than you."

She would tell Boris the truth. Hiding the facts would be pointless. Unless their mother had started having babies in her teens, there was no way she'd had all four of them. Maybe he'd understand and maybe he'd push her away like the others had. But maybe not, there was always a chance someone would understand what she'd done.

"We all have the same father but Mason has a different mother. She left him on our doorstep in the middle of the night. I was awake reading when I heard a car stop in front of the house, so I went to see what was going on. When I opened the front door, there he was, on the front porch in his car seat." She stopped talking and waited for Boris to say something.

"How do you know he is your brother?"

She looked away. "Well, there was the note from his mother and my dad admitted to having an affair with her. She was a riverboat card-dealer in Baton Rouge. But to be sure, mom had Mason's DNA tested."

"So, you kept him."

He maintained eye contact with her and didn't flinch. She figured the silence was his way of waiting for an explanation.

"Mom didn't want anything to do with Mason, so I took care of him. He's always been mine since I was twelve." She stared at Boris daring him to contradict her.

"You are very good sister to take care of baby brother."

She didn't know much at all about this guy and she wanted to change the subject. She didn't like talking about herself.

She asked, "What's it like living in Russia?"

There. That ought to keep him busy talking for hours. She breathed a short sigh of relief.

"Much like here. Work, eat, sleep and sometimes go to parties with friends. In the summer, we go to the beach for holiday if we are lucky. Water is very cold all year."

"Oh, right. I guess it would be cold that far north. It's warm in the islands. It's nice." She smiled at him.

"Mason says you dive on old wreck." Boris shifted, leaning more in her direction.

"Um. Yeah. It's what I do. I find old stuff, or pretty shells and sell it. People like to collect old pieces from sunken boats. I pay our bills with the money. I need to get back out to that site before someone else finds it."

"Misha will fix your boat. It takes time." He kept his eyes fixed on her.

"Great. Yeah. Um, how long have you known him?" She needed to know more about the man working on her *Lucky Desperado*. If he messed up, she could end up drowning.

"He is my cousin. He worked in Russian Navy shipyard before he worked with my unit. We talk about coming to America. We work, save money, that takes us a long time but we get here. Annie's grandfather gave us good jobs. Good man, Captain Coldwell. We teach Annie how to work on tugboat. She went to college to learn to run company and be a captain."

"I like her. She seems nice." Sahara was out of ideas to talk about. "Um, I guess I'm more tired than I thought. I'm going to bed." She got up. "See you in the morning."

"*Da*. In morning."

She wandered down the hall to her room. Great, no door. She wanted some space to herself. Something was really wrong and she had a feeling it was Alessia's curse. It was more complicated than stopping Balboa's heirs from finding true love. She wasn't finished but if she'd translated it correctly so far, it went more like the person with the heart-shaped locket, Salvatore's Heart, will find their true love. Salvatore's Heart was in the drawer under her bunk when she'd found Boris.

She'd do what she could to stay a safe, emotional distance from Boris and hope like hell that Misha could get her boat fixed soon—real soon. There was a possibility that if she put a couple hundred miles between her and Boris, the curse would wear off.

Or not. Better not to think about that. She needed to rein in her wandering emotions and stay focused on her salvage. That would fix a lot of their problems and with luck she could get herself a life. Not the one she'd had when she was in college but something where she wasn't wandering the seven seas and one dive away from being dead.

Falling in love with Boris was going to have to wait. But she'd put it on her list of things to do. Men like him didn't come along every day. If she wasn't mistaken the curse was already taking effect. Damn.

CHAPTER 7

On Sunday morning, Sahara woke to the aroma of French Vanilla coffee drifting down the hall and into her room. Yum, it smelled delicious. Wait. Hold it. Something was wrong. No, it couldn't be. Had Boris fixed it for her? He said he would but she didn't think he'd meant it. This guy was good at doing what he said he'd do. Amazing.

She rolled over and glared at the open space where a door used to hang. "Alessia, you have to do something. I can't fall for this guy." *Like I haven't already. Who am I kidding?*

No answer. Imagine that. Humph.

Every day of the past week, Boris wheedled his way a little deeper into her good graces. Mason was happy at Niko's. They both had roofs over their heads, food on the table, and beds to sleep in. North wouldn't find them any time soon.

With her eyes closed, she stuck the toes of one foot out from under the covers checking the temperature. It was okay. She stuck her other foot out to be sure. Maybe she'd get up.

Boris's voice boomed in her ear. "*Kroshka*, I have breakfast ready."

"Ahhh!" she yelped, jerked her feet back under the covers, and glared at him standing in her doorway.

He grinned. "You come eat. Sunday is good movie on TV. I put pillows and a nice blanket so you can rest on the couch."

"Okay, give me a minute and I'll meet you in the kitchen."

He nodded and disappeared down the hall.

It was a set up. It had to be. No man in his right mind did all this for a perfect stranger. Sure, maybe they weren't total strangers but still, who was he trying to kid?

A few minutes later, Sahara padded barefoot into the kitchen wearing an old, well-worn Springsteen concert t-shirt and sat at her seat at the kitchen table. It wasn't really hers but it was where he'd put her their first morning so she'd kept on sitting there, in her designated spot. If she moved to another chair would he throw a fit? Hmm? She moved over to the next chair, sat down and waited.

Boris turned from the stove with two plates in his hands. Without missing a beat, he walked to the table, put their plates down and smiled.

"Good. I like you to sit closer to me." He grabbed their forks and put hers next to her plate.

Oh hell, she'd really gone and done it. Sure enough, she'd moved closer to his seat at the table. *Just shoot me now.*

He sat and ate. Between bites, he said, "Tomorrow you go with Annie. She has big, new tugboat. The *Santos* is very strong for heavy ships."

"She said she named it after her husband. She must really love that man." Sahara waited for an answer. Alessia had forsaken everything and gone away with Salvatore. Annie had married Santos who was not, in any way, a seafaring man.

"They have been in love since high school but could not get married until she came back." He raised one eyebrow, looked her direction for a brief moment, and went back to eating.

"I don't get it. You want me to work with Annie's crew?" She wasn't sure she liked that. It sounded like he was getting rid of her. It hurt. It shouldn't but it did. Yeah, Alessia's curse was definitely working overtime. There had to be a way to make it stop.

"It is good for you to learn different tugboat. Annie is very good captain. You will like her." He kept smiling and chewing.

"Okay, if it makes you happy, I'll do it." She couldn't manage a smile so she brought her coffee mug to her lips and hid her disappointment behind the rim.

She still wasn't smiling when she put the mug down, but hopefully she didn't look like she was about to cry. She never cried.

Boris stopped eating. "*Kroshka*, what is wrong?"

"Nothing. I'm tired is all." She was up and moving quickly down the hall, trying not to run. Hell, the house wasn't that big. She made it to the bathroom, slammed the door shut, and leaned against it.

"*Kroshka*, open the door."

"Go away, dammit." She stared at the floor. She couldn't, wouldn't, fall for Boris. Yeah, like she had a choice.

"Okay. You come watch movie when ready."

She listened to his footsteps padding down the hall. What was up with that? Usually he was so quiet she never heard him. He could beat any cat when it came to walking silently.

She had to pull herself together. She was being silly. She unlocked the door and followed him to the kitchen.

From the set of his shoulders, she was pretty sure he knew she was standing there. She couldn't fool him to save her life.

She softly said, "I'm sorry. When I get this tired, I'm not myself."

"*Kroshka*." He stood and walked over to her. "Okay. You want to watch movie? I put blanket on couch for you."

"Sure." She walked to the couch and settled in with her head on the pillows that smelled suspiciously like Boris. Had he taken them off his bed for her to use? She reached for the blanket but Boris beat her to it.

He spread it over her and tucked it in. "All good for having nap and watching movie."

"Thank you." She looked up at him.

"Okay." He held her gaze. "I would like you to tell me what I did wrong."

"Nothing. You didn't do anything wrong."

He took a step back. "I think maybe I make your coffee too strong or you are tired of scrambled eggs."

"That's not it." She inhaled in a shaky breath. "You don't want me on your boat anymore. I get it. I'm not much help."

"I want you to learn new boat. Maybe I get one, if you like it. Annie can show you how large tugboat operates." He grinned.

He had to be kidding. "You can't get a new boat because I like it. They're very expensive and there's nothing wrong with *Connie*. You're fine with the boat you have." She mashed the pillow down and resituated her head on it. Great! Now she could smell him even better. God, she loved the way that man smelled. Clean with some king of exotic spice, the kind of scent that could melt a girl's panties in a flash. So not fair.

She asked, "What movie are we watching?"

Boris settled in his recliner. "*Overboard*."

CHAPTER 8

Misha worked on the *Lucky Desperado II* for three weeks and still had lots more to do. Sahara came by every few days to check on her boat and Boris was always with her. They looked like they had an uneasy truce keeping the peace between them.

The rumor going around the Riptide was that Boris had taken the doors off the bedrooms in his house after she'd barricaded him out of her room. Everyone was dying to know the real story and nobody was brave enough to ask.

Misha laughed to himself and glanced over at the yellow cat sleeping on his work bench. Some things required patience. Boris was not known for having much of that. Misha secretly hoped that for once his cousin would rein in his dominant side and let the woman come to terms with him.

He turned back to the project at hand. It was slow going on her old boat. The *Lucky Desperado II* had been built for speed and to handle the rigors of the sea, not bullets. The builder had meticulously put it together to be strong and fast. The broken pumps, tanks, and wiring were taking time to fix. He could order replacements for most of it but he was going to have to make some pieces himself.

He'd found some hidden compartments. Before he went any

further, he called Boris to take a look. They stood in the late afternoon shadows staring up at the hull.

"I wanted you to come alone so you can see this. Most of the damage is here." He pointed starboard side of the hull. Somebody tried to stop the *Desperado* from sailing."

Boris turned, half-facing Misha. "This boat is not worth much. Sashara only has diving equipment."

"It was very expensive when new. Now it needs more work than it is worth. There are a few, small, soft places in the wood. Okay for maybe one more year then she needs newer boat." Misha reached up and rested a beefy hand on the side of the hull. "I can salvage some of the fine hard wood and brass from inside if you want."

"I will talk to her later."

Misha nodded in understanding. "I found hidden compartments. You want, I can open?"

"*Da*, I found some inside the cabin when I was looking for supplies. I did not open, not my business then. Now, I think we need to know what is going on."

They climbed aboard and went inside. It didn't take long to get the first compartment open. A couple of seconds passed in silence as they stood staring at the contents. It looked like something out of the movies. Pirate treasure. Gold jewelry, very old coins, ropes of pearls, tarnished silver, and precious gems all piled together. They closed it up like they'd found it.

"She is pirate?" Misha looked at Boris.

"*Nyet*. She found sunken ship."

"Someone wants to take these things from her." Misha blinked and grimaced.

"You take long time to fix boat. Do the best you can for now." Boris frowned. "Tell no one what we found."

Misha could do that but the *Lucky Desperado's* days were numbered. He exhaled the deep breath he hadn't realized he was holding as he watched Boris walk away.

Misha spent the rest of the day wondering what kind of trouble his friend had gotten himself into. Pirates and their treasures generally came to a bad end. At least that's what he'd always heard.

He ate his dinner and locked his place down for the night. One more day same as the last. He took a shower and laid down on the mattress in the corner of his workshop.

He lived and worked at his boatyard. There was no point in having an apartment. Even when he'd had a room in a tiny apartment back home, he'd slept on a mattress on the floor, same as his brothers. His family had never had much.

Long ago he'd made peace with the probability of spending his life alone. He didn't like it but there was no help for it. Boris and the people that had become his new family were all he had in the world. Galveston was his home. He saved his money and promised himself that someday he would build himself a small house on the cliffs over Sea Wolf Bay.

Misha stared up at the heavens through the skylight in the roof. He could pretend he was far away, someplace where he wasn't the ugliest man alive. He was strong. He was good with his hands, good with wood and machines. He could repair ships and build fine boats but he couldn't undo the explosion that had wrecked his face. One look at him and women turned away. He'd grown a full beard and moustache to hide the worst of it.

And he was still a man. A lonely one and that wasn't going to change. He fed the stray, yellow tabby cat and it slept in the shed out back. It had hissed and spit at him ferociously when they'd first seen each other but the scrawny animal had been more interested in eating than fighting so they'd come to an understanding. It kept the rodents away and Misha fed it and had some company when he worked.

He shifted his weight and pulled his briefs loose. Yeah, he was in the mood to relieve some tension. An hour later, he still couldn't sleep and he was staring at the stars when a shadow fell across the skylight. What? There were no clouds in the sky. It was a crystal-clear night. Maybe he'd imagined it. But no. There it was again.

He got up to take a look. Something had been bothering him all day and maybe this was the reason for his restlessness. It had been getting worse since sundown. He pulled on his jeans and slipped silently out the back door. Hidden in the darkness of the shadows along the edge of the building, he waited to see what was going to happen next.

Sure enough, shapely legs came over the edge of the roof and started down the rope hanging along the side of the building. From the shape of the ass, it was definitely female and she'd knotted the rope at intervals perfect for her height. A professional burglar? But he had nothing valuable someone her size could carry. He watched as she silently touched down, let go of the rope and looked around.

Dressed in black, she slipped through the shadows heading toward the dry dock. The only boats out there were the *Lucky Desperado II* and the one he was building for himself. It didn't have a name yet.

He had concertina wire around his dock. Nobody was getting to the boats. Not from the outside once he closed the gates. She had taken the only other route after hours. The roof tops. The treasure was the only answer.

She climbed aboard the *Desperado* like she knew exactly what she was doing and where she was going. The half-mask hiding the top half of her face also held her dark hair back and it hung in a long braid down her back. Who was this mystery lady?

He made his way along slowly and quietly on bare feet. Getting on board was going to take some doing without alerting her. He was no light-weight and aged wooden boats tended to creak and squeak complaining like old women.

He could hear her rummaging inside the cabin. The noise made it easier for him to climb up the ladder without being heard. He made his way to the cabin door and stood there waiting for her to turn around. She wasn't getting past him with whatever she'd come for because it looked like she'd found it. She closed the middle smuggler's compartment and put everything back perfectly on the outside. No one would guess she'd been there from looking. She was that good. But he couldn't let her out of there with the *Desperado's* treasure.

She tucked something small into the pouch hanging at her side, stood up and turned.

She took one wild look at him and muttered, "Holy shit!" She looked him up and down. "I guess your stress wasn't relieved enough earlier. Either that or you're a very light sleeper."

"What are you doing here?" He eyed her backpack.

"Oh, I just came to pick up some things. I've got 'em, so I'll be leaving now." She glanced around the cabin.

Misha grinned knowingly. There wasn't another door and the ports were too small to fit through. That only left the doorway he was standing in or the overhead hatch that was locked. He had her well and truly trapped. "*Nyet*. You give me what you take."

She shook her head once. "Um, sorry, no can do."

"*Da*, you give."

"Stubborn, aren't you?" She grabbed the strap of her backpack and shifted her feet. "I'm gonna ask you nice to move. Please, get out of my way."

"*Nyet*." He wasn't moving and she wasn't leaving.

"O-kay. Sorry about this."

She ran straight at him, dropped to the floor and slid like a runner stealing home plate, taking his feet out from under him.

Misha hit the deck flat on his face with the woman squashed under him. He shifted to one side and looked down at her. All he could see were her whiskey-brown eyes and pink lips. The mask still covered her upper face. She was looking up at him and frowning.

"Time for me to go." She pushed him to the side and attempted to roll him off.

He braced his hands on either side of her chest and grinned. "*Nyet*. Not done yet."

She kicked and bucked to get free. "Oh, yeah. We're done." She scrambled to get up and barely moved an inch.

Misha settled in tighter on top of her, fitting his hips between her legs. She went still under him. He'd squashed her. He was at least one hundred pounds heavier than the woman glaring at him. Reluctantly, he pushed himself up raising his chest from hers. She needed to breathe. He liked resting between her legs but it wouldn't be good if she suffocated before he could memorize the sensations of her laying under him. It wasn't likely to ever happen again. He'd have to live with only the memory for company.

She pulled her arm back and punched him in the eye. He jerked back and she crab-crawled backward to get out from under him. "God, you're heavy." She got to her feet. "Now, stay down. I don't want to hurt you."

"*Nyet*." Misha was up and reaching for her. He might be big but that didn't mean he was slow. He had ahold of her. Maybe not the best plan.

Before he realized what was happening, she clawed her way up his body, wrapped her legs around him, dragged him to the deck and rolled him. Back on her feet, she swung her heavy backpack and hit him hard in the stomach, knocking the wind out of him.

"I said, stay down. Why are men so stubborn?"

She flung her backpack over her shoulder as she disappeared into the night. "See ya, big guy. I'll be back for some of that mattress action."

Misha sat up, sucked in what air he could and choked out, "*Da*, you come back, we fuck good."

He heard her call out. "You got it."

She blended into the darkness while he struggled to his feet. He knew better. Chances were, he'd never see her again. Everything he was ever going to get from her, he'd already gotten. He touched his eye carefully trying to assess the damage as he walked back to his shop.

The rope was gone. He could have convinced himself he'd imagined the whole thing if it wasn't for his painfully throbbing eye.

He called Boris.

∽

Sahara's phone vibrated and she answered. "Yeah."

"I got it. Now what?" Lona asked, sounding somewhat giddy and a little breathless.

Sahara smiled into the darkness at her end of the conversation. She kept her voice low and whisper soft, not wanting Boris to hear her. "Sell most of it and deposit the money in your account. You can wear the prettier pieces. Some of it was in a small, metal chest, probably Alessia's." She slid off her bed and hunkered down on the far side, away from the doorway.

There were no damn doors on her room or his. This was crazy

annoying. Who the hell lived like this? And it made it hard to keep secrets. Next, she'd be hiding under the bed to use the phone.

Lona teasingly said, "Okay. Hey, you might have told me that Misha guy lived in the shop and he's like the size of King Kong."

"I didn't know he lived there. How'd you find out?"

Lona sounded irritated when she bit out. "What do you think. I saw him through the skylight. Hell, it was hard to miss."

"I don't know what you're talking about. What was hard to miss?"

"He sleeps there if that mattress is any clue. And he jacks off before he goes to sleep. Except tonight he didn't go to sleep. I sat up there on the damn roof over an hour waiting. I thought he'd finally dozed off. But hell, no. He followed me out to the boat."

"But you got away."

"Of course, but it wasn't easy. He's got the grip of a boa constrictor and weighs two tons."

"Never mind all that. When the *Desperado* gets fixed, we'll go back and get the rest of the salvage. Can you stay gone till then?"

"I'm already at the airport."

"Can you take pictures and make an announcement that we've found *El Anochecer?*

"Sure, I'll take some of it to the maritime museum to have it verified first. That'll help lock down our claim."

"There's a lot riding on this. We can't lose it," Sahara hissed into the phone. "We won't have to worry all the time. Mason can go to college and you can get your beach cottage." She chuckled softly and added, "And have regular foot treatments."

Lona snickered. "Leave my poor, mangled feet out of this. I'm still standing on them. It's going to work out. How about you get a bigger, better boat to live on and we'll make sure Mason is safe? I'll put out the *word, The Sundown* is our salvage."

"Lona, I think we have a bigger problem. I'm afraid Alessia's curse is real and it's working."

"What the hell are you talking about now? The curse can't be lifted without the locket and I've got it."

"Not that part. The other part where the people that have the locket will find their true loves. Did you have Salvatore's Heart with you when you ran into Misha?"

"Yeah. And you had it when you took it from *The Sundown* and you haven't found your true love. Right?"

Sahara grinned. Lona got all tongue twisted saying, *El Anochecer,* and used the English translation, *The Sundown.*

"Um, well, maybe. These last few weeks have been kind of crazy but I'm getting sort of attached to Boris."

"No. Can't be. You don't mean it." Lona whined. "You never get attached."

"It could be. It feels funny. I like him, a lot. He really does it for me."

"Well, stop it. Whatever *it* is, this is not the time for that kind of insanity. We need to sell the locket to the Count's last male heir. Without it he has no chance of lifting the curse and marrying for love. He's getting desperate. We're his last hope. Alessia really must have hated his family."

"Yeah, well, she was heartbroken. Revenge was all she had left." Sahara's sadness for the lost lovers drifted around the room and over the airwaves. "Knowing she was losing Salvatore crushed Alessia. She'd did the only thing she could to make sure the men responsible paid, forever. She took Salvatore's precious gift to the depths so they would never be parted."

Sahara exhaled a mournful sigh.

"The locket's been found. So, unless there was more to the story, the curse should be broken when it's returned to Balboa." Lona scolded, "If this doesn't pay off, we'll have to go to plan B."

"That's a lousy plan. I hate Plan B. B is for bad. We could come up with our own curse and disappear," Sahara suggested.

"What kind of curse? It would have to be a really good one so we'd be famous for it. And it would have to keep North away from all of us."

Sahara wasn't sure that would work either. Lona had the locket on her when she found Misha. It was probably too late.

Barcelona Starze was going to find true love with Misha if Alessia's curse was holding true. And Sahara had every reason to believe it was. She was falling fast for Boris even if he was crazy bossy. He was getting closer every day to being her one and only. But what he didn't know wouldn't hurt either one of them. Right? It didn't count if you never said it out loud.

"Lona, you gotta marry for love. The rest isn't all that important."

"Yeah, right. And what about you? You'll be diving for conch to keep that ancient raft of yours afloat until it finally sinks for real, if this doesn't work. We need guys that can pay the bills and keep North scared off. Love is a fairy tale. This is reality." Lona sounded pretty sure of herself.

"I don't think so and Alessia didn't think so either. For hell's sake, she ran away with a corsair because she was in love with him. That has to mean something." Sahara was trying to make a point without Boris hearing her waxing philosophical about love and romance. She didn't think he even knew the words in English and probably not in Russian either.

"Un-hunh. And look what it got her. Dead. That's what. She died a bad death over that nonsense. I can't think of anything worse than drowning." Lona sounded so sure.

"She didn't want to live without him. She shot herself." Sahara sighed quietly and tried to push aside the unaccustomed sense of loss that had crept over her. Alessia lost her love and her life. In the end, what was one without the other?

"What are you talking about? The story goes she went down with the ship cursing the Count de Balboa and her father."

"Alessia held Salvatore in her arms while he bled to death and *El Anochecer* was sinking. She cursed the Balboa family and her own." That's the story everyone tells." Sahara dragged in a ragged breath. "But what they don't know is she scribbled her last thoughts in her diary and left it with a priest on the island. She was afraid of drowning and she was terrified of what Balboa would do to her if he got his hands on her. She had Salvatore's pistol and she planned to shoot herself if Balboa caught her."

That was the part of the story nobody knew except Sahara and now Lona. She had the proof in her backpack. Lona had the gold locket Salvatore had given Alessia, but Sahara had her diary. It had been wrapped tight in several oilskins and shut in a locked, tarred wooden box and given to the priest at Governor's Harbour church. Alessia wanted someone, someday, to know what had happened to her.

"So, did she? Did she shoot herself?" Lona's voice came out of the phone sounding like she was excited to hear the sorrowful details.

Softly Sahara uttered, "I think so. There're parts of the diary I haven't been able to translate. Some of the ink is smeared. I'm still working on it."

"Oh my god! She blew her brains out over that worthless pirate!" Lona shrieked and broke down laughing.

"Really? You think it's funny? I gotta go. Boris is probably awake and listening to every word I say. I swear the man can hear a mouse pissing in the attic." Sahara sounded tired and a little disgusted. Didn't anyone care that Alessia had risked everything for the man she loved and she'd lost everything, including her life?

She wasn't sure if it was Lona or Boris who had her at the end of her patience but it was time to hang up before things went to hell.

When Lona was in one of her moods there was no reasoning with the girl. She was coming down off an adrenaline rush from sneaking into Misha's and it would be a couple hours before she got back to some semblance of normal.

Sahara disconnected the call, crawled into bed and stared at the ceiling. The curse said the person with the locket would find their true love. The locket had been in the compartment under her bunk when she'd sailed into the Gulf of Mexico and found Boris. It also said if they followed Alessia's tears they would discover the real treasure. So far that was looking to be true.

She'd been running from North when she found Boris. He was kind to her. They were falling in love but she was going to have to leave him or lose everything her brother and sister needed to survive. It was building up to crying time for sure.

Why, oh why, did it have to be him? He was everything she'd ever dreamed of. He was big, strong, easy on the eyes, hard-working, steady, and had one hell of a sense of humor to put up with her silliness. She wasn't in any hurry to run away anymore but she couldn't stay. Her brother and sister needed her to make the salvage. They counted on her to take care of them.

Her only hope was that Boris wouldn't fall for her. And that wasn't looking to be the case. No, he was stuck to her like a barnacle on a hull. The worst part was she was getting used to it. She liked having the big guy around. He'd watered down her coffee and started putting sugar and creamer in it so she could drink some of it during the week and true to his word he made her special vanilla coffee on Sundays. He did his best to feed her things she liked and he cooked a perfect steak on the backyard grill.

She could see herself happy with Boris if her twisted excuse of an older brother would go the hell away and leave her family in peace. North had gotten too close this time. He'd found her in the Bahamas.

She rolled to her side and hugged the spare pillow to her chest. She imagined how it would feel if she was holding Boris. He was hard bodied and warm.

She was in so much trouble. *Thanks a lot, Alessia.* There had to be a sea goddess to save her from this maelstrom. She'd have to check on that in the morning and start praying.

CHAPTER 9

The next afternoon, Sahara sat with Annie and Lulu at Annie's kitchen table. She'd never had girlfriends or people to eat lunch with for the sake of having fun. She'd just taken a big bite of her club sandwich when a scowling young woman walked in and threw her purse on the counter. She had dark, almost black hair and a strong resemblance to Boris and Niko.

"Hey, Annie. Uncle Nikolai told me this woman is here and I want to talk to her." She glared at Sahara and sat on the closest chair.

Looking at Natasha, Annie asked, "What's up?" Then she turned her attention to Sahara. "This is Natasha, Boris's daughter. We grew up together."

Sahara gave Natasha a closed lipped smile. "Nice to meet you."

Annie nodded. "Boris has been like a dad to me since I was ten and went to live with my grandpa. We're family."

"Gotcha. That's great." She still didn't have any idea what she'd done to irritate Natasha. She'd never even seen the girl before this minute.

Natasha glared at Sahara. "You leave my papa alone."

Annie sat back and stared at Natasha. "Whoa! What are you talking about?"

Sahara hadn't seen this coming. She put down her sandwich and wiped crumbs off her fingers with a napkin. "Boris is a grown man. He definitely makes his own decisions."

"You are treasure hunter—a gold digger—that takes advantage of a lonely, old man. You want him to support you." Natasha enunciated each word carefully with a derisive edge. "He has been alone a long time and he does not need you."

Sahara glanced at Annie and then Lulu. They were part of Boris's family and she wasn't. She was outnumbered. Would they turn on her? It was time to find out.

"Have you talked to him about this?" She looked pointedly at Natasha. "It's his decision."

Annie focused on Natasha and added, "Think about this a minute. Papa knows what he wants. It's not right to interfere."

"He is an old man. He should look for a woman his age with a good job, not treasure hunter with broken old boat." Natasha tossed a copy of an old newspaper article onto the table.

Sahara pushed the paper away. "I salvaged *The Venetian*. It paid for my sister's college education. It put a roof over Mason's head and food on the table."

Annie and Lulu remained silent. Not smiling or frowning but they were watching and waiting for what would come next.

"You go now, before you break his heart." Natasha leaned back in her chair.

"I can't go anywhere. Misha hasn't finished fixing my boat."

Natasha took her phone out of her back pocket and placed it on the table. "I will call Papa and tell him you spend lots of money on your sister so she can go to expensive nightclubs around the world."

Sahara narrowed her eyes on Natasha. "Leave Lona out of this. No one picks on my kid sister. She deserves to have some fun."

"You can pay for party, you can pay for motel. You get out of Papa's house."

Sahara pushed the phone closer to Natasha. "Go ahead. Call Boris. Tell him you're taking me to a motel. I'm not stopping you."

Natasha picked up the phone and pushed the contact for Boris. Annie scooted back from the table while Lulu got up and settled a few feet away with her back against the kitchen counter.

Sahara sat back in her chair and waited. This would take it out of her hands. She'd be fine in a motel. She'd wait for the *Desperado* to be repaired and haul-ass back to *El Anochecer*. She'd put Galveston behind her. Done deal.

Natasha put her phone on speaker and waited for Boris to pick up the call. The confident quirk of her lip was like a cat about to eat a canary.

Boris answered, "*Da.*"

"Papa, I have talk with Sahara. I will take her to a motel. Okay?"

There was dead silence for two heartbeats. "*Nyet*. She comes home. No motel. You take care of Ivan. I take care of Sashara."

The quiet calm in his voice was terrifying. Lulu cringed. Annie winced. Sahara frowned.

Natasha yelled, "*Nyet*. You are an old man fooled by a younger woman. I will find you a good woman, not a treasure hunter."

"I am busy. We will not talk about this anymore. Sashara comes home." He yelled before the phone went quiet. Conversation over.

Natasha muttered, "Foolish old man."

She grabbed her purse, gave the women in the kitchen the evil eye and left.

Annie cleared her throat, resumed her place at the table and took a sip of her iced tea. "Well, that settles that."

Lulu sat down. "I'll take you home after lunch."

Sahara mumbled, "Wow, that man sure can yell."

"That's nothing. You should hear him and Niko go at it. That's yelling." Lulu giggled between bites.

"I'll keep that in mind. I'm more into to the quiet of the open sea." Sahara took a bite of her sandwich and reached for her peach-flavored iced tea. Somewhere along the way she'd grown a fondness for the stuff. Probably more of Lulu's influence.

She swallowed. "There's no guessing where I stand with Natasha."

Annie looked from Lulu to Sahara. "I've never seen her act like that before. I'm not sure what brought it on."

Sahara talked around her food. "It doesn't matter. I'll be leaving as soon as my boat is ready to sail. We have to keep moving. Lona travels a lot. Mason and I move every year when school gets out since North was released from prison. It keeps us one step ahead of him."

Annie asked, "Can't the police keep him away?"

"No. We tried that. All the restraining orders we've gotten have never slowed him down. He's gone by the time the cops arrive. If they don't catch him on-site harassing us, it doesn't count."

Lulu spoke up. "Please don't leave. Niko says he hasn't seen his brother this happy in years. Boris isn't sleep-walking through life since he found you."

"If it was only me, I'd stay. Natasha's right about one thing. I'm pretty much broke these days and I have Lona and Mason to take care of. They're depending on me. I can't let them down."

Annie sat back in her chair. "What if you could take care of them and give this thing with Boris a chance to see where it goes?"

"Let me know if you figure out a way to make that happen. I'm willing to listen." Sahara took another bite of her sandwich.

~

Boris disconnected Natasha's call. He didn't need his daughter treating him like he was some senile, geriatric, old man that had to be watched. She had chosen her husband whether or not he liked the man, so whatever woman he wanted was none of her business.

At the moment, he and Misha had a table to themselves at the Riptide. He studied his friend's face. He looked a little worse for wear. His nose appeared slightly swollen and he had a shiner of a black eye.

"She give you that?"

"*Da*. Strong woman. Krav Maga or Mixed Martial Arts, maybe both. Very good." Misha took a long swallow from his schooner of draft beer and pressed a baggie of ice against his eye.

"How old?"

"Her face was covered with mask. I could not see good but not old. She has long, dark hair in braid and she moves fast. Maybe she hurt her foot when I fell on her. She had small limp when she ran away from me." He grinned. "I feel her under me. She is very strong. I like."

"She punches you in the eye and you like her?" Boris looked harder at his cousin.

Misha had lived a lonely life. If this mystery woman made the man feel good, he'd help him find her. Problem was they had very little to go on other than she'd known about the smuggler's compartment on the *Lucky Desperado II*.

"*Da*. I must find her. She says she will come back for me but I don't believe that." Misha adjusted the ice bag.

Boris brought his mug to his lips and took two slow swallows. He lowered the mug and said, "Okay, we will find her."

"She is a thief. When I bring her here to live with me, she will not have to steal anymore."

Boris contemplated the situation while staring at the door. A young woman who was familiar with a smuggler's sailboat, treasure valuable enough to have people shooting to get it, and Sahara. It added up.

He looked at Misha. "Sahara has a younger sister. I hear them talking on the phone late at night."

Misha leaned in closer and lowered his voice. "Where? I will go get her."

"*Nyet*. We wait. She will come back. My *Kroshka* will bring her sister to us."

"Will she do it?" Misha winced and rearranged the ice bag.

"She will want sister at wedding." Boris grinned. "Every woman wants her family to come to the wedding."

"What wedding? You are going to marry Sahara?" Misha's brow wrinkled and he winced.

"*Da*. It takes me a couple more weeks to convince *Kroshka*. She is very headstrong woman. I must be patient." He grinned at Misha. "And you will have to convince her sister to marry you. We cannot kidnap women. That is very bad thing to do."

"Maybe her sister is not a thief? Maybe Sahara gives treasure to her sister?"

Misha looked and sounded more hopeful than Boris had heard him since they got word they were cleared to go to America.

Boris looked at the table and slowly shook his head. "You want a woman that fights with martial arts and I want a woman that hunts for treasure. We are crazy men."

"Okay, fine. I am crazy. No problem." Misha finished his schooner.

"What she took from the boat must be important. We will find out." He raised his hand and called for another round. He looked back at Misha. "There is terrible curse on the treasure. I read about it in the old book *Kroshka* hides under the mattress."

Misha winced. "What curse?"

CHAPTER 10

The drive home from the Riptide wasn't far but it did give him time to think. Sahara was slowly driving him crazy. She invaded his thoughts constantly and that kept him semi-aroused all day and hard all night. He wanted her the way a man wants a woman, his woman, and not only for one night. No, this was the one he'd been waiting for. It was time to get it done.

He was sick and tired of hearing her vibrator humming in the late-night hours. He was right next door on the other side of the damn wall. All she had to do was ask. No need to wear out all those batteries. He had thought about hiding her adult toy, but first he'd have to find it.

She'd gotten good at hiding things from him. That was another game they played. That old book and her duffle bag were missing. There was nothing of hers in the closet or dresser. He'd checked the air vents and the attic. She kept her clothes in her backpack and it wasn't big enough for whatever she'd had in the heavy-ass duffle she dragged around with her. She was ready to run but she wasn't taking the heavy stuff. So, where was it?

She was the most frustrating woman he'd ever met in more ways than one. He couldn't up and straight out ask her to fuck. American girls didn't like being asked like that. She'd be all insulted and he'd blow his chances of getting her into bed.

Lulu said he had to call it something else and make it sound nice. She'd made him practice saying stuff like, go to bed, sleep with me, roll in the sheets. That sounded stupid. Why not get to the point?

What he needed was an opportunity. Something where he carried her down the hall and he'd ask nice. When she agreed, he'd put her in his bed and that would be that. Problem solved.

He shut off the radio and parked his SUV. He was halfway to the front door when the first rain drops hit him and thunder rolled somewhere in the distance. He grinned. Perfect. Nothing like a rainy night for fucking, having sex, rolling in bed, more fucking. *Da*, yes, he was getting laid finally, hopefully. He couldn't take much more waiting, hoping, wishing, and masturbating.

He shut the door and looked around the living room. No sign of his *Kroshka*. He headed down the hall and stopped when she came barreling out of her room wearing one of his old t-shirts. He braced for impact when she flung herself against him and wrapped her arms around his neck.

"I'm so glad your home." She hugged him tight and pressed herself against him. "I hate thunder and lightning."

He smiled over her shoulder at his good fortune. "Okay. All good."

Sahara hugged him tighter if that was possible. "It's not good. I saw it hit a mast in St. John's Bay and damn near blow the boat out of the water. Lightning is dangerous. What if you got hurt? What if you got killed?" She didn't loosen the grip she had on him. "I was so worried."

Boris wrapped his arms snugly around her and hugged her back. She smelled so good, fresh and citrusy like she'd recently taken a shower. He'd missed coming home to the smell of a woman in his house. He liked her sleepy face at breakfast and the way she sat close to him at the Riptide.

He walked toward his bedroom with her body plastered to his and her toes dangling off the floor by several inches. "No problem. We are safe here."

"How can you be sure?" It sounded like she didn't believe him. Not completely.

Her head rested tucked up on his shoulder and her breath feathered over the skin on the side of his neck. It was warm and sent heat straight to his groin. He'd waited so long for the right woman to come fill the empty places in his soul. This little one was perfect.

He said, "This is a good strong house. I know." He stopped at the side of his bed. "You sleep with me tonight. I will keep you safe." He let her down slowly till her feet touched the carpet.

"Boris?"

She bit her lip and looked at him with wide eyes. He didn't like that look. She had to be sure or this wasn't happening.

"*Da*. What is wrong?" He really wanted to get the words right. His army training kicked in and he observed her carefully for any telltale clues he was messing up.

"Maybe it's not a good idea."

He had to think fast. There couldn't be any doubt between them. For him, this was for all time. There was nothing temporary about it.

His voice came out harsher than he intended. "What is not good? You think I am too old, not man enough?"

Well, he'd gone and said it. Shit! How did she always manage to bring out the brute in him?

"What? No. I don't know what you're talking about." She stepped back, bumped into the mattress edge and ungracefully sat down.

"I am not deaf. I hear fine. Every night." He stared at her. "You think I don't know what a vibrator sounds like?"

Had she broken every filter he'd ever had? And he'd never had many to begin with.

Her face puckered up before she fired back. "It's not every night and you're supposed to be asleep. If there were doors on the rooms like normal people..." she sucked in a deep breath, "and if you were sleeping like you're supposed to be, you wouldn't hear anything. Just looking at you is enough to melt any girl's panties. It's nobody's fault but your own."

He was out of patience. "I wait for you to want me. Instead you only want fuck? Okay. You want vibrator, we can use. Go get it."

She stared daggers at him. Oh hell, she was never going to get in bed with him now.

"No! How rude. I do not want fuck. You can damn well sleep

alone." She stormed past him muttering, "Of all the nerve. That's the least romantic thing I've ever heard, Cossack."

"Russian, not Cossack. I tell the truth. You do not like hearing it," rumbled out of him.

She yelled down the hall. "Just shut up."

∽

Sahara turned off the lights in the kitchen and the living room before she flopped down on the couch. Sitting cross-legged, she stared out the window at the storm rolling in. Talk about exasperating. That man was the embodiment of the word. They should put his picture in the dictionary next to it.

If lightning did manage to hit the stupid house, she wasn't going to be hiding under her bed. Hell, no. Even if it electrocuted her, she'd meet it head on, like everything else in life that had come her way. It was better than hiding like a coward.

She'd faced down every obstacle life had thrown at her, everything except Boris. Him, she was dancing around trying to avoid the obvious. She was falling for him. Correction. She had fallen for him and now she needed to get over it. He was so not into her. What kind of man asked a girl to fuck? Uncouth Russian, that's what. *Miserable barbarian. Cossack!*

She grumbled under her breath, "Do I want fuck? What kind of awful question is that?"

Great. Now, she was talking to herself. She flinched as thunder rolled over the house rattling the windows.

"Not awful. Honest." His voice came from the side of the couch nearest the hallway.

Sahara damn near levitated off the cushion. "Ahh! You scared me. You shouldn't sneak up on people like that."

He sat next to her. He was only wearing grey microfiber briefs that left little to her imagination. Was there no part of this man that wasn't huge? His chest was covered in curly, black hair. She could get into running her fingers through it. He was a walking, sex fantasy that invaded her dreams at night and her daydreams during the day.

His voice was as soft as she'd ever heard it. "I want we can sleep together. We roll in the sheets. You come to bed, yes?"

He inhaled deeply and let it out slowly. His eyes stayed glued to hers.

She didn't have an answer for him. Not a good one. "I want to but I'm afraid we'll be sorry in the morning."

"Why sorry? I want. You want. All good."

She scooted away from him to get some breathing room. The heat coming off his body was too inviting. It was all she could do not to jump on the man and do him right there in the living room in front of the picture window.

She had to tell him the truth before they were too far gone to turn back. "There's this curse and I think it could be the reason we're acting like this. These feelings might not be real."

Lightning flashed out in the street and thunder rolled over the house rattling the windows again, only worse this time. Sahara cringed and tried not to let on she was terrified.

Boris opened his arms. "Come, *Kroshka,* I will hold you."

Sahara didn't waste any time crawling over to him and straddling his lap. She squeezed herself as close to him as she could get. They were belly to belly and face to face with her arms around his neck. She wanted to love the man so bad and all he wanted to do was fuck. Not the ideal romance. She wanted more from him.

His breath whispered across her skin. "What are you talking about? What curse?"

If he really wanted an answer, he'd better be ready to listen to a long and complicated bedtime tale of sorrow.

"It's a long, sad story." She rested her head on his shoulder. "This feels good."

Her hands glided down his arms and wrapped around his powerful chest. This might be the closest she'd ever get. She inhaled his scent. Perfect. Yeah, she had it bad. Just like poor Princess Alessia. Falling for the right man at the wrong time.

He settled back and got comfortable. Guess they weren't going to bed any time soon. Maybe that was a good thing. At least for now, while she got a grip on what she wanted.

He rubbed her back gently. "You tell me story. I listen."

"Well, it was a long time ago. I was taking a tour of an old palace in Genoa. Some pretty, little things caught my eye and I saw a letter left by the last princess saying goodbye. She was running away with her true love." She sighed and fingered the hair above his nipple. It looked coarse but it was soft to the touch.

"Alessia had lots of long, golden-brown hair. She would tie it up with silk ribbons and strings of pearls and the tiny golden charms like the ones in the display case. One day this young man showed up in the local market selling beautiful things from far away. Things that she'd never seen before. His name was Salvatore."

She yawned and snuggled down deeper against his thighs, letting his heat radiate into her. If she could stay this safe and warm forever, she'd be happy.

Boris smiled at her story or maybe to himself. She couldn't tell for sure. She caught the corner of his mouth curving upward. It made her happy to see it for no other reason than he looked pleased. Lately it had been happening more often.

"*Da*. I am listening."

"Well, they met in the market every chance they got. And they slowly fell in love. But her father had arranged for her to marry a wealthy Spanish count, the Count Augustin de Balboa." She shuddered at the thought. "He was a cruel man. I checked. Alessia was right to avoid him. She pretended to be sick with girl problems and kept putting off the wedding."

Sahara yawned again. Thunder rumbled in the distance. She wiggled her center over his growing erection and got comfy. It was so fine having him tucked up under her. He fit her perfectly. Boris was meant for her. The sea goddesses had provided the answer to her prayers. She didn't want to fight it anymore. There had to be a way to work it all out.

"Salvatore was handsome and dashing and strong. But he was poor with no family. He wanted to marry Alessia but if he got caught, they'd hang him. Salvatore was actually a corsair." Sahara sighed against Boris's shoulder. "He was a bad man who'd done terrible things but Alessia loved the tiny bit of good still left in him. They married in secret. Then, when the time was right, she snuck out to meet him on the docks and they sailed away on his ship, *El Anochecer, The Sundown*."

She rubbed her cheek on his shoulder, like a cat claiming its territory. "The Count was furious when he found out and he followed them for months. He caught up to them in the Bahamas. There was a terrible battle between the two ships and Salvatore was mortally wounded. Alessia refused to leave him. As *El Anochecer* was sinking, Alessia put a terrible curse on the treasure and both families, hers and Balboa's."

She pressed tighter against Boris if that was possible. He was so cuddly and warm she couldn't get close enough. He was also an alpha male, and he'd absolutely go ballistic if he knew she thought he was perfect for snuggling. He had the right touch. His arms were strong and safe, not the smothering kind that threatened to squeeze the life out of her.

He was getting harder by the minute. She could feel him swelling against her. Yes, he was right between her legs the way she'd imagined he might be someday. And someday was now. She couldn't stop herself from rubbing slowly against his erection. She wanted him so bad.

"*Da, Kroshka*, then what happened?" he rumbled.

Her hand stilled over his rapidly beating heart. She'd done that to him. Was there a sea goddess to pray to that would fix it so he'd fall in love with her? She'd have to check on that in the morning.

"Um. Oh. Well, anyone that has the gold locket, Salvatore's Heart, will find their true love like they did. But the men in both families will never find any love at all until they have the heart. It went to the bottom of the sea with Alessia and Salvatore. Her family died out, and his is down to the last male heir."

"But you found it." His voice came out soft and a little breathless.

"I did. I had it and now Lona has Salvatore's Heart." She exhaled slowly against his neck.

"You touched it?" he asked.

"I had to pick it up and put it in my belt bag." She kissed the side of his neck and licked her lips. "You taste good."

Boris swallowed hard. "This curse says you meet your true love, not fall in love with first man you meet. Yes?"

"Not exactly. It says, you will find your true love. That's different than meeting your true love. I found you out there in the Gulf of Mexico. Salvatore's Heart was under my bunk. I opened my eyes and there you were."

"I am lucky man. Fine good curse." He stood with Sahara wrapped in his arms and her legs around his waist. "We go to bed now. We find this love they lost. *Da,* okay, yes?"

"*Da.* But only if you talk nice to me." What on earth was wrong with her? She was starting to talk like him.

"Okay, kiss good, fuck good, you will like very much, very nice."

"Right." she murmured. The man was impossible. Impossible for her not to love him, broken English, and alpha-maleness aside. The goddesses had to know she'd tried not to fall in love with him but some two-hundred-year-old curses couldn't be broken. Leave it to her to find that one. She and Lona were doomed as doomed could be.

Boris carried her to his bed. No detour. She untangled herself from him so she could sit down and scoot back closer to the middle.

This was the first time she'd gotten a good look at him without his pants on. He had muscular thighs and chiseled calves. Definitely not skinny bird legs. Was there no part of this man that didn't turn her on and leave her breathless?

She asked, "When you were snooping on my boat did you touch Salvatore's Heart?" She needed to know. The curse could be on him, too.

"*Nyet.*" He peeled off his trunks. "Misha and I found your smuggler's hiding places but we did not touch the things inside." His erection jutted up powerfully.

He caught her off guard when he reached out and pulled the borrowed t-shirt over her head.

Sahara covered her breasts with her arms. "Excuse me. I like that t-shirt. It smells like you and I can take off my own clothes."

"*Nyet.* That is my shirt." He inclined his head toward her. "And I want to see you."

"No. Turn off the lights." She aimed a stern glare at him. She needed to set some boundaries on this guy or he'd run all over her.

"Better with lights on." He grinned.

"It is not. You don't have a romantic bone in your body, do you? Whatever happened to soft music and candlelight?"

"Not necessary. We fuck now."

Thunder rolled, the lights flickered and went out.

In the darkness, Sahara mumbled, "Thank you, Alessia. Some men are simply heathens. Us civilized girls gotta stick together."

The mattress jiggled and Boris's hands touched her.

"See, you didn't need the lights on to find me."

He pulled her down and rolled on top of her. "I like." He kissed her neck and kneaded her breast. "Very good. Take long time. Lights come on before I finish." His lips found hers.

The man could kiss. Who'd have guessed his lips would be so soft and coaxing. She parted hers and let him in. His way of silently asking was irresistible and she wasn't inclined to challenge him. She'd spent hours imagining this very moment.

She pulled herself together long enough to say, "I can shoot out the lights." It wouldn't do to let him think he'd won so easily.

She wrapped her arms around his neck and kissed him back. She would lose the light bulbs when he wasn't around. Change to lower watts, put in soft colors. Pink would make a soft glow. In the meantime, she'd take full advantage of the dark and of him. A hard man was good to find in bed.

She expected to be mauled by the bear of a man that everyone saw but instead she got big, warm hands touching her with reverence. She buried her hands in his hair but there was no holding his head still. His tongue invaded her mouth and for all that she was teasing him with hers, he was in control.

Fine, she'd let him have it his way, for now.

She got her lips free only to catch her breath as he moved down her body to suckle her tits. Oh, heavens, it was too good. She was restless and wanting him to get on down to the real deal. And like he'd gotten the message, he moved lower. His greedy hands blazed a trail down her sides with his beard rubbing against her skin, signaling his intentions.

It was awfully hot in his bedroom. She wanted to turn the ceiling fan up or the air-conditioning down. His next kiss at the juncture of her thighs incinerated all thought, leaving her only with the weight and feel of Boris ravishing her body. Her soul was already gone, captured. His.

She'd never ever wanted anything this much. Boris was born to please her. His fingers caught her thong and it was gone without ceremony. Nothing was getting in her man's way.

His mouth covered the soft warm folds between her legs, making her shiver with anticipation. Her breath caught when his tongue licked slowly over her clit, again and again. It was too damn hot in that room. It was plain he planned on keeping it slow and her on the edge until he was ready to take what he wanted most.

She moaned, "Please, I want you."

He continued his slow, seductive assault.

She begged, "I need you inside of me."

He apparently wasn't going to following instructions. He continued taking his time until she grabbed a handful of his hair and pulled, hard. His head came up and she looked into those laughing eyes. "Now, dammit."

Boris grinned. "My name is Boris, not Dammit. What you want? You tell me."

"You, deep inside me. That's what I want."

He slipped a finger in, working it around to her sweet spot.

She gasped. "Oh, yeah, that's good, but your cock would be better."

"You want fuck?"

"Yes, that's what I said. Weren't you listening?" She was short of breath and out of patience. Her heart pounded at an rapidly escalating rate while her body strained to find release.

She brought her heel up and rubbed it over his butt cheek wishing she had a good sharp pair of spurs. That would get him moving.

He kept looking at her like he was waiting for detailed instructions, so she gave him one.

"Boris, sweetheart, be a dear and fuck me. Now!" She groaned as he gently rubbed her sweet spot. "Please."

The clouds parted and the moonlight was enough to make out the smug smile on his face. Great. She'd created a self-satisfied, sea monster and an expert at getting his way with her.

He crawled slowly up her body until he loomed over her. They were back to being face to face. She was going to get what she'd asked for. This was not some casual hookup. He was going to take what he wanted, just like she'd asked him to. She'd gone past the point of no return with him, and she wasn't sorry.

He was positioned to be buried balls-deep with one good long push and there'd be no turning back. She didn't need to hear the words to know what he was all about. The man had made up his mind.

His cock nudged her entrance. He growled, "You want?"

This was it. "Yes. I want you. You're the one."

He pushed forward slowly at first. She inhaled at the sensation, she could tell he was going to knock the breath out of her. His thick cock filled up every last bit of her core and stretched her to the max. It was sooo good. She'd never get enough of him.

Her fingers twisted in the sheets as her hips bucked to meet his thrusts. Yes, she was going to take all of him and come back for more. They had all night long to get this done.

She grabbed his arms and wailed, "Oh, hell yes. Harder. Do it. I need you."

After she uttered those famous last words, her world went on tilt and she got everything the man had to give. Flesh slapped together and her boobs jiggled to the oldest rhythm on earth. They shook the bed and rocked the house with their pent-up longing finally set free.

He was true to his word. He took his time pushing her over the screaming edge. His resounding roar followed by a rush of hot wetness flooded deep within her core to complete their union. Nothing would ever be the same. Boris would always be a part of her. He slowly moved off to the side and collapsed next to her.

Thank goodness the lights hadn't come on. She didn't need him seeing what a hot, sweaty mess she was. He'd rocked her world.

He looked at her, wide awake, his hand resting on her hip. "We are together now."

"Yeah, I think you're right." She wasn't panting anymore but she was still not back to breathing slow and easy.

She rolled to face him. "It's never been like that for me."

His lips curled into an easy smile. "It will get better."

"I might not live through it, if it gets any better. I think my heart stopped." She brushed his cheek. "What am I going to do with you?"

"Sleep in my bed every night and I will show you." He pulled her close and draped his leg over hers.

A little while later, he was sound asleep. She cleaned up and flipped the light switch off on her way back to bed. She didn't need to come awake to the overhead ceiling fan lights blasting her in the eyeballs at some unholy hour of the night, morning, whatever.

If she'd been tired before, she was completely worn out now. He, on the other hand, would probably bounce out of bed a whole new man at the first hint of dawn. Well, she'd see about that.

She crawled back into bed, snuggled up to his side and draped her arm over his waist. He was amazing. Best sex ever. Who knew? The Russian boys had it going on. When the word got out, none of them would be safe. Girls would be hunting them mercilessly. She'd get Lona on it first thing in the morning.

Hello, Misha.

CHAPTER 11

*B*oris woke up when the bed moved. He held back his smile and watched through barely open eyes as his *Kroshka* padded across the room and disappeared into the master bathroom. She came out a few minutes later and flipped the light switch off.

When she didn't go back to her room, he let himself relax. She accepted him. Now that they'd gotten past their first time together having sex, there was hope for a future together. The first time was always the scariest. If it didn't go well, relationships tended to die by morning. Nobody wanted a repeat of lousy sex.

And even though she'd been hot for him, she'd been scared. He got that. His heart had damn near pounded its way out of his chest. A man's greatest fear is being unable to sexually satisfy his woman. That got worse with age. He had no idea what she liked or what she expected of him. Women expected more from men these days. Once her soft moans turned to cries of pleasure, his confidence was restored and all that remained was to make it the best she'd ever had.

He didn't understand what was so wrong about having sex with the lights on but apparently it bothered some western women. Lulu had told him that, too. No problem. They had the rest of their lives together for him to work on it. She'd come around to his way of thinking. Daytime, nighttime, anytime was good.

He closed his eyes and pretended to be asleep. The mattress dipped and then she was next to him all soft and warm. Perfect. It had been a very long time since he'd shared his bed. Too long. Thank goodness he hadn't gotten too clumsy to please his *Kroshka*. And he was determined to make her want him so much that she'd never look at another man ever again.

Hell, while they were sitting on the couch the heat coming off her had penetrated his skin. She only had a thong for panties and his trunks were made for comfort. They kept him cool when the days were long and sweltering. Every rising degree between her legs and her wet heat had throbbed against his shaft. When she'd rubbed her sweet pussy on his cock, hell, yes, the girl was ready for him. He got that message loud and clear. It had been all he could do to hold out long enough for her to finish the damnable story.

That was nothing compared to how hard he was for her by the time they'd gotten to his bedroom. He'd never been that hard in his life. It was to the point of being painful. He needed to get off so bad but at the same time it was so damn good he didn't want to let it go.

When he finally gave in and turned himself loose, he couldn't hold back the shout followed by the groan that tore out of him. Her wailing had likely awakened the neighbor's dog. The mutt barked like a horde from the Steppes was invading. He wasn't taking the blame for that racket. *Nyet*, that was all her fault.

He grinned into the darkness on his side of the bed. He might have to get a house with more insulation and a bigger yard so the neighbors wouldn't hear them having sex at all hours of the day and night. And there was going to be a lot of sex. It was time to get a new and bigger bed.

If he took her to Sea Wolf Bay, he could make her scream long and loud over and over. The only thing she'd disturb would be the local seagulls. He liked that idea. And he would make her scream. Thinking about it made him hard, again. At the rate he was growing, he would need relief soon.

He rolled over and softly said, "*Kroshka*, I need you."

It wasn't all that much later and the damn dog was howling loudly.

～

For what had to be the first time in her life, Sahara woke up on her own at six o'clock in the morning. And she was in the mood to ride Boris. The man had a voracious appetite when it came to her, which he'd demonstrated all night long. Along the way, he'd awakened a craving in her that hadn't existed before. So, now it was her turn.

He rumbled and blinked while she played with his cock and balls. He was all man and loved being gently stroked, licked, and sucked. His eyes fluttered open and the look in them told her what was happening registered with his brain, the one in his head, not the one in charge of his dick. That one had been on board from the beginning.

She stopped licking and smiled at him over the expanse of his abdomen, stomach and chest. "Good morning, handsome. How about you take it easy and let me go for a nice ride?"

"Good, yes. You ride. I watch." His head dropped back and his legs parted a bit more giving her better access.

"Perfect." She hummed with her mouth wrapped around his cock.

He fisted his hands in the sheets but couldn't suppress a moan.

She listened to him moan and let out the occasional grunt as his thigh muscles bunched. She was going to make damn sure he was hard and ready to rock when she climbed aboard. When he finally arched off the mattress, she stopped humming and crawled up his legs and seated herself on the broad tip of his shaft.

"Are you ready to have some fun?"

"*Da*, fuck me very good."

His face looked strained. He was getting close. She'd make him wait a little longer. Anticipation was good. It made the release even sweeter. Or so she'd been told. It sure looked like it might be true.

She slid all the way down his engorged, pulsing shaft. "You're the one, the only one. It's you." There wasn't anything else to say. She rode him to the end, until they were sweaty and breathing hard. Before she could lay down on his chest, he sat up and wrapped his arms around her.

"You tried to kill me," he accused. "I like."

"Yeah, you would." She ran her fingers through his messy hair.

"You need a shower." She kissed him. "I'll make the coffee while you get cleaned up."

Before she could get untangled, he took her by the upper arm, stopping her. He brought her close and kissed her. But this wasn't his usual kiss. This was something different. She let him have his way and it was soft and gentle and loving. Gone was the barbarian. This was her Boris.

When he let her go, she asked, "What are we gonna do?"

"We stay together." He slipped his hand between her legs and lightly brushed his fingers over her clit.

Sahara shivered. "Your daughter hates me."

"You are my woman now. Natasha will get used to it." He grinned. "No problem."

"Right. No problem. And you're delusional if you believe that." She gave him a quick kiss. "I'll get the coffee started."

Oh, God. She was in so much trouble. She was crazy-obsessed with the man. One touch from him and she wanted to tie him down and do it all over again, and again, and again. Better to get her mind out of his bed, or the gutter, or wherever it had gone and back on track.

They needed to go to work. That meant breakfast. She definitely needed a shower. She'd get the coffee started and he could handle the food. She could finally make his kind of coffee. The stuff was evil and dentist's nightmare of stains and damaged enamel. But it did get the eyes open.

The man was growing on her.

Finding her true love was one thing. Keeping him was another. She didn't know how to do that. And she had no idea how to settle down and stay put. The closest she'd come to having a home was her mail box in Neptune Beach and the *Lucky Desperado II*.

She had to put Mason through college, Lona needed regular foot massages to minimize her limp, the *Lucky Desperado II* needed a captain at the helm, and *El Anochecer* needed to be salvaged. She had absolutely no idea how she was going to tell Boris she had to go back to the Bahamas, soon. Time was running out. She could come back after she got the salvage sold, right? That could work, if he'd wait for her. And that was a big *if*. The man had all the patience of a badger.

CHAPTER 12

A few afternoons later, down at the Riptide, it was quiet enough that Sahara and Annie had a table to themselves. The dimly lit, cool interior lent a peaceful air to their lunch. With no one sitting near enough to hear their conversation, they spoke freely while enjoying their wine coolers and wings.

Sahara washed down a wing with her wine cooler. "I'm not very good at this tugboat thing. I appreciate you letting me learn on yours, but once my boat is repaired, I've got to get back to work."

"Not a problem. I think Boris is looking for a reason to get something bigger and more powerful. I'm pretty sure it's a guy thing. Have you thought about running a party boat? You could take people sailing and fishing." Annie reached for another wing.

"I've checked around. It seems like there's lots of that already but you never know." She dipped a wing in sauce. "Misha seems like a nice guy. The work he's done on my *Desperado* looks really good. I wish he'd done the refitting for me the first time."

Annie grinned, chewed and swallowed. "He's kinda shy till you get to know him. But he's one of the good guys." She sighed. "Most people don't look past the wild hair and scars to see the real man."

Staring down at the table, Sahara softly said, "I think my sister, Lona, likes him."

Annie's head popped up from studying the wing bowl. "Really?"

"Yeah. It's Alessia's curse." Sahara met her gaze. "After she put Salvatore's Heart in her bag, she found Misha. Every time I talk to her, all she wants to know is stuff about Misha. I'm afraid he's her true love and neither one of them has a clue what they're up against."

Considering North knew about the treasure, there was a very real possibility he'd ambush her out on the open sea. She might not make it back. Somebody needed to get Lona to come to Galveston where she could meet Misha in the usual way. And not by assaulting him in the middle of the night. There had to be a way to give him a chance to know the real Barcelona Starze and fall in love with her.

"I've never heard of Alessia's curse." Annie shook her head. "I've listened to a lot of sea stories, could it be called something else?"

"Princess Alessia fell in love with a pirate, a corsair named Salvatore. His ship was *El Anochecer*. After all the bad things he'd done, people said he was a heartless bastard. When he met Alessia, he changed. He fell in love with her."

Annie nodded. "Okay, this is starting to have a familiar ring to it. Go on."

"He had a big, beautiful, gold, heart-shaped locket he'd sworn to give to his one true love. It was worth a fortune. He gave it to Alessia so she'd always have his heart." Sahara let that sink in.

"Holy shit! You found *The Sundowner*." Annie's eyes were all but popping out of her skull. "Alessia was the stolen princess bride of Genoa. Some filthy pirate snuck into the palace and stole her right out of her bed in the middle of the night."

"That's her but that's not what happened. I have her diary: she ran away with him. I've been doing my best to translate it, but between the old words I can't find translations for and the way she wrote, it's very slow going. I'm stuck with simple stuff like, 'the small stones he gave me are the colors of spring flowers, and today I discovered he has given me the most blessed gift of all,' what the hell does that mean?" Sahara shrugged her shoulders and took several swallows from her bottle. "She put a curse on her father and the Count de Balboa before she killed herself. I found the locket Salvatore gave her to seal their love. The Balboa heir needs it to lift the curse. I gave it to Lona."

"Wow. What a story. And Lona knows about Misha?"

"Yeah, but she might not give him a chance to know her."

"And you're telling me because..." She let it hang there in silence.

"My boat is almost fixed. Salvaging is dangerous. Between poacher's, pirates, sharks, and my older brother, North, there's always a chance something could happen and I won't make it back. And I can't tell Boris."

"Can't tell Boris what?"

"He doesn't know Lona was here and ran into Misha on the *Desperado*." Sahara exhaled slowly. "Lona picked up the locket so she could sell it to Sebastian de Balboa. She needs the money."

"Ah. I get it. If all goes well, you'll invite Lona to come for a visit. I'll throw a party and get Misha to come. We'll get them together in the backyard and voilà. They find each other." Annie grinned and grabbed another wing.

"Great, but if all doesn't go well, you'll have to get Lona here for some other reason. There are some things of mine at Boris's house. You can tell her she has to come get it in person." Sahara picked up another plump piece of chicken. All the scheming was making her hungry. "But for now, you can't tell anyone Lona was here." She bit into the tender wing. Their plan might work. It was better than nothing.

Annie nodded. "Okay. So, how are you and Boris getting along?"

"Good. Better. I get that Natasha's trying to protect her father. I can't blame her for that. But I'm not a thief. That would be my older brother, North. After our parents died, he burned through his money. When it ran out, he forged documents to steal money from our trusts. It got ugly."

Annie looked solemn and reached for her cooler. "Family fights are the worst. Believe me, I know." She took a drink and put the bottle down. "Did it work out okay?"

Sahara sat back and nodded. "We got by for a while. But North was wiping us out faster than I could stop him. Things got tight and I dropped out of college." She swirled a wing through the Riptide's special sauce. "I'd spent a lot of time with my folks hunting for lost treasures. I knew how to do it, so I did. *The Venetian* salvage got us enough for Lona to finish her college degree and get her feet fixed. It's kept us afloat while I get Mason through school. But now I need to get Mason through college."

"Wait, back up. What's wrong with her feet?"

"North is a mean drunk. He stomped on her with his cowboy boots and broke a bunch of bones. She was an amazing acrobat and ballet was a breeze for her. She couldn't dance anymore after that." Sahara drew in a deep breath and let it out slowly. "She has to have foot massages and she uses one of those spa machines at home every night."

"I'm so sorry. It must have been hard for all of you."

"I'm fine. But Lona not so much. It took some time but when she could walk again, she went and signed up for martial arts classes. Nobody's ever gonna hurt her without having a fight on their hands. She's an expert now. She teaches in the winter and spends the summers someplace fun and glamourous. She doesn't stay in one place long enough for North to find her." Sahara took a couple swallows and finished off her cooler. She waved it at the bartender, she needed another one. "This round is on me."

Annie asked, "So, what are you gonna do now?"

"Get Mason to graduate high school and get him into the best college I can afford." She smiled as the waitress put the frosty, fresh coolers on the table. "He deserves a shot at a better life. He's a good kid."

"And Boris? What about him? I'm sure if you explain it, he'll understand. He's pretty amazing that way."

Annie had a vested interest in Boris, so Sahara had to be careful what she said next. "He's wonderful. He sure didn't have to help me and Mason. When I get the salvage sold, I'll pay him back for the room and board. When Natasha sees I'm not taking his money, she might back off."

"He won't take it. He's not wired that way. In his world, men take care of their women and family."

"Yeah, but we're not his responsibility. He's done way more for me and Mason than anyone ever has."

"I'm sure he only did what he wanted to do. You're not going to find a better man." Annie stopped eating and stared at Sahara. "Unless you don't love him."

"That's the catch. I do love him but what if it's only the curse? What if it's not real and it wears off? The *Desperado* hasn't got many more years left. It's old and I'll need to get another boat to keep working or change my line of work." She looked around the diffusely lit room. "I can't keep diving. I'm worn out, exhausted. I promised Lona I'd get her enough to buy a small beach cottage somewhere North can't find her. After that I'm not sure what I'll do. It wouldn't be fair to drag Boris into all that mess."

Annie nabbed another wing. "Life's not fair. You know that. I think you should stay right here and let Boris help you. We can build a nice, little place for Lona. I know a spot hardly anybody else knows about. It's a Tugger's secret hideaway."

"What are you talking about?"

"There's an out-of-the-way place not far from here. She might like it there. And if things go right, your brother would have to get past Misha." Annie smirked. "What are the chances of that happening?"

"From what I've seen of Misha, not good." Sahara pointed a wing at Annie. "You know, this might work."

Annie was a few years younger than her. If Annie could settle down after years working as a deck officer on merchant freighters roaming the seas, there was no reason Sahara couldn't.

Sahara giggled. "You know I had the locket under my bunk when Boris came aboard the *Desperado*. I found him. Of course, if you ask him, he'll say he found me sinking into the Gulf."

With her eyes perusing the wing bowl, Annie said, "He's my papa. Always has been since my biological father dumped me off on the dock to live with Grandpa. I've seen Boris through a lot of sadness." Her lips drew to one side while she contemplated the remaining selection. "He took it hard when my grandma Connie died. You've come along and put a smile on his face I haven't seen in years. You're good for him. That's what I know."

Sahara tried not to cough when she nearly swallowed the wrong way. "Your grandma?"

"Oh, crap. Here we go again." Annie put down her wing and wiped her fingers. "Who gives a damn how old the lady was? She was what he wanted. They were good for each other. For a few months there, they had the world on a string." Annie picked up her cooler and took a drink. "I'm really done with this hang up people have about age. If it works, it works." She glared at Sahara. "Is there a problem with that?"

Sahara shook her head. "No, no problem. It's all good."

"Glad to hear it." Annie picked up the fat wing she'd been eyeing and asked, "If the curse works, then is Boris the man for you?"

Sahara put her food down. "It only says you'll find your true love. Not that they'll love you back or that it will turn out to be happily-ever-after. Alessia found Salvatore and they died running for their lives from a monster. There was no happily-ever-after for them."

Annie quit chewing. "But you love Boris."

"Not my fault. Nowhere in the curse does it say that the love would be returned. That's the catch."

"But Boris does. I know it. I can see it when he looks at you." Annie leaned into the table.

"Men change their minds all the time." Another swallow of cold wine cooler and maybe the lump in her throat would go down.

"Not Boris. He's not like that. He loved Connie. He waited for her. He never gave up on them being together."

"Sounds like she was his true love. I'm glad he found her. But that kinda leaves me out." Sahara downed the last of her cooler and the lump was still threatening to strangle her. "It really is a curse."

"No, that can't be right. Grandma told me she was only keeping him company until the right woman came along. I know he's in love with you. You're the one."

Sahara talked around a mouthful of chicken. "Why don't you try making heads or tails out of that damn diary, and then we'll see what's what."

It was all going to turn out fine for Lona and Mason. She'd done her best to make sure of it. If anyone could bring Lona to Galveston, Annie could. She'd do it for Misha. He was family.

As for herself, that was another story. She was afraid she was going to end up like Alessia. The right man, the wrong time, and the watery grave of a love lost to the sea. She waved at the waitress for another round. She wasn't going down without a fight. Or a drink.

CHAPTER 13

The morning sun peeked through the blinds, waking Sahara. Boris slept quietly next to her. She took in the sight with an appreciative eye. No man had a right to be so handsome at that hour. A couple weeks had passed since her conversation with Annie. Every night she tossed and turned, haunted by *El Anochecer*. Then Boris would rest his arm over her and she'd settle down, temporarily safe and secure in his protective embrace.

She fell deeper in love with him daily. He was definitely her man. How would she manage without him to see her through thunderstorms and long, cold nights sleeping alone on the *Desperado*? They didn't make a blanket that would keep her warm like he could. She couldn't imagine loving another man so deeply, ever. Not the way she loved Boris.

How much gold would it take to fix the pain of leaving him? That was the burning question she asked herself a dozen times a day and she was pretty sure the answer was, all the gold on Earth couldn't fix a lonely, broken heart. Apparently, Alessia had come to the same conclusion. Instead of staying warm in her fine home, surrounded by the wealth and security of her family or her soon-to-be husband, she'd run through the dark streets of Genoa to be with her true love, the pirate who had captured her heart.

Sahara shook off the sad thoughts. She wasn't giving up, she was stronger than that. She would love on Boris every chance she got until time ran out. Those memories she would keep for the rest of her life or until he took her back. However long that was. Considering how stubborn he was, it might be a while.

After she salvaged *El Anochecer*, she would come back and they could pick up where they'd left off. She'd be careful with her money and get a local job to pay for Mason's college. It could work: if North would leave her alone and if Boris would take her back. Those were two big ifs, and the odds were not in her favor. *Hello, Alessia. I get it. You love them so much you step out onto thin air and hope the fall doesn't kill you.*

Sahara brushed her hand up his chest. She loved the feel of his chest hair under her fingers. The man was a beast. Her beast. She was so in love with him and she didn't have the guts to even start that conversation, never mind the one with her going back to *El Anochecer*. No, that was something for another day.

If she blabbed that she was hopelessly in love with him, she'd seal her own doom. She'd never have the strength to leave him, and he'd know it and use it against her. So, she kept it to herself, protecting her way out. She could deny being a fool for love and he'd never know the difference.

In the soft morning light, she reached for what she wanted most. Her hand rested over his beating heart.

He grumbled, "*Kroshka*, you make me want sex."

"Hm, that's the idea. I want you to want me." She inwardly grinned at his new way of speaking. He'd mellowed from wanting to fuck, to having sex. He was changing.

He rolled her direction. "I want you very much."

∽

They got a late start but no one seemed to mind. And by the time they tied up at the dock that evening, they'd worked more than enough to call it a very good day.

She was caught off-guard when he released the crew and turned around wearing a wolfish grin. "I have a surprise. We stay on board."

"What surprise?" She watched everyone else disappearing, headed to their cars and trucks. "What's going on with you?"

"Come, I fix good food and we stay here." He held out his hand. "Come. I show you."

She took his hand and followed him into the cabin. It was so unlike him. He usually couldn't wait to get her home. He was insatiable, like he couldn't touch, hold, and kiss her enough. Even when they were too worn out to have sex, he still wanted to be close to her. She'd discovered that he liked to touch and be touched. She would never have guessed it when they first met.

He had no problem pulling her onto his lap while sitting in his recliner. He liked holding her. Had they broken the mold after they made Boris, because she'd never heard of this kind of behavior in men? She liked it fine but he was uncharted waters on her map.

What was going to happen to him the day he came home and she wasn't there? This was not the time to think about that.

Once inside, he gently put his hands on her shoulders. "I fix special dinner. We eat, then we are together. I turn off lights and put candles. I make you come very long time and no dog barking tonight. All good, yes?"

"Yes, it's good. You're the best man a girl could ever have." She hugged him tight. He was giving her the romance and candlelight she'd accused him of not knowing a thing about. She had been so wrong about him so many times, but she was learning.

In that moment, she desperately wanted to tell him how much she loved him but that would put an end to her salvaging days and *El Anochecer* would be lost. Lona would likely go and do something stupid. It would be a shipwreck. She couldn't let that happen.

She rested her ear snugly over his beating heart. He was her everything. He listened and heard her. In his own way, he'd given her what she'd asked for. No one else had ever done that. Boris worked every day to support his family and business. He wasn't the kind of man to let his woman go sailing off alone. She had no choice but to leave him, go salvage *El Anochecer*, and take care of her family.

If it came down to him or the treasure, the treasure would win. That thought was enough to put her appetite in the crapper. Well, tough. She would damn well pull it out of the crapper and put a smile on her face. She was not going to wreck her dream-date on the water with Boris.

They ate dinner on deck under the stars. Candles flickered on the table and romantic music wafted over the air. Wow, he really knew how to impress a girl, including serving the perfect white wine to go with the chicken in his secret recipe cream sauce.

That was another thing she was learning about him. He was more than capable of getting what he wanted. He wanted to have a romantic evening with her and it was happening. She looked down the dock at the other boats.

"Is that Annie's boat with the lights on?"

Boris glanced over his shoulder. "She likes to stay aboard with Santos. She had a special, sleeping space made for them."

"Oh, so that's why her cabin is so different. That sounds romantic and like something she'd do."

"There is nice place not far, Sea Wolf Bay. You will like it there. Very romantic, very private." He rolled the stem of his wine glass between his thumb and fingers. "We stay all night."

He had that look in his eyes and her girl parts were definitely onboard with a sea cruise. Actually, she didn't see any reason to wait that long or leave the dock.

∽

Boris watched his *Kroshka* sip her wine. He'd been in love before but never like this. There was more in his heart than having sex could convey. Making love with her wasn't enough. His feelings had grown way past that. There were times he'd look at her and forget to breathe. He needed her in ways he couldn't put into words.

"Come, I put blankets on deck and we look at stars. There is full moon tonight." They'd eaten dinner but he was hungry for more than food. His heart, his soul, ached to be close, to be joined in a way that could never be broken. He was desperate to show her all the things he didn't know how to say.

"You've thought of everything." She followed him to a spot on the deck with several blankets and pillows.

Laying side by side, they could whisper secrets to each other like children after the lights were turned off.

"This is perfect. It's so clear. The stars look like they're so close I could reach out and touch them." She wrapped her fingers though his. "Thank you. This has been the best romantic date ever."

He couldn't take his eyes off of her. "I have never seen anything so beautiful." He took her in his arms. "We stay here all night. I will keep you warm."

"People will talk."

"It does not matter. We are together." He kissed her slowly and thoroughly. He pulled back and asked, "You are happy, yes?"

"Yes."

His heart beat a little faster and he steadied his breathing. As long as she was happy, his world was fine, better than fine. He didn't give a damn what anybody said. Captain Boris was making love to his woman on his boat.

He pulled a light-weight blanket over them. He didn't want his *Kroshka* to hold back worried about being seen. They were outside, under the stars and that was enough. He toed off his boat shoes and pulled off his shirt. When he reached for his belt buckle, her hands beat him to it.

"Here, let me. I like helping you out of your jeans. It's like unwrapping a hot, sexy present." She brushed his hands away.

He was good with that. He'd unwrap his present next, prop her hips up on a nice, soft pillow and make love to her all night long. He would not leave any bruises on her backside from the deck. That would not do. He wanted her to enjoy the night so they could do this many more times. Her, the rocking of the boat, the stars overhead for romance and he planned on giving her lots of that. He would do anything for the woman he loved.

He eased the tank top over her head. "Ah, so beautiful. I want kiss you all over." He reached for her waistband of her cargo pants. "This must go." He pulled them down her legs as she shimmied out of her thong." He quirked an eyebrow at her bold move.

"They only get in your way." She slipped her hands around his chest. "The air is cool. Why don't you come closer? You promised you'd keep me warm."

"Yes, very warm." They sank into the pillows. He slipped lower while easing his way between her legs. "I want very much to kiss you here." His finger brushed over her clit.

"You'll make me scream. It's so good when you do that."

"I like."

"People will hear me." She tried to clamp her legs together.

His shoulders didn't give. He wasn't going anywhere. He was right where he wanted to be. "There is no one to hear."

She groaned. "Annie and Santos are a few slips over."

"They are busy, no problem." His mouth closed over her most sensitive area and his tongue licked her clit.

Her fingers threaded through his hair while she held his head in place. "Oh god, yes," she moaned. He liked listening to her sexy noises. It let him know he was doing things right and it made him hard thinking about what was to come. Time slipped away lost in the pleasure he was giving and receiving.

She caught her breath, grit her teeth a few molar grinding seconds and yowled, "Ah, yes!" Her thighs clamped tight against him. He kept licking until the lingering ripples and trembling stopped.

He watched her chest rise and fall with every breath she took as he eased his way over her. "You are ready for me?"

Her lips turned up in a satisfied grin. "I'm always ready for you."

His pupils dilated and an animalistic growl rumbled through his chest as the swollen head of his cock slid through her wet slit and sank into her tight heat.

He wanted to take his time but the blood rushing through his body wasn't going to let that happen. The hot friction combined with her inner muscles massaging his cock drew a hoarse shout from his throat. His balls tightened and he couldn't hold back his body's demand for release. Jets of warm cum pumped from his pulsing cock.

His touched his forehead to hers. "I wanted to go slow." He soft chuckle escaped between drawn breaths. "You are evil woman. Why you try to kill me?"

"You tried to kill me first. It's only fair I return the favor. And you did say we had all night and I'm not exactly done with you yet." She rolled toward him and hooked a leg over his hip. "Let me know when you're ready."

CHAPTER 14

For the last three months she'd slept with Boris, worked with Boris, lived, and breathed for Boris. She'd put off leaving as long as possible. The weather was changing and she was running out of time. She loved the man, but family responsibilities came first. She still hadn't found a way to tell him she'd be sailing away the minute the *Desperado* was sea-worthy. It didn't take a genius to know that day was coming very soon. Too soon.

Misha was almost finished. Actually, he was finished and he was stalling. She was letting him get away with it because she couldn't bring herself to say goodbye to Boris. That was gonna cut like a porcelain knife with razor-sharp precision.

After another long day working on the *Connie,* she sat next to him at the Riptide listening to the crew telling tales and laughing at the crazy things they'd had to deal with all day long. She leaned against his shoulder and looked around table. For once in her life she didn't feel like an outsider.

Annie sat next to Santos leaning into his side. Sahara watched them and wanted what they had. Captain Annie was in love with a biker. He had the look of a man in love with his wife. It was so obvious that they belonged together. It scared her to think that they'd almost missed being a couple. The odds had been so badly stacked against them.

When Sahara looked at Boris, there was the same devotion in his eyes. The guilt of holding back her feelings from him chewed at her. She didn't dare put into words how she much he meant to her. She couldn't make a long-term commitment to him yet, no matter how badly she wanted to. Mason and Lona needed her.

Alessia's curse was terrible and more far reaching than it seemed at face value. Finding a true love came with a price. Alessia had paid with her life. Sahara was afraid she would spend the rest of her days living with regret in the land of no return. She'd found her true love but she was going to lose him for all time. Boris wasn't the kind of man to wait patiently at home while she dived for lost pirate booty. Great. She needed another drink.

Her wandering mind was unceremoniously jarred back to the present when Annie pointed at the TV in the corner above the bar. "Isn't that your sister? The caption says Barcelona and Sahara Starze found *El Anochecer*. Look. That's a picture of the *Lucky Desperado*."

Sahara stared at the screen. Sure as the sun rising, there was Lona standing in front of the maritime museum with a Jolly Roger flag draped over one shoulder. So dramatic. Leave it to Lona.

"That's an old picture. The *Desperado* has taken a lot of damage since then. Now that the word is out, we'll have to salvage the wreck before someone else does. We've got a claim to it but if we don't get it done soon, the scavengers will." She looked around the table. "Misha says my boat's almost ready. I'll head out in a few days."

Boris instantly went stone cold and silent. His expression had no hint of any emotion, good or bad. This was not the way she'd pictured doing this. She wasn't sure exactly how she'd hoped it would go, but this definitely wasn't it.

Annie stared at Boris. She didn't smile, she didn't speak, it was way past ominous the way she silently watched him. Those two went way back. He was the dad that had taken her in. Hurt him and she'd be your enemy for life. At the first sign of pain, all hell would break loose.

Sahara needed damage control quick. "Once I have the salvage finished, I'll be back. I'll get Mason into school since he likes it here. And Lona will need a pedicure from the best salon in Houston. I won't be gone long." She patted Boris's arm. "You won't have time to miss me."

The broadcast went on to the next story and Niko changed the subject at the table. He must have sensed his brother was not happy with Sahara's news. For once she was grateful for his interference. Go Niko. How about those sports scores?

Hell, she wasn't thrilled with the news either, but there was no help for it. The rest of the evening was quieter than usual. Lona had thrown a very wet blanket, Jolly Roger flag, on their group. The Tuggers extended family was ready to shut her out if she hurt Boris. Natasha would probably come down to the dock and wave goodbye. Shoot her the finger was more like it, but for sure she'd be glad to see the *Desperado* heading for the horizon.

It wasn't exactly unexpected and there was nothing she could do about it, but she sure as hell didn't have to like it.

She'd talk to Boris when they got home. Wow, going home. That was a new script. She'd never had a real home, someplace she felt comfortable, until Boris. She corrected herself: she'd talk to him when they got to his house. There, that was more like it. Her home was floating, tied to Misha's dock. The *Lucky Desperado II* was finally back in the water where it belonged.

Their evening ended sooner than usual with a silent walk to the parking lot. No holding hands, no small talk, no questions, no nothing. She couldn't get a read on his mood. Only that he wasn't happy.

Boris sat silent as the Sphinx on his side of the SUV.

Sahara tolerated the quiet for about five minutes. Enough was enough. "We need to talk about this."

"There's nothing to say. You are leaving." He stared straight ahead.

"Lona registered our claim to *El Anochecer*. It's ours but the scavengers are already circling. They don't wait."

"Okay, fine. You go."

"I'll be back and I won't be broke. I'll have money for my share of things." She turned toward him. "I'll be able to pay for Mason's college."

"Okay, fine." He pulled into the driveway and got out.

Sahara followed him inside. But instead of going to the kitchen to fix their dinner, he went to the garage, brought in his bedroom door, put it back on its hinges, and closed it.

Sahara watched and waited in the hall. The ache in the vicinity of her heart, and the cold fear sitting in the pit of her stomach, was something she had never experienced before. Damn. Why did it hurt so bad?

He didn't even look at her when he shut the door. She hit it with the side of her fist and shouted, "What are you doing? We need to talk about this. Lona's trying to protect our salvage rights. It's not a big deal."

No answer.

So, there she stood listening to the lock click the closing note on their romance. He'd shut her out. Out of his room and probably out of his life, if she had to guess. Talk about being over, his cold shoulder and locked door said it all.

She grumbled under her breath, "Fuck you, Alessia. Your curse just hurt a good man."

Sahara trudged to the kitchen and dug around in the refrigerator. She needed food to settle her stomach so she could take something for her headache.

More than anything she needed Boris to come out and tell her everything was good. A tear rolled down her cheek and she brushed it off. It was not good and not going to be good. Ever. Never. She was cursed.

"Stupid." She could mutter to herself all night long and nobody would hear her.

But that's what she was, plain stupid to let herself get sucked in to this condition. She'd never find another man like Boris. Well, shit, that was the problem wasn't it? He was her one true love and she'd screwed him over but good. *Find me, take care of me, tolerate my crazy, show me how good a man can be, and in return I break your heart and leave you behind. Great, just fucking great.*

She'd have to settle for something less. *Thanks a bunch, Alessia.*

That had to be the worst idea she'd ever had. It sounded like something Lona would come up with.

She found some left over mashed potatoes and some green beans. It would squelch the noises her stomach kept making. She fixed a small plate and microwaved it. It didn't have to taste great. It only had to work good enough so she could fall asleep.

A few minutes later, she put her dirty dish in the sink and walked down the hall. She stopped in front of Boris's locked door. He could pound on doors and so could she.

She hit it hard. "Open the door, dammit. We're not doing this. I'm coming back for your ass, so get ready." She kicked the door for emphasis. *Take that stupid door*.

Nothing. Not a peep or a squeak on the other side. Damn.

She'd call Lona in the morning.

Boris shut his bedroom door and locked it before he said something he couldn't take back.

He'd found out the hard way that his dreams of having a loving wife and warm home were not going to come true. Sahara was going to sail away and he couldn't stop her. It wouldn't be right to stop her. She had family to take care of and so did he. He couldn't leave and she couldn't stay.

She'd come back long enough to take care of Mason but it would only be temporary. He'd been in the business of ferreting out the truth too long to be fooled. They were all but over. There were only hours left and she'd be gone.

His phone rang. Niko. Of course. Boris answered. If he didn't, Niko would be on his front porch in five minutes pounding on the door and disturbing the neighbor's noisy dog.

"*Da*. What you want?"

"Lulu wants me to call, make sure you are okay."

"Fine. See you tomorrow morning." There was nothing left to say. How fine was a matter of opinion. He was still breathing.

Niko shouted, "Wait."

Boris disconnected. He didn't want to hear anything. He didn't want to think about anything. He wanted the pain in his heart to stop. He shut off the lights, shucked out of his clothes and lay down on his empty bed. Same old bed. He hadn't gotten the new one yet. He'd wanted Sahara to go with him to pick out their bed. All good. One less thing for him to do now.

His phone rang again. He glared at the screen. Misha this time. "*Da*. What you want?"

"What you want me to do with *Desperado*?"

"Finish it."

"It's ready. You are sure?"

Boris grunted. "*Da*. All good." No one could help him with this.

He disconnected the call and wished he could disconnect the weight crushing his hopes and dreams as easily.

It was not all good. His *Kroshka,* the woman he'd found clinging to the *Desperado's* wheel for dear life, was not his, never had been, never would be. He'd been fooling himself. She was going after *El Anochecer* and leaving him behind.

He stared at the ceiling, his mind working overtime. He was not a man who gave up easily. There had to be a solution he could live with. Experience had taught him he'd have to fight for anything and everything that was good in life. But what would he be fighting for with her? Nothing, that's what. She'd never come right out and said she loved him.

He struggled to get comfortable in his cold bed, only to be interrupted by her pounding on his door and yelling. He was not in the mood to listen. She'd ignored him and, by damn, he'd ignore her and see how she liked it.

At two o'clock in the morning he gave up, got up and walked down the hall. She was in her room asleep, curled up facing away from the doorway, softly snoring and clutching a thick pillow to her chest.

There was still a chance he could fix things.

He padded silently across the floor, slid into bed and wrapped his arms around her. He needed to hold her, even if it was only for a few more hours.

His voice came out rougher than he intended. "*Kroshka*, I cannot let you go."

"Um. What?" She tried to turn but he didn't budge. "Dammit."

He had her stuck right where he wanted her. "My name is Boris, not Dammit."

"Oh, not this again." She huffed out a breath. "I know your name. If you didn't make me so mad, I wouldn't have to cuss you."

He put one of his legs over both of hers. "I like. Feels good like this. Maybe we get smaller bed. Sleep close."

"We sleep plenty close when you don't lock me out of the bedroom."

She pushed her butt against his growing erection. "You plan on using that hard-on you've got there?"

"*Da*. If you ask me nice." He kissed the back of her neck.

∼

This was it. Her one best, last chance. It was now or never. "Will you make love to me?" She didn't like the way it came out, both needy and breathless at the same time.

Dead silence hung in the air. She was afraid she'd screwed up this time for sure. The man never, ever talked in those terms.

He growled softly in her ear. "I thought you would never ask. I like very much to make love to you."

"Oh, thank God. I was so scared you didn't want me anymore."

"I always want. You are my *Kroshka*." He moved only enough to let her roll toward him. "We are together always. Yes?"

"We can try." It was enough to scare her to death. Always was a long time and it sounded like something Alessia had said. And just look how that had turned out.

CHAPTER 15

Sahara woke up the next morning to a silent house. She finally had the freedom she'd so desperately wanted a few weeks ago. Only now it didn't feel good. *Well, there you have it, girl. Be careful what you wish for because you might get it.*

She sat down at the kitchen table and wished Boris was there, cooking her breakfast. She'd eat it. All of it. If he'd just be there. It had never been so quiet and she didn't like it. At sea, there was always the swish of the water brushing the hull and the wind blowing through the rigging. Being alone had been safe.

Sniveling in his kitchen wasn't going to fix anything. She got up and made a small pot of his awful coffee, in case he wanted some when he got home.

After she fixed herself a cup, she called Lona and put the phone on speaker leaving her hands free to drink the now familiar bitterly strong coffee. The carefree voice of her sister came in loud and clear. "Hey, good morning. How's life in Galveston?"

"It sucks." Sahara sniffled back the emotions that were getting ready to overwhelm her.

"What? Are you okay?"

"Not really but I will be. We have a shipwreck to salvage." Sahara did her best to put a happy note in her voice. Fake it until you make it happen.

Lona bounced back in true Lona style. "Great. Once we get paid, you can go back to your tugboat captain. It's not like he's going to find anyone better than you in a couple of weeks. He'll be amazingly happy to see you after doing without." Lona giggled. "Lay him down, ride him hard and he'll forget all about you being gone. Baser instinct always wins. He'll be fine."

Boris was not that kind of man. Last night, she'd half expected him to come drag her out of bed and carry her off to his room like the Neanderthal she'd accused him of being. Instead he'd slid into bed with her and given her what she'd asked for. He'd rocked her world, again, some more. But this morning she'd woken up alone. Not good.

"Um, I don't think that'll work on Boris. I've got to get that damn salvage in the bank. I've been thinking about starting a tourist gig here. I can take people out sailing." She looked up at the ceiling. "Or I could go back to school and finish my accounting degree. His daughter, Natasha, says I don't have a real job and I'm using her dad."

"His daughter? Good lord, how old is this guy?"

Staring at the ceiling wasn't helping. She turned her attention back to her coffee. "Just right for me but she doesn't think so. She found the crap story from the Venetian salvage and showed it to Lulu and Annie. Then they saw you on TV last night. Everybody knows I'm a treasure hunter."

"So? You didn't do anything wrong. North was wiping us out. There wouldn't have been anything left if you hadn't stopped him. The *Venetian* kept us from having to eat corn flakes three times a day to survive. If they believe that melodramatic crap, then you're better off without them."

"But the tabloids have made us sound like fortune hunting villains." Sahara inhaled in a quivering, deep breath. "Look, we gotta get *El Anochecer* salvaged and I'll sort this out with Boris later, if he's still speaking to me."

"He'll be speaking to you or I'll beat his ass till he does. You're my sister and I take that shit seriously. Nobody disrespects you. Not after everything you've done for me and Mason."

"Speaking of Mason, I'm leaving him here with Niko and Lulu for now. He loves living with them and there's no point in hauling him away when he's finally getting settled in. He needs something steady."

"Great. The weather report is clear so you should make good time. I'll be ready and waiting. We'll knock this out and be home in time for supper." Lona laughed. "And then I'm gonna get myself some of that Misha for dessert."

"I've been hoping you'd give the man a chance. He's one of the good ones. Annie agreed to give a party so you can check him out like normal people and not a cat burglar."

"Oh, hell yes. Sounds great. He's so well hung I've got him on my list of things to do. He's built for fun. I know for a fact he can handle a hard ride and keep on pleasing. And with the payday from *The Sundown*, I can afford to enjoy him. Like indefinitely." Lona snickered. "There's a lot of that man to enjoy. Know what I mean?"

"I'm getting a picture I don't need running around in my head." Sahara shifted on the kitchen chair. "Misha is not your run-of-the-mill plaything. You need to treat him right."

Lona let out an exasperated sigh. "What is wrong with you? I've never heard you this down. What has that man done to you?"

Sahara lost it. She wailed into the phone. "He left me. I was asleep. He didn't say goodbye or anything."

"Fine," Lona huffed. "I'm gonna help you this one time. When we get to Galveston, we'll lock him up and tie him down till he comes to his senses. Convincing him will be up to you, but I can give you some pointers. We can tie him to the bed or hang him from the rafters, if there are some. That way everything is reachable."

Sahara almost choked. She was trying to stop crying and not laugh at the same time. The picture of Boris tied up was too funny and too awful to even contemplate. He'd rip the house apart and the bed wouldn't survive a minute. There'd be splinters and stuffing everywhere.

"Ah, no, we're not tying him up. He wouldn't take that well at all." She was still trying to wipe the tears from her eyes, only now they were from laughter.

"Fine. You figure it out. Get him naked and send me pictures."

"No, and hell no. You can look at Misha if you want to look at a naked man." Sahara giggled and sniffled some more.

"Look, see there, you're feeling better. Mission accomplished." Lona laughed. "See you in the Bahamas."

"Yeah, see ya, soon." Sahara disconnected. Wow, her day had taken an unexpected turn. Lona had a point. She'd told him she'd be back and by damn she'd show him. He'd better be ready to drop his pants and get fucked, all, night, long. And maybe all day.

Natasha could take her best shot.

∼

Boris and Niko sat across from Misha, staring at a map spread out on the scarred and worn, work bench. Niko looked at Boris and grinned. "See. All good. You go with Sahara and keep women safe."

Boris shook his head and glared at his brother. "What's all good? I have business to run here."

Niko chuckled. "You need vacation like good American. Lay on beach under palm tree. I want picture. I will ask Sahara."

"*Nyet*. No picture. Not happen," Boris snarled but there was the beginning of a grin on his face.

Niko kept smiling. "Ivan will take care of your boat and Annie will take care of business in the office. You help Sahara get treasure so she can marry you. Mason can go to school and Lona can marry Misha." He looked at Misha. "You get haircut and trim beard so she sees you are not caveman. Everyone happy. Okay."

Boris turned his attention to Misha. His cousin tended to take things seriously. Too many bad things had happened to him before they left Russia.

"You are okay, yes?" Boris studied Misha and grinned. "We see Bahamas and have pretty girlfriends."

Misha's wrinkled brow relaxed. "Okay. We go and keep women safe. I get to know Lona." He rubbed his eye. "Maybe, she doesn't hit me this time."

Niko snorted and chuckled. "She sees you cleaned up and likes big cock. You have good vacation."

Misha turned red from his neck to his hairline and muttered, "*Nyet*. American girls do not want me. She sees me in the dark. In daylight she won't like."

"Very dark at sea after sunset. All good. Pack what you need. We go." Boris laughed softly under his breath as he walked away, leaving Niko chuckling and Misha wide-eyed and speechless.

Boris drove straight home. He'd gotten up early, called Niko, and gone to Misha's. The *Desperado* was not sailing without him aboard. They needed supplies and he'd given Misha the list.

The girl had finally asked him to make love to her. He'd given it everything he had and was planning to do it again when he got home. He wasn't alone anymore. Whatever lied ahead, they would handle it together. He wasn't backing down or backing off.

His home had been empty for years until he'd found Sahara. She was his and it was going to stay that way. He looked down the road and turned into his neighborhood still smiling. At long last, Misha had been noticed by a pretty girl. What Lona saw in him was a mystery but it didn't matter as long as she liked the man and treated him with some kindness and respect.

Boris parked the SUV and walked in the house, feeling pretty damn good about where his life was going. The idea of a vacation, treasure hunting, and sailing with Sahara in the Bahamas was working for him. He'd turn forty before they got back but he was not an old man. One more damn day on earth did not make him old.

"*Kroshka*, where are you?" He walked toward the kitchen.

"You came back!" She came running down the hall in one of his worn-thin t-shirts and flung herself into his arms. He wrapped an arm around her and hitched her leg up over his hip. He liked it when she wrapped her legs around him.

She mumbled into his shoulder. "You're home. I was so scared."

"*Nyet*. Why scared?" He held her tight. Not letting go. He had a good hold on her. All the better to keep from being hit and kicked when she got mad at him. Experience had taught him to expect that the next few minutes were going to be tough.

"You left me. You weren't here when I woke up." She sniffled.

"I went to talk with Misha. *Desperado* is ready. We will go to the

Bahamas. All of us. I have never been on an island vacation. Good time to go now." He tightened his grip.

She went tense and tried to push away from his chest. "Let go."

"*Nyet. Desperado* is nice big boat, lots of room. Me, you, Misha, we go get treasure and have nice vacation. You salvage sunken treasure. Misha takes care of boat. I take care of you. All good."

"No. Not good. You can't go." She struggled to get free but quit squirming when she it proved pointless.

"Why is not good? You tell me." He waited patiently to hear the words come out of her mouth so they could clear the air and get on with the more important things he wanted to do. Like take her back to bed.

"You have to work. You're the captain of the *Connie*. You can't leave."

"I am captain. And I have good first mate. Ivan can work boat. If there is problem, Annie and Niko can fix it."

"Um, Annie needs you here to help run the company."

"Annie is smart. She can run company fine." He was sure Sahara was running out of excuses and would have to tell him the truth any minute.

Sahara sighed. "Fine. Natasha says I'm taking advantage of a lonely, old man. I don't want to come between you and your daughter. You can't come with me. When I have plenty of money, then I can come back and everyone will see I'm not using you." She pushed at his chest again but didn't get loose.

"I am not lonely anymore. You fixed already. And I am not old." His grin turned into a wicked smile.

"My brother, North, did a lot of bad things and I put him in prison. Some people think that was mean of me." She watched him intently. "Natasha wants you to have a nice lady, someone closer to your age with a good job."

"Why?" He had to ask so she wouldn't figure out he'd checked into her background the night he'd brought her home.

While she'd slept, he and Niko ran every background check there was. They had dug up everything there was to learn about North Dakota Starze. He liked gambling but he wasn't any good at it. He was in serious trouble and owed a lot of money to some extremely nasty people.

Boris and Niko were familiar with the kind of men North owed money to. They understood the danger even if Sahara and Lona didn't. North had to pay back what he owed or his lenders would get it from his sisters.

Boris could not let her go out sailing alone. Misha was concerned for Lona. Together they would keep their women safe. Niko would look out for Mason.

"You don't want to know," she lowered her eyes. "It was bad, that's all."

"*Nyet*. You are my woman. You tell me. No secrets." He wanted to shake the truth out of her but wasn't about to try it. Knowing her, he'd end up with two black eyes.

She looked straight at him. "You won't like me after this. You can forget your vacation."

"You tell me. I will decide."

She chewed on her lower lip and waited a few seconds before going on. "Lona was a beautiful dancer. North broke her feet. I caught him hitting Mason. I stopped him both times but I was always too late. I should have found a way to protect them from him."

"Without you there, he would have hurt them more. I believe you did the best you could."

"My best wasn't good enough. I took shooting lessons and practiced everyday so I could kill him if I had to." She was still staring straight at him without blinking.

"Good. You defend yourself. Strong woman. Go on."

"He stole from our trust funds and I pressed charges. North went to prison long enough for us to get away and straighten out our lives. But he's free now."

"Okay." He waited patiently, keeping his impatient impulses under control.

"He wanted *El Anochecer's* salvage and he shot up the *Desperado* trying to get it. We couldn't get underway fast enough, so I shot him. I took a chunk out of his leg. He went down but he wasn't dead. It gave me and Mason time to get away." She pushed against his chest. "Now you can let me go. I'm cold-hearted enough to shoot my own brother. And I'd do it again if I had to."

"Good. You protect yourself and Mason. I like. Now we go to bed."

"What are you talking about? I just told you I shot a man and you want to have sex? Are you crazy?"

"Yes, okay, crazy. I like."

"Women with guns turns you on?"

He walked down the hall, still holding her tightly to his chest. "You are good for me. I see your fine rifle on boat and know then."

"So, I won't have to point a gun at you to get you into bed with me?"

"*Nyet*. I go easy, no problem." He grinned. "Maybe I surrender if you offer me good deal."

"I don't know. You're kind of bossy." She smiled enticingly at him.

He stopped next to his bed and let her slide down slowly over his erection. The friction made him harder. "I am captain that makes me boss."

Her fingers curled around the waistband of his jean. "Well, we're not on your ship right now." She slipped the top button loose and released the zipper. "You're so hard. You feel so good inside me."

If she kept talking like that, he was going to have to push her down on the bed and fuck her senseless without so much as a kiss first. "Take off panties. Lay down."

She tugged his pants down and looked up at him. "I'm not wearing any. How about I suck you till you can't stand up, Captain?"

"Okay, I like very much."

"Me, too." She pushed his jeans the rest of the way down his legs. "Come on and kick off those shoes. You won't be going anywhere for a while."

He stepped out of his shoes and pulled off his shirt, leaving only his form-fitting, black briefs.

"We are together." It was all or nothing. His fingers wrapped around her wrist stopping her from stroking his erection. "You are sure?"

He held his breath and waited for the answer.

"Yes."

She freed his erect cock from his briefs but the cool air did nothing to relieve the throbbing ache. The soft touch of her fingers encircling his shaft along with her warm breath flowing over the swollen crown made his heart skip a beat in anticipation of her wet tongue and lips sliding over him. He sucked in a deep breath and held it while his cock disappeared past her soft lips.

If there was a heaven for men like him, he was there. Her warm, and wet tongue slid over sensitive nerves on the underside of his cock. His knees almost buckled and his hands fisted in her hair.

"You must stop. I can't last long like this."

She retreated over his length, slowly skimming her lips over the crown freeing him from the warm confines of her mouth and looked up. "Tell me what you need."

"You. I need you." He reached for the t-shirt she was wearing. "Take off."

"But it's daylight." She reached for the edge of the covers.

"No more hiding under the sheets. You see me naked many times."

Boris lifted the shirt over her head. He loved looking at her bare skin but he loved touching it even more. She was soft and smooth. Nothing compared to the feeling of her skin next to his.

"Come lay down here with me. We take our time. I want to make love to you very slow."

He grabbed the pillows and dragged them to the middle of the bed. There would be no hiding herself from him this time. He patted the pillow closest to her. "Here, I make nice and soft for you."

A slow smile crept across Sahara's face. "I like it better when you are nice and hard."

∼

By the time he slid off to her side, he didn't think he could go again. She'd worn him out. He wasn't as young as he used to be, apparently.

She wore a satisfied smile.

"What? Why you smile like that?"

"You look so good with your hair all messed up. I like looking at you." She traced his moustache and gently combed her fingers through his beard. "And this feels amazing between my legs."

"*Da*, I like."

"Yeah, me too."

He pulled her close until they were nose to nose. "I go with you. We find treasure, then we come home and you marry me."

"What? I...I don't know. I mean this is way too soon."

"You tell me rest of story. Alessia married Salvatore, *da*?"

"Yes. Of course, she did. I mean, in those days, nobody was getting under her skirt until the priest blessed their vows."

She looked confused for a second.

He grinned.

"How did you know?" She looked at him with narrow focused eyes.

"I read very old book when you were sleeping. Takes long time."

Her eyebrows furrowed and her nose wrinkled. "You can read Italian?"

"Yes. I speak, read many languages. I was in Army Intelligence. Sometimes we cannot wait for translator."

"Why would you care what happened to Alessia? It happened so long ago."

"She was a beautiful princess. Why would she run away with a pirate?" His hand rubbed gently over her shoulder. He had his own runaway to worry about. He needed to understand her.

"She loved him." She scooted closer.

He spoke slowly, hoping to get every word right. "He did not deserve her."

"But they were in love. It was meant to be." She rested her hand right above the crest of his hip.

"*Kroshka*, Salvatore was a very bad man. He took many women from ships he captured. He sold them in the East. She learned this after they were out to sea." He held her gaze. He wanted her to understand Salvatore was not good.

"I know but she forgave him. He'd changed. Love can do that. I read every word of that diary. I don't know all the words but what I could make out was so sad. He'd done terrible things to survive and he was sorry. She gave him a chance to be someone good." She tightened her hold on him. "They had a chance at love and happiness. They were going to start over together. They were going to live in the islands and be a family."

"Maybe you are right." He kissed her slow and gentle. Heaven help him. He had been a bad man; he'd done terrible things and he loved her so damn much. He had a lot in common with Salvatore. He'd do whatever it took to become the man she deserved so they could live on Galveston Island and be a family.

CHAPTER 16

Between her and Misha, they made good time with fair weather and steady winds in the sails. Misha showed off his masterful sailing abilities and he took pride in teaching Boris, who learned quickly. If those two clowns thought they were going to steal her boat out from under her, they were crazy. Mutiny was not happening. But it didn't hurt to have help. She'd learned that the hard way.

Sahara smiled at Misha as they neared the island of Eleuthera. He was going to meet Lona sooner rather than later. They would meet up with her and move around to the outside of the island and into the North Atlantic Ocean.

The abandoned pirate ship, *El Anochecer,* rested in international waters. That made it the property of the person who found it and that was her. All she had to do was salvage it. It would take a couple days to do it right with both of them diving to bring up what was left of the treasure and marketable historical pieces.

Salvatore and Alessia planned to settle down on a little plantation and live out their lives hidden away from the rest of the world. The crew would pick a new captain and take *El Anochecer* on new voyages.

Only it hadn't worked out that way. Everyone and everything was lost when *El Anochecer* went down. Balboa's crew made sure there were no survivors.

Once the *Desperado* was moored for the night, Sahara planned to call Lona and confirm the arrangements. They'd get a good night's sleep, and go out to the site in the morning. With the hired a salvage boat and crew to do the heavy lifting, the work would go fast. They'd be packed up and out of there before North showed up.

She didn't hear Boris walk up until he was right behind her. His arms snaked around her waist and he hugged her close.

"We made it here, no problem. You are good sailor. I like this boat."

She let out a soft laugh. "I should have made you work for your passage. Instead you got free sailing lessons."

"I supervised. Watched carefully. Made sure you and Misha did not get lost."

She wiggled around till she was facing him. "I never get lost. I have a very good sense of direction, a reliable compass, and don't forget the stars. They never let you down."

"Yes. Good compass. Points straight to me every time." His hand slipped between her legs and squeezed. The loose legs of the dark blue, cotton twill shorts did nothing to slow the man down.

"Stop that!" She pressed her thighs together. "Misha can see you." She only hoped Boris didn't sneak his hand up under her sunny-yellow tank top and grab one of her tits. He was obsessed with them in her opinion. The man had more arms than an octopus.

Misha nodded at them. Sahara tried to look innocent, like nothing had happened.

Misha tipped his head toward the land. "We have company soon."

Boris looked in the direction Misha indicated. "Looks like a salvage boat."

"Lona must be in a hurry. I was going to catch up to her once we got secured for the night." She raised her hand over her eyes to block out the glare from the sun. "Get my binoculars."

Misha stopped what he was doing and raced to the cabin.

Boris grumbled, "What is it? What's wrong?"

"I don't like the looks of that boat. It's in bad shape. Lona wouldn't hire something like that unless there was nothing else available. I don't trust it." She bellowed, "Misha, bring me my rifle."

Misha came back with the binoculars and three rifles. He handed the binoculars to Sahara. She peered through the long-range lenses. "Son-of-a-bitch. It's North and he has Lona."

She dropped the binocular's lanyard over her head and took her rifle from Misha. "And he has an armed escort."

Boris had already grabbed the rifle he wanted and was checking it. He chambered a round and rested the barrel casually across his chest. Misha did the same as the piece of crap boat carrying North motored closer.

They pulled up within shouting distance.

North wore a shit-eating grin. "Hello, sister. Glad to see you could make it. I brought some friends this time. I see you brought some friends too. Looks like we're going to have lots of help picking up my treasure."

Taking in the brutes standing next to North, Sahara had a good idea these were not his friends. Hell, he didn't have any friends. These were his loan sharks or whatever they called themselves these days. Basically, they there the men holding his debts and they weren't lightweights from the looks of them.

She shouted, "That's my salvage. I don't owe you anything."

"I'm your brother. We're family, and I promised my friends you'd give me my share. We're in this together. I want what's mine."

"It's not yours. You have zero claim. And that's what you're going to get. Zero."

North kept smiling. "I have Lona. What's she worth to ya?"

The goon standing over Lona with his rifle raised across his chest bumped her shoulder with the stock. She shouted, "Tell them to go screw themselves. Don't give 'em anything."

Sahara nodded once at Lona. "You heard her. You're not getting anything from me. I should have killed you when I had the chance." She raised her rifle to her shoulder. "But now will do just fine."

"Nyet." Boris slammed his rifle barrel down on the barrel of hers and pushed Sahara hard, sending her staggering. Misha caught her before she hit the deck and took her rifle. She grabbed Misha and used him to get back on her feet. What the hell was wrong with Boris?

She watched him turn stone-cold eyes on the man standing to the left of North. The man in charge. He shouted, "*Da*. You have one sister and I have one. Mine knows where the treasure is. We make deal."

Misha clamped an arm around Sahara's waist and muttered in her ear, "Keep quiet."

Game on. She didn't like it but she wasn't going to get caught in the middle of a Russian standoff.

∼

Boris stepped to the railing. "How much does that pig owe you?"

"Two-hundred fifty thousand plus this fishing trip. Maybe another thirty." The leader brought out his semi-automatic, nine-millimeter pistol from behind North's back.

Boris smirked. "You take half, we take half and girls."

"We take all the treasure and both girls. We don't kill you."

Boris kept his rifle ready and turned his left shoulder enough to expose his upper arm so everyone across from him could see the ink. "I don't think so."

He watched their smug expressions change to ones of horror.

The man poked North with the business end of the weapon. "You stupid bastard. You bring death to us."

North's face got red and he yelled, "That's my treasure. I'm the reason she went looking for it. I told you she'd find it. I want my share."

"*Da*, you give him is share." Boris stepped back and laughed.

"We take care of girls." Misha brushed the stock of his rifle along his zipper seam. "I go first." He flashed his wolf tattoo at the enemy as he walked toward the cabin, dragging Sahara.

Boris looked at the man standing next to Lona. "Take good care of my property. I won't like it if she gets used before me."

The man in charge swallowed hard. "I lock in cabin. No one touches her. You make that one tell you where the treasure is."

Boris grinned wickedly. "*Da*. She will beg to tell me what she knows. You follow us in the morning."

The man took a half step back and nodded. Boris waited, not turning his back on the enemy until their boat moved a reasonable distance away. Then he walked deliberately toward the cabin, looking like a man on a mission.

Boris stepped into the cabin and slammed the door shut. He looked over at Misha who was standing next to a red-faced Sahara. He was in so much trouble.

Misha asked, "What we do now?"

In a low voice, Sahara snarled, "Yeah. What are we going to do now that you've given away my salvage?"

Boris looked out the port at their new and unwelcome partners. "North is a fool. They will kill him and take everything."

Misha rubbed his tattoo. "Lona will not want me now. She will think I am bad guy."

"Nyet. Nobody is dead yet." Boris looked from Misha to Sahara. "Best I can do is take you and Lona away from them. They will take the treasure and North. Big win for them. That will make their boss happy and we go home alive.

"What the hell?" Red-faced and shuddering, Sahara reminded Boris of a volcano ready to erupt.

Misha stepped back.

Boris fixed his eyes on Sahara.

Her voice came out a muted growl. "Who put you in charge? I'm captain of the *Desperado.* This is my salvage. I make the decisions."

Misha took another step back.

"I keep Lona alive and get her back for Misha." Boris came toe to toe with Sahara. "They give us Lona. We give them the treasure."

"She would have gotten away. You shouldn't have done that."

"They are very dangerous men. I know this. They would hurt her, maybe kill her. We cannot take chance." Boris desperately wanted to make her understand. "North makes bad enemy. They enjoy killing for fun. Misha and I will keep you and Lona safe."

She glared from one to other. Boris watched several emotions slide across her face but the last one as the worst. She was pulling away from him.

"I'll do whatever I have to do. You get me and Lona out of this alive since it's turned into one big cluster-fuck, and you can keep whatever deal you made with those shits." She took a deep breath and let it out. "You save my sister and you take care of Mason if I can't. There's enough from my first haul back at your house to pay for his room and food. You owe me that much. That's my deal. Take it or leave it."

"I take. We have deal."

"Why the hell didn't you stay home? It didn't have to come to this."

"Niko and I checked. North has no money to pay those men. They will take treasure, kill him, and sell you and Lona. I cannot let that happen."

"Yeah, well, North is a dead man either way. Hell, I should have killed him myself when I had him in my sights. This is what I get for letting that snake live."

"Those men would have come looking for you to pay his debts. He promised them the treasure. This way is better."

"Great. They get the treasure I found and North can run up another bill for me to pay. It's never gonna end."

"He is not free yet. Tomorrow it will be over. We take Lona and go home, no problem. They will get plenty of money from wreck."

"Well, I'm glad it's no problem for them. But Lona isn't going to be thrilled about this and I'm going to have to find another salvage after I drop you off in Galveston."

Boris shot her a no-nonsense look. "We go home. All of us go home."

Misha sat down across from Boris. "What we do now?"

"Wait for sunrise."

Sahara rummaged in the kitchenette cabinets. "We need to eat. Tomorrow is going to be rough and we're going to need our strength." She glared at them. "I'll dive on the wreck and help Lona load the nets. While they're hauling the salvage aboard, we'll have to cut and run."

"I will help you fix dinner." Misha volunteered.

Boris forced himself not to shudder at Sahara's steely look. The expression would have made lesser men run for their lives.

"I don't need any more help."

Boris didn't dare turn away. "Why are you so angry? You are okay. We get Lona back tomorrow and go home. All good."

"It is not good. Lona is stuck on that run-down boat with those bastards. You gave away *El Anochecer*. North is alive and well, probably laughing at me with his buddies because he's going to get what I've worked for." She braced both fists against the counter top. "This was supposed to be my last hunt. It would have put Mason through college and given Lona enough to take care of herself without having to marry for money. And I was stupid enough to believe I could settle down with you and finally have a home on dry land. You've ruined everything."

"North brought them here, not me. We are not ruined. We have good home. Mason can live with us."

She banged a pot on the burner grate.

Boris kept an eye on her while he and Misha formulated a plan to get Lona aboard and leave without being followed. Pulling up the treasure from the ocean floor would be more important to North's friends than chasing after two women.

Misha steeled himself before asking Sahara, "We need to get Lona aboard. Do you have way to make them let her go?"

"They'll let her go. They need her to dive on the wreck so we can get it loaded faster. North is afraid of the water. He can barely swim. I'll meet her at the wreck. We'll load up the net so it's good and heavy. While they're hauling it on board their rust-bucket, we'll swim to the *Desperado*."

"We'll climb aboard while you two unfurl the sails. I'll cut the anchor loose." Her eyes narrowed at Boris. "You'll owe me for the anchor."

About thirty minutes later, a small meal of canned chicken and noodles hit the table. Sahara sat down next to Misha.

Misha pushed a plate toward Boris. "Tomorrow is hard work. We need to be strong."

"Tomorrow we fix." Boris looked pointedly at Sahara.

Misha swallowed. "Why Lona has to marry for money?"

Sahara leaned back against the cushion on the wraparound bench. "North broke the bones in her feet ruining her chances at being a professional dancer. When she gets older, arthritis will set in and she won't be able to teach martial arts anymore. She thinks a rich husband is the answer. Someone that can afford to take care of her and keep North away."

Misha shook his head. "Rich husband will get pretty, young mistress and leave Lona home alone. Not good. She needs good, strong man to take care of her."

Sahara looked pointedly at Boris. "Well, there's a severe shortage of available, good, strong men these days."

Boris reached for her hand.

She pulled back from the table out of his reach. "Don't."

Without thinking he blurted out, "What about treasure you bring back in smuggler boxes?"

"Mason's share will get him through high school and buy him a decent used car. There might be enough for a junior college. Lona's saving up so she can build a small cottage by the sea where North can't get to her. She's afraid of being homeless." She looked at Misha. "Our parents moved around a lot. She hated not knowing where we'd sleep or what we'd eat and wearing the same old clothes every day."

Misha looked up from his plate. "Lona will live with husband in his house. He will take care of her. Mason can use that money for school."

Sahara stared at Misha. "What husband? I told you I'm not letting her marry for money. If I have to stand in the church with a shotgun and stop the ceremony I will. It's love, or nothing." She glanced at Boris.

"You will marry me. We will be happy."

"I can't marry you. Natasha will tell everyone I married you so I can live off you like a giant, blood-sucking leech."

He watched the emotions play across her face. She wanted to stay with him. That was the good news. She was worried for Mason. He could use that. Misha would take care of Lona. It would take time to fix but it was doable. He sighed and softly said, "Alessia forgave Salvatore."

"Yeah, and it got her killed."

CHAPTER 17

Boris watched the sunrise after spending the night on deck keeping an eye on their unwanted company. It had been quiet and uneventful. They watched him watching them.

With the soft breeze and clear skies, it was a beautiful day for sailing and diving. One more day to be near his *Kroshka*. He hung on to her admission of wanting to make her home with him. He could fix the rest with time and patience. Getting her to believe they could make it together and trust him to take care of her was going to be the hard part.

He looked at the salvage boat. They were up and moving around. He'd very much like to kill them all, but that would only bring their superior down on him and his friends. For now, he'd play their game and give them the treasure.

Misha came out and stretched his arms over his head. "I get boat ready. We go."

"How is *Kroshka*?"

"Okay, putting on wet suit so they can't see we did not beat her."

"Is she still angry with me?"

Misha nodded. "Not so much but it takes time. You be patient."

"How long?"

"We will go home. If Lona wants me, I have enough to build small house. I can fix nice place for us at Sea Wolf Bay. Mason can use that money for college. Not perfect but still good. Time can fix." Misha put his hand on Boris's shoulder. "Come, we go sailing, find sunken pirate ship, rescue pretty girls, and be heroes."

∽

Sahara woke up tired after spending a sleepless night tossing and turning on her bunk. She needed Boris to wrap his arms around her and tell her everything was going to be all good. And she needed to shoot him for everything that had gone wrong. She'd lost *El Anochecer* to her useless, thieving, older brother.

If those greedy bastards floating one boat over thought they were going to be swimming in gold and jewels, boy were they in for a surprise. If they got good prices for what was left, it would cover North's debt with a little left over, but the best pieces were already gone, safely tucked away back in Galveston.

That ship, the *Lucky Desperado II,* had sailed. Literally.

Getting Lona back alive and getting the hell out of there was the top priority. North could stay with his buddies. She didn't care what happened to him. Whatever it took to make him leave them alone was fine with her. He was a born opportunist and a survivor. He could talk his way out of anything.

Lona was a fighter and a realist. She'd come back from this, figure out a way to put it all behind her, and move on. Hopefully, she'd take a serious look at Misha. The man had come along to protect her. The least she could do was give him a chance and let the locket do its magic.

Mason always looked for the good in people. He'd learn the ways of the world with time and experience. But in the meantime, Sahara would have to watch out for him.

That left her to be the look-out and provider. *El Anochecer* was supposed to give them a shot at living like normal people, not treasure hunters. There was still a chance she could make it work.

Falling in love with Boris was a priceless gift from the sea. She'd found a home. For a couple of months, she'd gotten a taste of what a life with him would be like. She wanted that life. The prospect of losing it only emphasized how much she'd come to love Boris and the people he called family.

It wasn't over yet. They'd dive on the wreck, wrap what was left of the deteriorated, water-logged chests in nets, hook them to the retrieval lines, and let go. She had no idea how she was going to explain to Lona that they were going to need a new plan, but she'd figure it out.

This latest chapter in the Starze family saga wasn't over yet. Sahara tugged her wet suit over a teal, one-piece swimsuit. Her arms, legs and back were covered. She could be black and blue underneath and nobody would know the difference. She'd walk slow and look pitiful, like she could barely move. Her kohl eyeliner was smudged and looked like she had two black eyes.

She hobbled out on deck and handed Misha the coordinates. He could sail the *Desperado* as well as she could.

Hiding a smirk, her mouth barely curled up as she watched him walk away with one of her better Browning rifles slung over his shoulder. It looked good on him. He was quiet and moved with unusual grace for an extra-large man. For all his many scars and scary wolf tattoo, he'd shown himself to be a straightforward man who was patient and slow to anger. All good qualities that he would need to deal with Lona—

She looked up long enough to check the location of North's boat. She muttered under her breath, "Oh, hell and damnation." There were three more salvage boats waiting for them. As soon as the *Desperado* dropped anchor their divers would hit the water. *Lousy bunch of scavengers!*

Sahara stifled a laugh. Good. Let them fight over it. Once in the water, Lona could swim to the *Desperado*, they'd throw caution to the wind and race for home. North and his pals could stay and shoot it out.

Focused on the horizon, she gauged the wind and estimated the time it would take to get to the salvage site. She could take her time getting ready. After she slowly ambled around behind the cabin and out of sight of North's boat she could move freely. She opened the forward equipment compartment and pulled out a rope ladder made to hang over the side from the anchor bolts screwed into the hull. No sooner had she secured the ladder than Boris came up behind her and wrapped his arms around her.

"I am sorry you are losing treasure. Misha will take care of Lona. I have good, strong tugboat. I can take good care of you and Mason. All okay."

"It is not okay. People will talk about me. They'll say I tricked you. One day you could wake up and wish you'd never met me."

Boris grunted. "Maybe you will wake up one day, look at old man next to you in bed, and wish for younger man."

"I'd slap you for that, if I could reach you. You know damn good and well you do it for me perfectly. You're it for me."

"Good. We make a good life together. Why should we care what Natasha and other people say?"

She couldn't help but grin at the man's stubbornness. "That's a discussion for another day. Right now, I need to get my sister off that floating death trap." She wiggled to get loose.

Boris relaxed enough to let her turn in his arms. "She is locked in cabin. We wait. I tell them you dive with her to load nets."

"There isn't a lock Lona can't pick. She's probably been in and out of that cabin all night long. They have no idea the trouble they're in. We need to keep those bastards busy watching you while I finish here."

"You are sure?"

"Yes, I'm sure. North use to lock us in our rooms and we always got out. We can climb up and down damn near anything, including this rope ladder. I'll drop it over the side when we get to the site."

Boris turned to go.

Sahara grabbed his arm. "Remind Misha we're going to cut and run. He'll know what to do." She let go and turned away.

Sahara got her diving gear, checked her watch, depth gauge and knife. She was ready. There was nothing to do but lean back against the bulkhead and wait. It wouldn't take long to get to the site. They'd practiced their whole lives for this. Picking locks, sneaking in and out of the house, and climbing makeshift ropes and ladders were games they played when they were young.

Boris returned and stopped a few feet away from her. "They want to see you get in the water."

"Fine." She carried her equipment to the other side of the boat with Boris standing over her like he was giving the orders. Right. This was a one-time thing, so he'd better enjoy it while he could.

Lona stood across from her at the back of the salvage boat, ready to step off into the ocean. Sahara strapped on her weight belt and fins. Then came her tank and mask. She raised her arm signaling Lona and the both stepped off into the air.

Sahara hit the water and headed for the bottom. She met Lona and they descended to the ocean floor. They were alone down there. Something must have scared off the other divers. Imagine that, Russian loan sharks were scary out of the water.

Lona had the net with her as they moved toward the dark outline of *El Anochecer*. Waterlogged rotting timbers were about all that was left. A few chests were still caught in the wreckage along with loose items scattered on the ocean floor. She and Lona tugged, dragged and hauled till there was enough to make it a heavy load.

They also stuffed a few small pieces into their belt bags for themselves. It wouldn't save the day but it would buy time.

Sahara gave Lona a thumbs-up and they released the yellow flag, signaling the crew to bring up the net. When the rope tightened and the net secured the load, they took off swimming for the *Desperado*.

While watching the time and cautiously ascending to the surface, Sahara unfastened her weigh belt and let it sink. Getting up the ladder with full gear would waste precious time. Stuff was replaceable, Lona wasn't. She let her fins go and climbed the rope ladder. She got over the edge and peered over the side. The top of Lona's head popped out of the water.

Sahara called down to her. "Come on, hurry." She shucked out of her tank harness.

Lona looked around before scrabbling up the ladder. "Cut us loose."

Sahara grabbed the machete and scrambled forward, keeping low till the last minute. She stood, raised the machete high over her head and bought it downward with every ounce of strength she had. The heavy rope sliced apart and disappeared into the ocean.

She yelled, "Now, Misha, now! Get us outta here." Sahara ran back to the ladder and helped her sister crawl aboard.

Lona flopped onto the deck belly-down, unfastened her tank, squirmed free and rolled over. They locked eyes and broke out laughing.

"We did it." Lona giggled.

Sahara plopped her butt down next to her sister. "Yeah, we did. Are you okay?"

"Fine. Boris put the fear of God into those goons. I don't know what the hell he did but they were scared shitless. They locked me in a stuffy little closet of a cabin and left me there."

Sahara lost her grin. "I have no idea other than he showed them the evil wolf tattoo on his upper arm."

Lona reached out and patted her sister's leg. "Whatever he did, worked. We're okay."

The smile slipped from Sahara's face. "Without *El Anochecer*, we're gonna be living on a really tight budget. I can try to find us another wreck but it's real slim pickings."

Lona sat shoulder to shoulder next to Sahara. "So don't. We'll get by. Let this be the end of salvaging."

"Are you sure? I wanted better for us."

"I'm sure." She grinned. "I saw Misha. I think he's grown since the last time we ran into each other." She snickered, "I really laid the man down that time."

"With a rifle slung across his back he looks like something out of the history books. A resistance fighter. Super-hot."

"Hey, I got first dibs on him." Lona bumped her shoulder against Sahara's.

"He's all yours." She pulled her arms out of the wetsuit and worked the rest of it off. It was too hot to wear it out of the water.

Lona sighed. "It's time we quit running. You're happier since Boris came into your life. Don't screw it up now. My offer to help you tie him up and change his attitude still stands."

"You have no idea how badly that won't work." Sahara let out a soft chuckle. "Give it time; you'll see what I'm talking about."

"Since when do you run from a challenge? Who the hell are you? And what have you done with my sister?"

Sahara looked out over the horizon. "I'm not running. But he's not exactly getting a good deal. I don't have much."

Wrinkling her nose, Lona whined, "That's like so old-fashioned. You've been reading too many history books."

"History books are where people write about lost treasures. So, yeah, I read old books."

Lona rolled her eyes. "Have you considered reading something romantic with a gorgeous hero and a happy ending?"

"Gorgeous like Boris, and happy like living in Galveston with the man of my dreams?"

"Exactly. You could try it. If you don't like it, the sea will always be waiting to take you back." Lona unzipped her wetsuit.

"I'll think about it," Sahara answered wistfully.

"Have you ever considered that having North for a brother damaged us? Every time we get settled, he comes along and ruins things." Lona pulled her wetsuit loose and wiggled out of it. "I've seen all the bright lights and they're starting to look the same. I think I'd like to be a mom and take my kids to play at the beach." She flung her suit against the deck. "I'm going to take your advice and give Misha a serious go. Money can't keep me warm at night, other than to pay the heat bill. With him around, I'd be plenty warm. See, I'll be saving money."

Sahara burst out laughing. "Only you could come up with something like gauging the male heat factor of Misha."

Lona smiled slyly. "That old boat those fools rented was piece of crap. It wouldn't surprise me if something happened to it."

"Like what?"

"I don't know, something."

Before Sahara could open her mouth to ask what Lona was talking about, a loud boomed sounded in the distance. She gasped, "What did you do?"

"Nothing too bad. But it sounds like they might have just lost their engine." She shrugged. "Oops."

CHAPTER 18

An hour later, with no sign of trouble following them, Lona sat on a brightly colored beach towel rubbing her left foot. It was trying to kill her. The cramp had started slowly and wasn't backing off. Any second, she'd be crying and yelling for Sahara to help her.

Misha's feet appeared in her line of vision a split second before he dropped to his knees. She'd barely registered what was happening when he reached for her foot and brushed her hands away.

He said, "I will fix,"

"No, you can't." She swatted at his oversized hands. "The bones were broken so you have to be super careful."

"*Da*, I know. Sahara tells me." He looked straight at her. "I fix."

His fingers rubbed gently between the bones kneading the knots in her muscles. His warm hands and nimble fingers worked miracle after miracle, massaging away the searing pain.

Lona relaxed and leaned back. "Okay, it's getting better. Just don't get over-excited and break anything." She could already feel the cramps easing. She could get real used to his miraculous hands. "Yes, yes, that's it. Okay, yes."

She dropped her head back, and moaned, "That's so good. Oh my god. Don't stop. Never stop. That's perfect. Do that some more. Please."

~

Inside the cabin, Sahara stood at the counter fixing lunch and listening to her sister. She silently snickered to herself. Her sister was never going to let Misha get away. His hands had signed him up for a life sentence to be served at Lona's feet. He should run the minute his feet hit dry land.

People joked about toe-curling orgasms. Sahara chuckled quietly to herself. She'd read about nerves connecting the pelvis to the feet. So, signals can go in both directions. Rub the feet and, voilà, the nerves in the pelvis wake up. Lona was definitely having a wonderful afternoon. If Misha wasn't careful, he might be in for a surprise.

Sahara's boat wasn't big enough for all their fooling around. She wanted to yell, *"You kids quit that!"* but it wouldn't do any good. Lona would for sure be inspired to find a way to get into Misha's pants. Better not to incite that kind of mischief.

Still smiling, Sahara watched Misha carry Lona across the cabin and carefully deposit her at the table. He waited until she scooted in along the bench before sitting next to her. Yeah, this was the beginning of something. He had that that smitten look. Locket magic was working. Wouldn't it be wonderful if it all came true and they fell in love? Lona deserved a kind man that would love her for herself.

All Sahara's worrying and planning to get Annie to bring Lona and Misha together had been for nothing. Well, better safe than sorry. It could still be a great party.

She picked up the plate she'd fixed for Boris and carried it outside to him. He was at the wheel, using what he'd learned about sailing to take them home.

"I brought you a sandwich. You should eat something." She put it down on the ledge, next to the rifle he kept with him. He'd grown attached to her Weatherby. Imagine that. He and Misha had no trouble picking out her best weapons.

"Where is yours?" He enunciated each word like he was in language class.

"Inside. I'd better get back in there so Lona doesn't take Misha on the kitchen table."

Boris grunted, stifling a laugh. "*Da.* Good for Misha."

"Yeah, it would be good for both of them, but the table might not survive." She giggled. "I guess he could build me a new one."

"Yes, a very good strong table. I like. I will tell him."

"Maybe later. I think he's busy getting acquainted at the moment." There were so many things she wanted to say. "I'm sorry. I never meant for you to get caught up in this."

His grin disappeared. "Are you still angry with me?"

"No. You did what you thought was best. Thing is, Lona and I have been scared of North for so long. We want to stop running and hiding. The salvage would have helped us do that."

"Those are very bad men. I did not want to take a chance with your life or hers."

"I appreciate that. It worked out okay, except for the salvage."

"Too many other boats were there. North had to choose the treasure or you and Lona. We got away easy."

She nodded slowly. "North probably got drunk and told the world I was coming back to work the site. They only had to watch and wait for him to rent a salvage boat. He's stupid that way."

"You forgive me, yes?" His voice was hopeful.

"I forgive you. But I don't know how I'm going to earn a living in Galveston. I can't let you support us. I'm going to have to think about this." She stood up.

Boris reached for her. "*Kroshka*, wait."

"We'll talk later."

She walked to the bow and sat staring out at the horizon. If she could walk on water, she'd have kept going. Walking helped her think. But thirty-two feet was as far as she could get away from Boris. It was hard to concentrate around him. All she wanted to do was crawl onto his lap and let him fix it. This was her problem and she needed to figure out the solution.

Real treasure hunting wasn't like the movies. It took a long time to find lost treasures. Most of the clues were dead ends. And half the time the stories were figments of someone's imagination. The *Desperado* might not last long enough for her to go on another fruitless adventure. She didn't need Misha to tell her that.

Lona had her share from the first haul. She'd need it if things didn't work out with Misha.

They'd emptied out the smuggler's box at the dry dock to make room for more. The first haul was tucked away in Galveston. What she'd hidden at Boris's house was hers and Mason's. It would hold them over for a while and give her time to work things out. At least it was something.

Alessia had taken everything of value that was hers when she went to meet Salvatore. Considering women didn't own much in those days, it probably wasn't a lot but it was something. That was the way of the world. Women went to their husbands with a dowry or at least a hope chest full of useful household items. Sahara had the *Lucky Desperado II*.

Times may have changed but people's beliefs and opinions hadn't. Thanks to the stories regarding the *Venetian* salvage and North, she'd always be considered a money-grubbing, gold-digging, schemer.

The truth was an ugly animal. As long as she was sailing the *Lucky Desperado II,* she'd always be a treasure hunter. Greed was relentless, it never gave up: if North wasn't dead, he'd come back around.

She couldn't sit there all afternoon. She got up and walked back to the cabin door and peeked in. The table was in one piece, and the curtain that hung across her bunk for privacy was closed. It was very quiet. Oh, hell, no. Were those two love-sick fools fooling around in her bunk? Oh, man, she did not want that picture running around in her head. They'd better not wreck her favorite blanket.

She turned to the stern only to meet Boris's gaze. He grinned at her. Maybe she should throw herself overboard and hope for the best. At this rate, it was going to be a long trip back to Galveston.

∼

That evening, Sahara steered them toward the last glimmer of the setting sun while Misha and Lona sat in the bow so he could show her how to navigate using the stars in the heavens. Sahara figured it was more like stargazing because Lona was more interested in looking at Misha than she was the constellations. It was definitely a first. No man alive had ever held Lona's attention for more than one drink, never mind a lecture on celestial navigation.

Boris settled next to her on the bench seat. Great, she was stuck between him the edge. If she scooted over, she'd land on the deck. "If the wind holds, we should make Galveston tomorrow." She glanced his way.

"Good. We go home. Lona can stay with us if she wants."

He was doing his stoic man thing with his voice and facial expression or lack thereof. Sahara recognized it from her early days of staying with him. "I think Lona is going to stay aboard or with Misha till we figure out what to do next."

"It's not safe to stay aboard."

"It'll be safe enough for a couple nights until I can get her taken care of. We'll be fine."

"I want you to come home. I am asking nice."

Sahara turned a cheeky smile his way. "Yeah, you did ask nice. But the *Desperado* is seaworthy and I can't let you keep taking care of me and my family. It's not right. We're not your responsibility."

He gripped his thighs. "I find you sinking in Gulf. I take care of you. We have sex. We agree we are together. We will get married, so no problem."

"It will be a big problem when my money runs out."

"No more talking about money. You work on tugboat with me. We have money."

"Not enough to send Mason to a college or university."

"I talked to Annie. He will get good education." He dragged in a ragged breath. "You tell me the truth." He turned his complete attention on her. "Do you love me? Yes or no?"

Oh shit! She needed a diversion. "It's probably Alessia's curse."

"*Nyet*. True love cannot be changed. You answer me."

"Fine. Yes, I am completely in love with you." She unclenched her jaw. "And I'm afraid one day you'll get tired of me and my family. North isn't going to stop coming and I can't have you getting in the way. It'll be Alessia and Salvatore all over again."

Apparently, she'd gotten loud because Misha and Lona were looking at her like she'd lost her mind.

Self-justifying, Sahara threw up her hand. "What? You know it's true."

Lona shrugged. "Alessia wasn't an expert marksman with a high-powered rifle. She shot herself because she couldn't shoot Balboa."

"None of that saved Salvatore."

Misha didn't let go of Lona's hand when she stepped closer. The slow smile on his lips gave away his new-found happiness. But Sahara also caught the concerned look in his eyes. He was waiting to hear more about Salvatore. Fine. She'd give it to him.

"Salvatore gave his heart to the wrong girl. They spent their last days running from a monster. Finding their true loves killed them." She sniffled. "I can't do that to Boris."

Lona and Misha sank to the deck and Misha rearranged himself so they were sitting hip to hip. Sahara couldn't get a read on his expression. He wasn't grinning and it wasn't his usual poker face. Something was up with Misha.

Sahara mumbled, "What?"

Misha rubbed the wolf tattoo on his upper arm. "We are good at killing monsters."

CHAPTER 19

Sahara's restless thoughts made for a long and sleepless night. She'd never been so glad to see sunrise and she was even happier to see Galveston Island. She was home. She wanted to crawl into bed, lay down next to Boris and never leave. Not that she was ready to admit it out loud.

Lona paced the cabin pouting because Misha had disappeared the minute they had the *Desperado* tied up to the dock. Give her a minute and she'd flop down at the table and stare out the port. This pattern had already been repeated several times. Boris stood firmly planted in the cabin leaning against the door, refusing to leave without her and Lona.

Sahara fell back on what she knew how to do, and that was find a lost treasure to pay the bills and make everyone happy. For all that she'd spent the last two hours staring at her list of known shipwrecks, nothing had come together. She'd crossed them off one by one over the years as they'd been found. The Florida coast was used up and the Gulf Coast was off-limits, taken by the surrounding states. She was not, repeat not, under any circumstances, diving on sunken river boats in the Mississippi River. Whatever was down there could stay there with the alligators and snakes. The thought alone made her shiver.

There might be something in the Carolinas. She pulled that map from the pile.

Someone, a woman, by the sound of the voice, yelled loudly, "Permission to come aboard?

Sahara pushed past a scowling Boris and walked out on deck. Yeah, that was definitely Annie standing on the dock in her usual faded, blue jeans and navy tank top. Even from a distance, she looked pissed.

"Permission granted." Might as well face her and get it over with.

Annie boarded and held out a bottle of Grey Wolf Vodka. "You got some shot glasses?"

"No, but I have regular glasses."

"Fine. Let's go." She pointed the bottle in the direction of the cabin.

"What's going on? Why are you here?"

Annie thunked the bottle on the cabin table. "I'm here because we need to celebrate your safe return."

Lona studied the bottle, her eyes teared up and she left the table. She crawled onto Sahara's bunk and curled up with her head buried in the pillows.

Sahara pulled four short whiskey glasses out of a cabinet. "That's a matter of opinion."

"So sit down and explain it to me." Annie slid onto the bench and rested her folded hands on the table.

Boris grumbled, "I am going home. Turn down air-conditioning so house gets cool, then I come back." He tipped his head toward Sahara. "You and Lona be ready. We go home tonight."

Sahara slid into her usual spot and shoved the papers over, clearing a space on the table. Lona lifted her head off the pillow, sniffled, and curled up tighter on the bunk if that was possible.

"I lost the salvage. North was there and screwed it all up. The men holding his markers took the salvage to square his debts."

Annie poured vodka into three glasses and took a sip. She tipped her head toward the bunk. "I'm assuming that is Lona?"

Sahara swallowed a mouthful of vodka and wiped her mouth with the back of her hand. "Annie, meet my sister Lona." With a nod in Lona's direction, she said, "Lona, this is Annie. Come get this drink. It'll help."

"No, it won't." Lona looked from Sahara to Annie and sniffled. "Hi, I've heard a lot about you. Thanks for helping us."

"Yeah, no problem. So, how did it go? Everyone looks okay but you're all acting like it's the end of the world."

Sahara tapped her glass on the table. "Boris traded my salvage for Lona."

"So, you got your sister back and gave up some soggy loot at the bottom of the ocean. Big deal. She's more important than those old trinkets."

"Those trinkets were worth a lot of money. Enough to take care of Mason and Lona, with maybe a little left over for me. I wouldn't be some destitute treasure hunter taking advantage of a lonely man." Sahara swallowed the rest of the vodka in her glass.

Annie finished hers and refilled both glasses. "Natasha shouldn't have said that. Boris knows what he wants. He's always known. Nobody's fooling him." She threw down her shot. "He's never settled for less than what he wants."

"I'm not so sure about that." Sahara downed half the contents in her glass. "Lonely men do stupid things same as lonely women. I don't want him to wake up sorry one day."

"That won't happen. He doesn't do sorry. He fixes things and goes on. Go home and let him fix whatever is holding you back."

Sahara put her hand on the pile of papers and maps she'd pushed aside earlier. Time for a distraction. "During the Civil War, Galveston became the main port after New Orleans was captured in April, 1862. There's nothing here I can go after." She shuffled the pages around until an old yellowed map surfaced. "But off the North Carolina coast, no one has ever found the *CS Annabelle Lee*. She wasn't a steamer so people haven't paid any attention to her. She sailed out of Wilmington and went missing. I think she probably went down off Topsail Beach. The captain of the *USS Iroquois* noted he'd fired on the *Annabelle* but she escaped by sailing into a fog bank. Without the noise from a steam engine, he couldn't follow her. That's all I've got so far."

"Forget the *Annabelle* and go home to Boris. Make yourself a good life with a reliable and honest man."

"I've been thinking about it. Mason likes it here and Boris said he could live with us." She glanced over at Lona. "He could go to college in Houston."

Annie's fingers played with her glass. "What if he doesn't want to go to college? What if he wants to go to a trade school?"

"He's too smart to throw his life away at some two-bit job working like a dog for minimum wage." Sahara rubbed the back of her neck. "I've worked hard so he could have a good life."

"Girl, you've done an excellent job. He's a great kid. Those trades are definitely not minimum wage. He'll be fine. I know we're not the normal family but we take care of each other. This a good place to settle down."

Annie sounded so sure, Sahara wanted to believe her. "What about Natasha? She really wants me gone."

"Hunh" Annie groused. "She'll come around. Boris and I will explain it to her."

Sahara was too tired to argue anymore. "Okay, we'll see. I'll sleep on it."

That was the signal for Annie to go home. They walked out on deck and Sahara spotted Santos leaning against a classic, red Mustang Cobra. He wasn't letting his wife drink and drive anywhere. Gotta love a dedicated man. She waved at him. "You're so lucky to have Santos. He's crazy in love with you."

"He's my everything, has been since I was sixteen." Annie kept her eyes glued to her husband. "Boris is crazy in love with you. Don't throw him away. I can tell you, love requires sacrifice but it's worth it." She ambled down the gangway.

Annie had made some good points. There was no harm in sleeping on it. Things might look better in the morning. Where had she heard that before?

Sahara went inside and closed the cabin door. Lona hadn't moved and the vodka was untouched. Sahara drank it and put their glasses in the sink. "I'm not wasting good vodka. Mind telling me what happened? This is not exactly the way I expected to spend my first night back in Galveston."

Lona sniffled. "Misha doesn't want me."

"That can't be right. He's been stuck like glue to you since you came aboard. The man fell at your feet literally. What the hell happened?"

"He says I'm too spoiled. He'll never be rich enough to make me happy."

"And you said?" Sahara planted her hands on her hips.

"You can't seriously mean that. Nobody could be that stupid."

Sahara gasped. "Oh, tell me you didn't say that. Misha is not stupid."

"I didn't mean it." Lona sniffled. "What am I gonna do?"

"Apologize. Start with that."

"What if he won't listen?" Lona hiccupped and caught her breath.

"Well, you can tie him up and explain it to him, slowly and very carefully."

Lona sat up. "That might work, but I'd have to take him down first. And this time he'd be ready." She fell back landing on her pillows. "It's hopeless."

"Since when do we accept that as an answer?"

"Never," Lona mumbled.

Sahara grinned. "Exactly."

CHAPTER 20

Boris sat in the driveway and stared at his empty house. In his younger days, he would have carried Sahara off the *Desperado,* put her in his bed where she belonged, and worked out the details later. But knowing her, if he tried that, he'd only make things worse. The situation called for tact. That was not his talent. But he knew where to get someone who could help.

He'd called Annie to handle the necessary diplomacy. Out of all of them, she had the best communication skills. She knew him better than most people. He'd helped her grow up into a capable, confident young woman and become a captain. She'd helped him understand Americans and cope with losing Connie. If he was being foolish, Annie would have been the first to say something. So far, she was all in on him being with Sahara.

Then there was Misha. He'd muttered something about not being good enough and walked off, leaving Lona behind. Boris couldn't fathom what was bothering his cousin. Had the whole world gone crazy?

His phone went off with an incoming call from Niko.

"What you want?" He grumbled at his brother, knowing he would understand.

"Glad you are home. Lulu tells me to call and make sure you are okay."

"North was there with his collectors. We got Lona and we got away."

"You come for breakfast. We will talk in morning. Yes?"

"Okay. Breakfast." He disconnected. There was nothing to do but go inside.

He slid out of the driver's seat, grabbed the few groceries he'd picked up, and trudged toward the front door. Some vacation! Never again.

Misha had taught him the beginnings of sailing. He liked the quiet and the feeling of the wind in the sails moving the boat over the waves. It was different from the growling engines of his tugboat plowing through the water.

It would be fine with him if they took the *Desperado* to Sea Wolf Bay. He'd pick a night with a full moon, put some soft music on, and make love to his *Kroshka*. Yes, he would very much like that.

After he turned on the lights and made sure everything was safe and undisturbed, he turned down the thermostat to make the temperature comfortable by the time he came back with Sahara and Lona. Tension was already running high, being overheated wouldn't help the situation.

He climbed back in his SUV and endured the short ride back to the dock. Along the way he hoped and prayed that Annie's visit had done its job and that Sahara would be ready to go home with him when he got there.

A few minutes later, Boris stepped inside the cabin and shut the door. "*Kroshka*, we need to talk."

"No, we don't. Not right now." She hitched her backpack over her shoulder.

"Oh?" He looked at her, his eyebrows knit and his eyes narrowed.

"You need to take us home. And you need to tell Misha to get his head out of his ass and play nice with Lona. She wants him. He's never gonna get a better woman, ever, spoiled or not. He can learn to deal with it. I'll put my own damn curse on him if he doesn't make her happy."

Boris grinned. "*Da*, I will tell him."

~

Relieved to be home and have Sahara with him, Boris walked down the hall to his bedroom. He took off his watch and put it in the bowl on his dresser. He wanted to take Sahara in his arms and never let her go, but Annie had warned him to give her some breathing room. So, he relaxed his jaw and hid his frustration.

Sahara flicked off the overhead lights and sauntered over to Boris's side of the bed. "I've got Lona settled in the guest room." She toed off her shoes. "It's good to be home."

His long stride ate up the distance between them. Screw the breathing room.

She reached for his t-shirt and pulled it loose from his jeans. "You look better without this," She pulled it off over his head. "Now, that's much nicer." Her hands rested on his chest.

Boris grinned. She wanted him for sex. He could work with that.

She ran her hands over his chest. "I had a nice talk with Annie."

"*Da*." He waited.

"I'll look for a job here."

"You will work with me. I have to keep my eye on you, so you don't run away with pirate."

She unbuckled his belt. "You're the only pirate I want."

~

With the first rays of daylight creeping around the edges of the blinds, he stretched his arms over his head and smiled. It had taken all night and devious, sexy methods but he'd convinced Sahara that they were meant for each other. They would work things out one day at a time.

He glanced at her sleeping soundly next to him. Perfect. He slipped out of bed and got dressed. He hated leaving her but he had business to take care of. He'd make it up to her when he got home. He drove to Niko's with the windows down and hummed along with the radio. He didn't need to be shown where love is, he needed Lulu's help getting

Sahara to the Justice of the Peace before anything else came along and wrecked his opportunity.

∼

Sahara woke up alone but this time she wasn't afraid. Boris would be back. He'd promised to never leave her and he always kept his promises. That was one of many things about him she had learned she could count on. She stretched and wiggled her toes. She ached nicely in all the right places. That was another thing she could count on him doing exceptionally well.

She crawled out of bed, desperate for a cup of coffee. There had to be some in the kitchen. She meandered down the hall blissfully floating on her Boris aftereffects.

Lona stepped inside the kitchen doorway and cleared her throat.

Sahara glanced over her shoulder and went back to digging in the cabinets. Lona looked like death warmed over. "Did you get some sleep?"

"Not much." She padded to the table and pulled out a chair. "What am I gonna do?"

"About what?"

Lona unceremoniously plopped onto the chair. "Everything. You got any coffee?"

Sahara found a new can of coffee and smiled; her man must have stopped at the store. "Yeah and I'm about to make some."

"Okay, black is fine."

"Do you mind getting us a couple cups? They're in the cabinet behind you." Sahara stared at her sister. The girl was a mess. Sahara shuffled over to the sink. "We're not going anywhere till you tell me what's going on."

"For the first time in my life I have no clue what to do."

"We'll have some breakfast and figure it out. One moody, Russian boat builder isn't gonna get over on us."

"Misha doesn't want me. I'm not sure how many more ways I can say it." Lona got up and trudged over to the cabinets.

"Lona, slow down. You're not making sense. I thought we had a plan last night."

"Assaulting the man is such a bad idea. I can't force him to want me. I'd like to leave and never come back." She leaned against the counter.

"You came aboard with your wetsuit and a bikini. Your passport is back in the Bahamas, if it hasn't been thrown out in the trash along with your credit cards and clothes. We need to cancel all that stuff."

"I know."

"We need to see about getting your bankcards replaced." Sahara tinkered with the coffee maker.

"I have emergency spares in the safe in Atlanta."

"Well, you can't go there right now. North probably has some low-life watching your apartment. We're safe here." She pushed the start button.

"For now. Do you really think he's going to leave us alone?"

"We don't know what happened to North. If his pals come looking for us, we're going to need all the help we can get." Sahara let out a long sigh. "Can you try to tell me exactly what happened with you and Misha? I thought you two were a done deal."

"He got all weird when I tried talking to him about going to his place when we got to Galveston."

"All right. I'm confused. What was weird?"

Lona went back to her chair. "He mumbled some nonsense about me needing a better man than him."

"What the hell does that mean?" Sahara looked away and then turned back. "Didn't you kinda already get together on the way back."

"No. He massaged my feet till I fell asleep." A dreamy look drifted briefly across her face. "He has the warmest hands. He stayed with me in case the cramps came back." She sniffled. "He fits against me all nice and snug in all the right places. I was hoping we'd go to his place and get together when we docked."

"It sounds like he got scared." Sahara quirked her mouth to one side. "Let's face it. You did black the man's eye last time you were under him."

"That was different. We hadn't been introduced, yet." Lona shook her head. "When we docked he kept avoiding me."

"Well, you did call him stupid."

"Not exactly. It was the stuff he was saying that was so ridiculous. Where did he come up with that dumb crap?"

"From years of being rejected is my guess. You're the party girl most guys wish they could get close to. He probably felt like you were a little out of his league." Sahara took her usual seat. "Come on, let's think this through. We can fix it. We're not going to give up without trying."

"I don't have a league and those men only want a one-night-stand. That's not my thing. I want Misha. When he wraps his arms around me, I'm right where I belong."

"How can you tell? You only spent a couple days in the middle of the ocean with him."

"Duh! The curse. You know, the one you dredged up. It's a feeling I get when I look at him. He's the one."

"Fine, blame it on me. But you're going to have to apologize to him."

"Can we just get out of here? I feel like I'm suffocating."

Sahara grinned. "I'll call Lulu and see if she can take us shopping. We'll start by getting you some clothes."

Lona kept fiddling with the coffee cups. "I finally find a guy I like and he walks out. I think there's something wrong with your stupid, cursed locket."

"Let's wait and see what Boris gets out of him before you do anything drastic."

"He's not cursed like me and you. You distinctly told me, it doesn't promise the guys we fall for will fall for us. I don't like Alessia or Salvatore. They needed to go to their watery graves and leave the rest of us alone." Lona poured herself a cup of coffee and landed in Boris's usual chair.

"Did you sell the locket to Balboa?"

"Of course. Maybe he'll have better luck with it." She took a drink and shuddered. "Damn, this stuff just stripped my enamel. Anyway, I think finding your true love is the curse."

Sahara sighed. "You might be right. Let's drink our coffee and go. We'll get some lunch in Houston and you'll feel better."

Lona breathed a sigh of relief. "What are you gonna do?"

"If Boris doesn't marry me, there's a wreck off the North Carolina shore, somewhere around Topsail Beach. It should have some silver on board. The planters were getting nervous about the way the war was going and sent stashes of silver dollars to the French West Indies for safe keeping in case the South lost."

Lona's mouth dropped open. "Say again. What's this about marrying Boris?"

"He's been talking about it but he actually asked me several times last night. I finally caved-in. It was the only way to get some sleep." Sahara giggled. "The man is relentless when he wants something. But he might change his mind now that the sun's come up."

"Don't you want to marry him?"

"What I want and what I get are usually two different things. You know that."

~

At breakfast, Boris and Annie sat across from each other while Niko sat at the head of the table. Niki sat wiggling in his high-chair next to Lulu.

"I'll be damned. Niki is looking more and more like Niko every day. Talk about handsome." Annie reached out and tickled him. "I love you, sweetheart."

Niki waved a chubby hand at her and spit out his cereal.

Lulu wiped up the mess. "Thanks, Annie. He's turning into an exact replica of his father." She glared at Niko. "Someone should have warned me about Russian DNA. He charms the women and only eats what he wants and nothing else. Stubborn and there's no changing it."

Niko laughed out loud. "He is a good son. I am very proud father."

Boris grumbled, "I marry Sashara and we have family."

"You need to learn to say her name right. It's Sa-har-a." Annie said, "Say it slow. Screw it up in front of everybody at your wedding and it won't look good."

"Sashara or *Kroshka* is good. She is the right woman for me."

"I've been researching wedding settings while you were gone on your crazy adventure in the Bahamas." Lulu offered Niki another spoonful of cereal. "She's never been married before. She deserves a nice wedding."

His hope for getting Sahara to a judge anytime soon was shot down before their breakfast toast was buttered. Annie and Lulu had their hearts set on seeing him married in style. He would wear his fine Russian coat that he'd worn to walk her and Lulu down the aisle.

Annie turned in his direction. "You and Sahara are going to have the finest Russian wedding Galveston has ever seen. You want to say her name right unless you want her to call you 'Dammit'."

"*Nyet*. Lulu already told me to get flowers and a nice bottle of wine. I have to ask again and make it romantic." He winced, thinking it sounded stupid, but he wanted to make his *Kroshka* happy.

"Oh. Sure, that will work." Annie eyed Boris. "You'll have to get her alone, someplace romantic."

"*Da*, okay."

"Great. When you've got her all to yourself, you propose again, formally, this evening."

As if on cue, Lulu's phone rang. "Hello, Sahara. Sure, I can take you two shopping. Let me finish feeding Niki and I'll be right over." She disconnected the call. "Why is Lona at your house?" She stared at Boris.

Boris looked at Annie.

"I didn't tell them. I was hoping Misha would change his mind."

"Not yet." Boris exhaled slowly.

"Then I guess Lona is gonna be living with you and Sahara." Annie's face brightened. "I know! How about Lona and Mason get an apartment together? He'll finish high school here and keep working on your crew part-time. That'll help him pay for trade school. Tuggers can loan him enough to finish if he runs short."

Lulu spoke up. "Excuse me, what did I miss? I thought Misha was on a mission to claim Lona's love and affection." She snickered. "As the old saying goes."

Boris eyed Lulu. "You know about Alessia's curse?"

"Sahara told me, there is a curse on the pirate treasure." Lulu put dry cereal on a plate for Niki to eat with his hands.

Annie groaned. "It's not the treasure. The curse is on the locket. Salvatore's Heart. Misha was on the *Desperado* when Lona picked it up and gave him a black eye."

Boris looked back and forth between the two women. "Misha is a good man but not handsome like other men. Not rich. He thinks Lona is spoiled and won't be happy with him. When he told her, she said he was stupid. After that he went home alone. I haven't talked to him this morning."

Lulu grumbled, "Well, that's just mean of her."

Niko blew out a breath and said, "I'll go by and check on him."

Boris nodded in Niko's direction.

"Last night, *Kroshka* tells me to think long time before I ask her to marry me in bright light of day. Very confusing American saying. What is, bright light of day?"

"It means men will say almost anything in the middle of the night to get sex. When the sun comes up, they have amnesia."

All eyes were on him. "I remember what I said last night. I will marry my *Kroshka*, Sa-har-a."

There, he'd managed to say it slow and correct. He'd probably never manage it again but for now he'd done it.

CHAPTER 21

That evening, Sahara and Boris walked into the *Desperado's* dim cabin. She clicked on the lights and asked, "What did you want to show me?"

"There is a nice bottle of wine in the refrigerator."

"Ah. That explains the wine glasses sitting on the counter."

"It is still light outside."

"Yeah, so?" She noticed him eyeing the shot glasses and half-empty bottle of vodka. "I have vodka if you'd rather have that. You look like you could use a drink."

He asked, "When did you start drinking vodka?"

"Annie brought it with her last night and left it. She said Mason wants to stay here and go to trade school. He likes working with Niko and Misha." She gave him the evil-eye. "I suspect you had something to do with that."

"He will work the tugs and earn money for school. He is good crew for Niko and good help for Misha."

She nodded. He had this all planned out. Of course, he did.

He poured two shots. "You should drink." He swallowed his in one gulp. "Before I come to America, I serve in special army unit. We get orders to handle problem and we fix. We all are in same unit."

"I already figured that out. You know too much about rifles and your crew works with military precision." She gave a short nod toward his shoulder. "Whatever that tattoo stands for, terrified those loan sharks damn near to death. It must be something really bad." She picked up her glass and gulped it down. "I don't care what you did in your old life. You're here now, living a new one."

He poured himself another shot. "I am older than you."

"You're the perfect age for me. Next?"

"I work here, live here. My crew depends on me."

"I'd forgotten how good a real bed feels. I like it." She winked at him. "Especially with you in it. All the treasure in the world can't buy that feeling."

"I am very old-fashioned man." He locked a steady gaze on her. "I want my woman to sleep next to me every night."

"Okay, but what about Mason? I can't put him out on his own. He's only sixteen."

"He will live with us. He likes staying with Niko, Lulu and Niki. Maybe he visits there sometimes, if he wants."

"So, what did you want to ask me?"

"Could you be happy married to me?"

"I guess there's only one way to find out." She slipped her arms over his shoulders and ran her fingers through his hair. "Captain Boris Rustov, will you marry me?"

"*Da*. Yes. Okay. We have fine Russian wedding."

His lips found hers for a toe-curling kiss.

When she came up for air she said, "With lots of candles and music." She had to get her request in early so she didn't end up in the dark like Alessia.

He smiled down at Sahara. "I will invite our cousin Alexandria. She helped us come to America. I would not have found you without her."

CHAPTER 22

Two months after she'd asked Boris to marry her, Sahara hid on the *Desperado*, barfing up her toenails. *Make it stop.*

Could her world get any worse? Well, never ever ask that unless you're ready for fate to hand you your ass on a platter. Sahara could hear the patter of Annie's boots on the deck. Sahara was on her knees with her head in the toilet. What better time for company?

She turned her head to the left and winced at the sight of Annie's knees in the doorway. "Good morning." She reached up and flushed the commode.

"Not from the looks of it. What's wrong? Didn't you get your flu shot?"

"Yes, I got my flu shot. This isn't that kind of flu."

"Well, what kind is it?"

"Boris flu."

"What?"

Sahara pointed toward the sink. "According to that stick thing, I'm pregnant."

Stumbling backward a couple of steps, Annie sank to the floor. "How'd that happen?"

"Are you kidding?"

"No. I mean aren't you on something?"

"I was. But the shot wore off and I don't have a doctor here. Then this started a couple days ago." Sahara waved at the porcelain fixture in front of her.

"I've got just the thing to get you feeling better." She swiped at her phone. "Lulu, I need you to go to the store. Get a six-pack of ginger ale and a box of saltines. Bring it to the *Desperado,* now."

Sahara shook her head. "That was not a good idea. Lulu will tell Niko, Niko will tell Boris, and I'm going to be in so much trouble. You should run before he gets here."

Annie stood and offered Sahara a hand up. "Come on. Let's sit out here at the table until Lulu arrives. She said she had everything at the house so she can be here in a few minutes."

After Sahara splashed some water on her face and rinsed her mouth, she slipped onto the bench seat across from Annie. "So, how are you doing? And what are you doing on my boat?"

"Mason asked me to check on you. He said you weren't eating and looked peaked. I figured that was some kind of code for not feeling well."

"You got that right."

"Why aren't you home where you can lay down and rest?"

"One, I didn't want Boris to find the pregnancy test. He's got some kind of built-in, stealth radar detection thing. He finds everything. Two, I wanted to know for sure before I said anything, and three, I wanted to see what I could do to fix up the cabin for me and the baby if he throws us out. We have to live someplace."

Annie snorted. "Boris would never throw you and the baby out. Not in a million years."

Lulu entered the cabin with a grocery bag. She pulled a can of ginger ale loose and set it on the table. "How pregnant are you?"

"Enough to feel like crap. This is what those frilly little sleep sets you made me buy got me. Are you happy now?"

Annie popped the can open and pushed to toward Sahara. "Try to sip some of this. It helps. At least, it helped Lulu."

Lulu patted Sahara's hand. "I have a great doctor. We'll make you an appointment. It's going to be fine."

"I'm thinking it's not going to be so fine. Boris already raised

Natasha and you." She looked pointedly at Annie. "I'm pretty sure he won't be thrilled having to start over again. It's not fair for me to do this to him. I'm the one that messed up. I can't make him pay for it."

Annie's head perked up. "You're right about one thing. He's not taking this well at all. In case you can't hear it, they're here."

Lulu squeaked, "Oh, no," as the door crashed open.

Boris shouted, "Why you did not tell me you are having baby?"

Niko put his hand on Boris's shoulder. "Stop, you are scaring them. Not good to frighten pregnant Sahara. Not good to frighten Lulu."

They ducked as a can of ginger ale flew across the cabin and barely missed Boris. Sahara shouted, "Get off my boat. Off. Now. Everybody."

She slapped the table top causing Lulu and Annie to jump and scoot out of the cabin, leaving Boris and Niko to face Sahara's wrath alone.

"This is my boat and I want everybody off of it. Off!" She dragged in a ragged breath. "I'm pregnant. So, what? Hell, when Mason was a baby, people thought I was underage and unwed. That was really fun. Now, get out. I want some peace and quiet."

Niko smirked at his brother, clearly enjoying every second of Boris's discomfort.

Annie dragged Boris down the gangway one step at a time. "It's okay. Pregnant women have mood swings. It'll wear off. You can talk to her later."

Sahara shut the door and picked up the soda can. That was exhausting and all she had to show for it was a sticky mess. She eyed her bunk. Clean up could wait until after she had a nap.

She curled up on her snuggly, worn-soft blanket and rubbed her tummy. "It's okay little B, we're going to be fine."

∾

Annie had trouble tugging Boris down the dock. He kept looking back over his shoulder toward the *Desperado*. Thank goodness Niko was latched on to his other side, helping herd Boris toward the Riptide.

Lulu brought up the rear so he couldn't turn around without running over her. His only way out was straight ahead.

Niko shoved Boris through the door and over to their regular table. "Sit before you do something stupid and get yourself in more trouble." His hand remained on Boris's shoulder until the man's butt hit the seat.

"Why Sashara did not tell me?"

Annie answered, "Because she just took the test today."

Boris glared at her. "I need drink."

"Niko is getting them." Annie swung her legs over the bench and got comfy. "You knew this could happen. You can't be mad at her. You're not exactly innocent, you know?"

Niko plunked down beer and wine coolers in the middle of the table.

Lulu picked up a bottle. "Cheers! Congratulations, you're gonna be a papa."

Annie watched and waited to see how Boris would respond.

Niko laughed. "All good. I like. I am Uncle Nikolai again."

Boris reached for a beer.

Finally, Annie gave up and asked the burning question everyone else was ignoring. "Do you want this baby?"

Niko grabbed Boris before he could launch like a rocket. *"Nyet.* Sit. We talk." He forced his brother firmly down onto the bench.

Boris's hands were shaking. "Why you ask?"

Annie shrugged. "Because you already raised Natasha and me. You were done raising kids and here this baby comes along late in your life. Some men your age don't want to deal with diapers and baby stuff."

"I am tired of hearing about my age. I am not too old to have baby." He grabbed a beer. "I want to marry *Kroshka* and have family. Maybe I have a son this time, but a daughter is okay too."

Annie tilted her head. "So why were you so angry back on the *Desperado?"*

His shoulders drooped. "If she does not feel good, she should tell me. I am her husband soon. She should take that test at home and tell me I am father. Not go to her boat and hide our baby from me."

She'd never seen Boris pout before. Doing her best not to laugh,

Annie said, "Okay. I get it but you're still going to have to apologize to her for upsetting her."

"*Da*. I will talk nice and make good food for pregnant woman so she can eat." He sucked down several gulps of his cold beer.

Lulu quirked her eyebrows at Niko and asked Boris, "How do you know what kind of food is good for a pregnant, upset stomach?"

"Natasha's mother is sick at first. But it gets better."

Lulu looked at Niko. "So that's how you knew I was pregnant."

He looked at Annie, exhaled and mumbled, "*Da*. I remembered what my brother told me."

Annie raised her eyebrows at Boris. "So, you had a clue Sahara was pregnant?"

"Maybe, but I wait for her to tell me."

"Let's drink to Boris. He's going to be a dad, again." Annie reached for a bottle. "I can't wait to tell Santos."

Lulu asked, "Okay, but who's going to tell Natasha?"

Niko flinched and they all shot questioning looks at each other.

∽

Boris walked back to the docks, leaving everyone at the Riptide to celebrate. He was going to be a father, again, at his age. Why did it sound like he was a hundred years old? He had to put that stuff out of his mind and enjoy the good news. He was having a baby with Sahara.

Yeah, he'd really screwed up earlier. But that's what men do. First, they have to make a mess so they can fix it. The *Desperado* came into view. Hopefully, she was over being mad at him.

He opened the cabin door and stepped inside. "Can we talk?"

Sahara looked up from the papers spread over the table. "Depends. Are you gonna yell at me?"

"*Nyet*. I am sorry."

She nodded to the space opposite her. "Okay, have a seat."

Boris settled in across from her. "What are these papers?"

"Business permits and applications. I need to start taking people out sailing so I can support myself."

"*Nyet*."

"Really?" She focused on him unblinking. "Is that like your favorite word these days? 'Cuz that's the one I'm hearing all the time."

Da, this is where she was going to rip him a new one. He put a hand over hers. "I can take care of you and baby."

"You didn't sound too interested in doing that earlier today."

"You tell me why you came here to take test. Why not do this at home with me, so we know at the same time?" That had hurt him. He was on the brink of being soul-deep in love with Sahara and she kept shutting him out.

"Because it's the last thing most men want to hear." She stared at him, unblinking.

He had nothing to do but to tell the truth. "You know I am not most men. Have you learned nothing from our time together? You can tell me anything." He settled his hand over hers.

"It took me a while to figure it out but there's a part where Alessia told Salvatore she was pregnant and he runs off and leaves her. What a rat." She rubbed her free hand gently over her tummy.

Boris nodded, the picture was getting clearer. "But he came back." His *Kroshka* was superstitious. He was going to have to be more careful where the curse was concerned. "I know what happened. You must not worry. I will not leave you." He grinned a very self-satisfied grin. "I like old story. Very brave pirate that dares to steal away beautiful princess."

"He wasn't brave, she was. She risked everything to be with him."

"If they catch him, they hang him. Not so good."

Sahara countered, "If they caught her, they'd throw her off the top of the tower wall. That's not good either."

"Come, we go home and make better end of story. I make love to my beautiful *Kroshka* and we are happy together forever."

"That's not the way it goes." She grinned. "We're supposed to live happily ever after."

"I like my way better."

"Of course, you do. But we still have a problem: Alessia's tears. If we don't follow them the real treasure won't be found."

"Okay. We will read book together and find answer."

~

They closed up the cabin and Boris helped her into his SUV. On the way home, he asked, "Where is Lona? She's not home all day."

"Ah, last time I talked to her she was busy at Misha's. Seems he's tied up while they're getting things straightened out between them."

"Okay. I call Misha if she is staying with him or coming home for dinner."

"Not a good idea. He probably can't come to the phone right about now."

"Why not?"

"I told you. He's tied up." Sahara smiled knowingly at Boris. "Like really tied up."

Boris's mouth opened and closed silently. Misha, his cousin, the scourge of their army unit, was tied up? He didn't know what to say.

As promised, he fixed their dinner when they got home and for the first time in a week, Sahara kept hers down.

After dinner, he sat in his recliner, still trying to puzzle out what happened to Misha. Finally, he gave up and asked, "How? Why?"

Sahara focused on him. "How what, and why what? What are you talking about?"

He frowned. "How could Lona tie up Misha? He is much taller and stronger."

"Uh, that would be lots of practice and leverage. I told you, she's an expert. International martial arts champion. Lona wasn't buying his, 'not good enough for her', nonsense. So, she's explaining things to him."

Boris scowled. "He will not like being tied up."

"There's being tied up…" She grinned and winked. "And then there's being tied up." She snickered. "I'm sure he's fine, better than fine by now."

Boris walked over and sat next to her on the couch.

He patted his lap. "Come, sit here. We talk face to face the way you like." He held out his hand to her. "I remember you like it when I hold you good this way. Yes?"

"Yes, it's my favorite." She crawled onto him, swung her leg over his thighs and rested her head on his shoulder. "What do you want to talk about?"

"I tell you story."

"I like stories." She nuzzled his neck.

She was everything he needed. He inhaled. "Long time ago, a man lives a hard life. He has to do many things he doesn't like to feed his family. Then he comes to America to make a new life. One day he goes fishing and finds a brave woman on sinking sailboat. He thinks he is a very lucky man and he takes her home. Maybe she will like him and stay with him. But it was a long time since he lived with anyone and he makes mistakes."

Sahara's arms wrapped around his shoulders and her one hand caressed the back of his neck. She rearranged herself and snuggled closer. "It's okay. Everyone makes mistakes sometimes."

"But he doesn't tell her he wants a family with her. When she gets pregnant she is afraid to tell him. This hurts his heart and he shouts at her. She sends him away. His brother tells him to go back and try to make it better."

"Sounds like he has a smart brother."

"What you think? Can he fix? Will she forgive him?"

"If she loves him even half as much as I love you, he's already been forgiven." Her fingers gently played with the soft hair at the back of his head.

"*Da*. Thank you." He hugged her closer, being careful not to squeeze too tight. "I make nice place for baby on *Connie* so we can all go to Sea Wolf Bay."

She kissed his neck right below his ear. "Me and Little B are tired. Can we go to bed now?"

"I will rub your back and we will sleep good. I will make you fine breakfast in morning." He carried her to their bedroom. It was way past time to make this arrangement permanent. All that was left to do was to wrap up the curse of *El Anochecer's* treasure and make an appointment with the Justice of the Peace to officiate at their wedding.

Boris put Sahara down on their bed and caressed her cheek. "We are lovers always."

She held out her arms to him. "You're my forever love."

Sliding into bed, he took her in his arms. "Come, I need you close with baby. We are family."

"I raised Mason but I didn't have him. I don't know how to do this."

"No problem. I can help and Lulu is good with having baby. I stay with you when baby comes. All good."

"Oh, no. Not all good. You don't want to see that. It's not pretty from what I've heard."

"You're always pretty. Besides, you don't tell me what I want. I want to be there for you and our baby."

Sahara chuckled but shook her head. "No, it's bad enough the doctor has to be there, and she's used to it."

"Niko stayed with Lulu." Boris gently rubbed her back. "Seeing his son being born was the happiest moment of his life."

"I'll think about it." Sahara snuggled into his chest.

Boris nodded. There was still time to convince her. He was definitely going to be there when their child came into the world.

CHAPTER 23

The next morning after breakfast, Boris put Alessia's book on the kitchen table. "Okay, we read book and fix curse."

Sahara fingered the cracked leather cover. "After her mother died and her father promised her to Balboa, Alessia spent most of her time worrying and crying. After she met Salvatore, she was happy, but she lost him."

He gently rested his hand on hers. "She had some good days with Salvatore. They were happy together."

"Sure, when he was in port or while they were on their way to the Bahamas. But in between it was terrible. She was afraid all the time." Tears pooled in Sahara's eyes. "She never knew if he'd come back. He could have been killed so many times."

Boris wrapped his arm around her and pulled her close. "It was dangerous on land, too. He couldn't be sure she'd be there when he came back. Her father could send her away. She could get sick and die. I think he was scared too."

She opened the book to the first page. "Okay. See here at the top of the page. This could be a small tear." She gently turned the pages until she got to another page with a similar mark. "Here's another one. If we read these pages carefully we might find the answer."

Boris started reading, "*I knew from the minute he touched my cheek, he would be my only love,"* He muttered, "Sounds like silly teenager."

"They died young in those days. By sixteen, her life was half over." Sahara patted Boris's thigh. "Keep reading, it'll get worse before it's over."

"I know." He turned to the next marked page. *"The winter storms are very bad and I am afraid all I love will be lost under the angry waves."*

Boris tried to keep himself from shedding unmanly tears over some long-dead girl's sorrows. Finally, he made it to the night they were married. *"The chapel was hidden down an alley on a street where only the worst business is done. No bells rang to announce our wedding, only the flickering light from cheap candles held back the darkness."*

At the choked sound that escaped Sahara, Boris paused. "Don't cry. I promise there will be candlelight and many happy songs at our wedding. Plenty of good Russian food, music and dancing for celebrating. Not like this pitiful, sad girl."

He wiped the tears from her cheeks. "Look, see this." He pointed to the smeared ink. "I think she cried when she wrote this. This is important page."

Sahara blew her nose in a paper napkin. "Let's get this done."

"I told Salvatore that I have missed my woman's time for several months and I fear I am with child. He did not appear to be pleased. For several days he has failed to meet me at our place in the market. I fear he has abandoned me. When my condition is discovered I will be put out on the street. There is no welcoming place for me to go." Boris glanced at Sahara.

Sahara ripped up another napkin. "Don't stop now." She dabbed at her eyes.

Boris read the next entry. *"Once again I waited in the market praying he would come. In the dying light of day he appeared and we made plans to leave tomorrow night. We will sail with the tide."*

The next tear appeared several pages later.

"We are two lost souls clinging to each other knowing our time is running out. Neither one of us can live without the other. We will face the end together. All my tears are stones that I carry in this book. I

leave it with the Holy Father to protect. I pray someday someone will remember me and my true love, my brave Salvatore. Once again we will ride the waves together and there will be happiness."

Sahara quit sniffling. "There wasn't anything with the book."

"Not with the book, in the book." Boris flipped back to the front and ran his index finger around the front inner binding. Then he flipped to the back but the pages were stuck together. "*Kroshka*, get me a knife, very sharp, thin blade."

Sahara hesitated. "What are you gonna do?"

"Pick up these pages and we see what is underneath."

Sahara handed Boris the smallest paring knife they had and he carefully peeled the edges of the paper until the pages lifted.

She gasped at the sight. "Oh my god! Are those real?"

Boris grinned. "*Da*, they didn't have fake jewels back then. These are the colored stones Salvatore brought her when he returned to her after each voyage."

Sahara sank onto her chair and stared at the gemstones in the diary's hidden compartment. "They would have been set for life if Balboa hadn't killed them."

"He had been promised a princess. He was not going to let some pirate steal what was his."

"He killed them for nothing. She escaped him in the end."

Boris raked his fingers through his hair. "We have the real treasure, but how does it break the curse?"

Sahara picked up the book, carefully poured the jewels onto the table and looked in the bottom of the well. "*Where he goes I will follow.*"

"They are both dead at the bottom of the ocean. It is done." Boris scooped the jewels into a pile in the middle of the table. "It was a bad end. I am sorry for them."

Sahara sniffled and cleared her throat. "I think we're getting a new boat."

"Why?"

She put the book down. "Turn back to the last page and read it again."

"There is nothing about the curse."

"*We will ride the waves together and there will be happiness.*" Sahara squeezed Boris's hand. "*Alessia n' Salvatore*. It has a nice ring to it."

"*Salvatore's Alessia* is better. He died for her."

"Is it your boat or my boat?" she asked, playfully elbowing him in the side.

"It is our boat."

Sahara kissed his cheek. "What kind of boat are we getting?"

"Misha will build a fine sailboat and I will have him put a strong engine for the times there is no wind. Okay?"

"That sounds perfect."

"I will go tell him to make a plan and put a cabin for us and one for our children."

"And a couple smuggler's compartments for treasures."

Boris frowned. "Are you going treasure hunting again?"

"I love you. I'm not going anywhere without you," Sahara flashed a mischievous smile. "But there might be some things we want to take with us that the kids don't need to know about."

CHAPTER 24

Later that day, while Sahara was shopping, Natasha barged into the house and threw herself down onto a chair at the kitchen table.

She glared at Boris. "Are you crazy, having a baby at your age?"

"I am thinking fine." Boris shook his head. "I like having a big family. My children, nieces, nephews and cousins, everyone comes to dinner. I will get a house with very large dining room so we can have big table for family dinners. Misha will build it. All good."

"Why are you doing this now? You are too old." She crossed her arms and glowered at him.

"Why do I have to explain to you?"

"I'm trying to understand why you are doing this. She is a treasure hunter with nothing but some rotting, old boat. She has a brother to take care of and now she is having a baby. You should have a nice woman your own age. Someone with a good job to help you and make your life easier."

"Sashara does help me. She helps me be a man with a family. She helps me remember I am a good man."

"You were always a good man and you have a family. Nikolai Annie, and I are your family."

Boris jammed his hands onto his hips. "I am still a man. I want sex with a pretty woman."

"There are plenty of pretty women your age that won't be getting pregnant and taking all your money for their treasure hunting."

"Sashara is finished with treasure hunting. She has me and soon she will have our baby to take care of. I will have Misha build baby bed on *Connie* so they can come with me."

Natasha's mouth fell open a half-second before she huffed, "You can't take a baby to work on your tug boat."

"Niko takes baby with him."

"He has Mason to watch Niki. Why can't you do like other men and pay her child support without getting married?"

"*Nyet*. I find Sashara. She reminds me how good living can be with right woman. I want her, she wants me. We are good."

Natasha leaned back and tapped the table top with her index finger. "What happens when she does not want an old man anymore?"

"We have very old curse on us. It cannot be broken. We are together always." He wasn't sure why they were standing in his kitchen arguing. He was not supposed to have to justify his decisions to his daughter.

"There is no curse. You are trying to live a fairy tale."

"I am trying to live." The determination in his heart poured out in his words. "I have found someone to love. Why you cannot be happy for me?"

"Because I'm afraid she will break your heart and I don't want to see you go through that again."

"It is a risk I must take."

"You could find someone else. Someone older, easier to live with. Sahara turns you into a crazy man." She flung her arm out in the direction of the bedroom hallway. "Everyone knows you took the doors off the bedrooms. They are all laughing."

"Good. I am laughing, too. It is good to be crazy sometimes, I think."

"You're going to be an old man trying to take care of a baby and support a wife who can't take care of you. Canned chicken and noodles in soup is not good food for a hard-working man."

"Who tells you this?"

"I asked Misha what happened on your vacation. He said she made a good dinner of chicken and noodles. He liked it and wants to have it again." She shook her head and sneered in disgust. "That's not real food."

"It tasted good and she fixed it fast. We were hungry."

Natasha leaned forward. "You're really going to do this, aren't you?"

"Da, I marry Sashara. We will take care of each other."

"Annie says we have to get new clothes for the wedding but you can wear your same coat."

"Okay, you wear pretty new dress and dance with Ivan. We have party with music and lots of good food and drinks for celebrating."

"Lulu is making the arrangements. She's talking about becoming a wedding planner but I think she wants to have more children."

Boris chuckled. "My brother is a lucky man."

"Are you sure this is what you want?"

"I am sure. You will respect my wife, yes?"

"Yes. For you, I'll do it, to keep the peace."

Natasha hugged him before leaving. He believed she would honor his wishes but it wouldn't be easy. His daughter got her stubborn streak from him. It would take time but eventually, when she could see he was happy, she'd accept his decision.

This was his life and his chance for happiness. He walked through the house, checking the rooms. He chuckled to himself as he passed the guest room. He had been so angry the day he'd taken the doors off. Sahara was his match in every way. He could not imagine his life without her.

∼

Sahara came through the front door carrying two shopping bags full of maternity clothes. Lulu had taken her shopping again. She was wardrobe-ready to be pregnant. The maternity support panties for her soon to be expanding abdomen were not sexy. Only the desire to avoid stretch marks convinced her to use them.

She'd snuck in a few baby things that had caught her eye. The soft, pastel yellow blankets would be good for either a boy or a girl. She peeked around the kitchen corner and didn't see Boris. His SUV was in the driveway so he was home. If she could get to the closet before he caught her, she'd be able to hide the bags.

Boris walked up behind her while her head was buried in the deepest, darkest corner of their closet. "*Kroshka*, why you did not call me to help you carry your packages?"

She squawked and got tangled in his shirts as she straightened up. "Sneaking up on me like that is not nice." She swatted at the sleeve still caught on her shoulder.

"What are you doing in my closet?" His mouth quirked up at the corners

"I thought it was our closet now that we're getting married."

"*Kroshka*," Boris said lightly, "You didn't answer my questions."

"What?" Her eyes darted around the room. "Your shirts attacked me. I didn't hear the question."

"Tell me."

She gave up stalling and blurted, "Fine. I bought some baby things." She crossed her arms over her chest. "There, are you happy now?" Saying the words made her pulse spike and the reality of the situation sink in.

Boris blinked. "Why you don't want to show me these things?"

"I don't want you to be mad at me. It's kind of early to be buying maternity clothes and baby blankets." She hated the tremor in her voice.

He pulled her close and wrapped her in a reassuring embrace. "Why would I be angry?"

With her ear pressed against his chest, she could hear the steady rhythm of his heart. "I don't know."

"Tell me what is wrong." He rubbed her back and pressed a kiss to the top of her head.

"I guess it's a habit. I always had to hide new stuff so North wouldn't tear it up and wreck it."

Boris brushed a tear off her cheek. "Forget him. I want you to buy the things you and our baby need. Show me what you bought."

"Your shirts grabbed me. I'm not going back in there right now." Her head bounced against his chest when he laughed.

"You sit and I will get the bags."

"Fine." Sahara plopped her butt on the edge of their new bed and let out a resigned sigh.

Boris backed out of the closet, holding the two bulging shopping bags. "Is this all of it?"

"Yes. For now." She raised her chin defiantly in his direction. She didn't need much but the baby would need plenty. He might as well get used to the idea.

He put the bags in front of her and sat on the bed next to her. He gently bumped her shoulder with his. "What did you buy?"

"Baby blankets, pacifiers, a rattle, and stuffed animals. Babies need toys." She did her best to blink back the tears threatening to erupt behind her eyes. "I can take some of it back if you want me to."

"We keep. No problem." He kissed her cheek.

"But you haven't even looked yet."

"It does not matter. You like these things, so I will like them. We will look together, later tonight." He stood and took her hand. "Come, I show you how we will fix room for Mason and we will put little B in the room next to ours."

She didn't know what on Earth made her do it but when they got to her old room, she said, "If we add a bassinette, I can sleep in here with the baby. That way we won't disturb you."

"Our baby will sleep in our room next to us. I will put good, comfortable rocking chair for us. Okay?"

"Sure. If that's what you want. But you work so hard and you need to get your rest. Babies can be fussy."

Boris lowered his eyes. "I was away in the army many years when Natasha was little. I want to be a father to our baby. Let me do this."

Sahara snaked her arms around his middle. "I'm so sorry. I had no idea you felt that way. You really do want to be a dad, don't you?"

"*Da*. I did not know how much until Lulu had Niki. It remined me of how much happiness children bring to a home."

He wrapped his hand around hers and they walked to the living room.

She settled on his lap in the recliner. "I never meant to turn your quiet, orderly world upside down."

"I did not like coming home alone every night to empty house. Now, it's good. You are here. Soon we have baby."

"It's going to get noisy."

"Very good. I like."

She curled up snugly against his chest. "I want to stay this way forever."

Boris hugged her and softly kissed her. "Me too."

"We're going to need one of those big recliners so we can all fit." She played with the button on his shirt.

He liked the idea of having his wife and child cuddled up with him watching TV or taking naps. He was ready to be a dad.

"Okay, we will get."

She slipped the button free and slipped her hand inside.

CHAPTER 25

Boris stared into his mug of ice-cold beer sitting on their table in the Riptide. He was getting married in two days. He still had trouble believing it.

Niko swallowed and put down his mug. "Congratulations, brother. You are very lucky man to get a young, pretty wife at your age."

"I am not old. I can still take you. We go to gym and I show you." Boris looked out the corner of his eye at Niko.

"*Nyet*. You are getting slow like old man. I will win." Niko snorted and laughed. "You need best man and ladies will not like it if we have black eyes for wedding pictures. Misha is too quiet and cannot make toast." He lifted his mug in salute. "You are stuck with me."

"Okay. Maybe we spar after honeymoon. That gives you time to get in shape." Boris picked up his mug and chugged several swallows.

Misha chuckled. "*Nyet*. You will be too busy making love to new wife to waste time on Niko."

"I think you are too busy with Lona." Niko grinned.

"Yes, I have very important thing I must do after the celebration." Misha blushed under his beard.

"And I have to take Lulu home after we clean the hall. I have to pack up all those candles. Why do you want so many candles?" He fixed his gaze on Boris.

"I made promise. I told *Kroshka* we would have music and candlelight for our wedding. She was sad for Princess that had to marry pirate in dark chapel."

Misha nodded. "Lona told me about the curse. I think I am sad for this princess." He looked up and grinned at Boris. "But I am glad for me. Without cursed treasure, I would not have met my Lona."

"You must build good, strong sailboat so we can fix this curse." Boris fixed Misha with a meaningful stare. "We have chance to make good, strong family."

"We will fix curse. I think this is better than I could have had back home. Back there, no Lona, no boatyard. Here, I can build house for my wife and have many children."

"I found Lulu without help from that cursed treasure." Niko's eyes focused intently on Misha. "Since when do you have a wife? You are not married."

Misha's smiled broadly. "I will ask Lona after the wedding. She will be in good mood from the party. Nice music and pretty flowers, room will look very good and I will ask nice. I practice all the right words like Lulu tells me."

Boris raised his mug. "This is for Misha and Lona."

Niko and Misha raised their mugs and said, "Misha and Lona."

They'd barely finished the toast when people rushed to look out a window.

"What happened?"

A Riptide regular replied, "A white limousine just pulled up in front of the door. Who would come here in a car like that?"

Boris avoided Niko and Misha's gaze. "Our cousin, Alexandria. Her father arranged the car to pick her up at the airport."

"What did you do? Why would she come here?" Niko swallowed hard and sat up straighter.

Misha looked up from his beer mug. "Our grandfather, Vasili, was captain of her great-grandmother's guards back home. She is family."

Niko cleared his throat and snorted. "That is your opinion."

"It's true." Boris tightened his grip on the beer mug. "When there was no hope of avoiding revolution, Vasili convinced Princess Charlotte to go to America. "She was pregnant with his child. He helped her escape from her husband and from Russia." He cleared his throat. "Alexandria is her great-granddaughter."

"How did she find out about us?" Niko looked from Boris to Misha.

Boris gazed at the table. "I needed help getting our papers to come to America. I called her mother, but Alexandria answered the phone. Her father is Marco DeAngeli, a man of influence. I did what I had to do."

Misha nodded. "Her father is opening the new resort and racetrack here. We would meet them someday. Better this way."

Niko looked from Misha to Boris and asked, "But why is she here, now?"

"I invited her to my wedding. It's time for both sides of the family to come together."

Misha stood. "I have never met a princess before."

Niko muttered, "Sit down. You are not going to meet one now. She is not a princess. They are gone since we had the revolution."

"I will let you tell her that." Boris chuckled. "She is a very successful fashion designer. Lulu will like her very much."

"You are making joke." Niko glared at Boris. "You are not funny."

Boris opened the door as a delicate, young woman approached. Not more than five foot-two inches tall and slender, petite didn't begin to describe her. She smiled at him at the same time the sun's rays glinted off the diamond barrette in her sable-brown hair.

He held out his hand to her. "Alexandria, I am Boris Rustov."

She rested her delicate hand in his. "I'm so glad to finally meet you in person. Call me Crystal. I haven't gone by Alexandria since I was a baby." She smiled up at him. "I've enjoyed our phone conversations. I hope you got the last shipment I sent. I had the tea cakes made at the best Russian Bakery in San Francisco. They were Grammie's favorite. I want everything to be perfect for your wedding."

"They arrived this morning. Please, come in and join us." He closed the door as she glided past him. The ruffles on her silk, turquoise blouse floating on the air around her. She was exactly as he'd pictured her.

Misha leaned forward, hunching his shoulders while simultaneously bending down to lessen the distance between his face and hers. Boris had to stifle a chuckle at the sight of her leaning back to look up at Misha. He was relieved to see her lips open into a huge smile. But he gasped when she reached out and hugged Misha.

"Misha, at last. You are the exact image of Vasili."

Boris's stoic cousin was not a man easily frightened but the way Misha's eyes darted around the room was reminiscent of a mouse looking for a bolt hole. And judging from the way his arms hung limply at his sides, he was too terrified to touch her.

Niko groused, "And how would you know?"

Faster than a king cobra could strike, Crystal turned and snapped, "I have Grammie's memory book. I've seen his pictures and I have his portrait." She gazed returned to Misha. "You're perfect."

Hoping to smooth things over, Boris interrupted. "Crystal, this is my younger brother Nikolai."

She released Misha and looked Niko up and down. "Ah, so you're the sniper."

"I am a tugboat captain." Niko snapped, "We are not in Russia."

Boris flinched and Misha took a half-step back. There was a change in the atmosphere. Even the bartender looked up from wiping the bar.

"You would make very good Chief of the Resort's Security Guard. I will mention you to my father." She cocked her head to one side. "It will require excellent security. You will do nicely."

Niko's clenched jaw and his red-tinged face was a tell-tale sign that the only thing he was likely to do was choke the life out of Crystal, if he got the opportunity.

Misha found his voice before Boris had to intervene. "I am master boat builder. I have a very fine, new sailboat. I can take you sailing before you leave."

"My bodyguard, Rafael, would have to go with us. My father and my husband won't let me go anywhere without him."

From where he stood behind her, Boris nodded at Misha.

"There is plenty of room."

"Oh, good. I love sailing." She tipped her head toward Boris. "Can I get a wine cooler, please?"

"I will tell the bartender." He didn't want to leave her with Niko. There was no telling what his brother would say or do next. Misha would have to protect her long enough for him to order her drink.

In less than two minutes he was back and putting the bottle and a cold glass down in front of her. Under his beard, Misha's mouth was turned up in laughter.

She looked away from Misha and stopped laughing long enough to say, "Thank you."

Boris choked down a chuckle. The old story must be true. Princess Charlotte was reputed to have charmed a Russian bear. Apparently, she'd passed the skill down to her great-granddaughter. Misha wasn't easy to make friends with and already she had him talking and laughing with her.

Boris took a seat at the end of the table where he could keep an eye on Niko and not crowd Crystal. She somehow commanded the space around her. Interesting. Not everyone possessed that kind of presence. He caught himself staring at the tanzanite and gold bracelet dangling off her wrist.

She must have caught his gaze and raised the bracelet toward him. "Grammie left me this. It was a gift from Vasili."

Boris had barely leaned his head down to look more closely at the bracelet when Niko leaned over the table, getting in her face, and snarled, "You lie. Vasili would never have given her anything like that. She forced him to be her consort."

Crystal grabbed her wine cooler bottle by the neck and met him nose-to-nose over the middle of table. She hollered, "Rafael!"

Boris grabbed Niko and hissed, "*Nyet.*"

The double doors of the Riptide slammed open, and a modern-day warrior in a black suit barreled into the dingy room. "Crystal, get behind me. Now!"

She let Misha take her bottle. "I'm not the one you should be worried about."

Rafael slowed his approach and stopped a couple feet from Boris and Niko. "Are you okay, C?"

"Yes, I was afraid you were going to have to save him from me."

She straightened her blouse and sat down. "Hmph, his manners need work."

Niko glared at her. "You are not my cousin."

She glared right back.

Boris didn't dare let go of Niko. Rafael stepped away but kept a close eye on them. Her bodyguard was a professional.

"Oh, but I am, and I have the love letters from Vasili to Charlotte to prove it. Be ready to apologize."

Misha stage-whispered to Boris, "She is fearless like Princess Charlotte. I like her." In a louder voice he said, "You will like Sahara, Boris's fiancée, she is fearless too. It takes a lot of courage to marry a man like him."

That made Crystal laugh and she sat down. Niko rolled his shoulders and stomped off to take a seat at the bar where he could sneer at them in the bar-back mirror.

Boris rested his hands on the table. "Try to be patient with Niko. He didn't have it easy when our unit discovered that Vasili had served a noble house. Family history still carries weight, good or bad."

She grimaced sympathetically. "I can't seem to escape mine no matter what I do. Still, I think Grammie was very brave to do what she did. She was definitely a woman before her time. I hope I don't let her down."

Boris didn't realize he was frowning as he processed what she'd said.

"Stop scowling at me. It's going to be fine. I'm good with my family's past. I'm stronger for it and so are all of you." She tipped her head in Niko's direction. "He'll figure it out. Give him time."

Boris mumbled, "Maybe."

Crystal lowered her voice to something barely above a whisper. "Think about it. It's family. We stand together, always."

"We can fix this." He raised his mug in a toast. "To family."

Picking up her glass, Crystal said, "To family."

Boris gulped down the last of his beer. "I think we should go with Crystal to meet our women. They are all together at the dress shop."

Misha nodded. "I will call and tell Lona we are coming."

∼

Sahara gazed at her reflection in the Russian dressmaker's mirror. She couldn't remember the last time she'd worn a dress. Annie and Lulu had gazed into the same gilt-edged, tri-fold, antique when they were fitted for their wedding dresses. She had never imagined her wedding dress would be a Russian version of an Italian princess's gown.

She was thankful that the empire style that hid her pregnant tummy was as classic as it was lovely. Her baby bump wasn't all that pronounced but it was there to her eyes. Her regular clothes were not as roomy as they once were.

She turned to one side and then the other, admiring the flow of the material when she moved. "It's beautiful and the Caribbean-blue is perfect."

No detail escaped Lulu's attention. "Okay, the scalloped hem is good for hinting at ocean waves. I especially like the seafoam, chiffon ruffles underneath. They move like waves when you walk. I think we've got this."

"It's like the old story, only instead of the princess being stolen by the corsair, it's a Russian sea captain." Annie sighed dreamily. "I'm so happy for you and Boris. It's so romantic."

"Boris thinks Salvatore was a hero of some kind." Sahara swayed, delighted by the way the dress swished back and forth. "He's determined to have the wedding they didn't get. Are you ready to call the fire department when the candles set off the smoke detectors?"

Lulu giggled. "There's not going to be any smoke. The smokeless candles arrived yesterday on a charter flight from San Francisco. It's going to be elegant with all the pastel colors glowing off the mirrors. Boris read the page to me about the cheap, tallow candles sputtering during Alessia's ceremony. Not romantic at all. We can definitely do better."

Annie smiled at Lulu. "You're really into this, aren't you?"

"Absolutely. I love weddings. Taking the pictures for the magazine was great but this is so much better."

Sahara rested her hand over her baby bump. "What's it like being married?"

Annie looked at Lulu. "You tell her."

"Me? Why me? You married Santos." Lulu shot back.

"You married Niko. That's more like being married to Boris."

Lulu conceded with a tilt of her head. "It's the best. They are all about family."

"Yes, that's true." Annie nodded.

Lulu frowned. "And they are alpha males to the max. Good luck with that. Some days you need a whip and a chair to get the lion in them to sit still, hush up, and listen."

Annie grinned. "No kidding. A bull whip could come in handy. I'll get you one for a wedding gift. Argentinian leather is the best."

Sahara's eyes darted back and forth between the two women. "You're kidding, right?"

Annie's smiled knowingly. "We're independent women and they sometimes need to be reminded."

Lulu snickered. "Once I tied Niko to the bed in his sleep and tickled him with feathers until he promised to quit being so stubborn."

Sahara raised an eyebrow. "And that worked?"

"All I have to do now is leave a feather on his pillow and his attitude adjusts super quick."

Annie and Sahara burst out laughing.

"I'll have to keep that in mind for the next time Boris gets grumpy." She looked at Annie. "I don't think I could bring myself to hit him, ever."

Lulu leaned back on the dressmaker's rose brocade, Queen Anne couch. "Oh, you'll get over that when you're in labor. You'll be envisioning all the ways you can beat a man. It might be the only thing that gets you to keep pushing after five hours. Those Russians do not have small babies."

Sahara looked at Annie with wide eyes. "Oh my god. Maybe I don't want to do this."

Annie patted her on the shoulder. "It's a little late for that. Now, me, I'm not doing the motherhood thing for a couple more years. I have a tugboat to operate and a Harley to ride. Santos can breathe easy for the time being."

"I saw Harley baby clothes at the dealership. Baby-biker-Santos would be so cute." Lulu offered. "Or baby-biker-Annie."

Annie frowned and snarked, "I hate you, Lulu. You keep your biker-baby ideas to yourself. Don't be giving Santos any ideas."

Lulu grinned back showing her teeth. "Too late. He's already seen the stuff. He was telling me they just got a new shipment of the cutest things for kids."

"It's not happening, so don't worry about being Aunt Lulu to my children any time soon. You hear me? Not happening."

Lulu raised her hands in surrender. "I hear you. But seriously…" she looked at Sahara. "Marrying Niko is the best thing I've ever done. And Niki is worth every minute of labor I went through. Boris is going to be a wonderful father."

Sahara sighed. "We were cursed the second his foot touched the *Lucky Desperado's* deck. More than anything, I want him to be happy."

"I don't know. As curses go, that one has turned out pretty good for everyone, so far." Annie said with all sincerity. "And this is the happiest I've seen Boris in years."

They all turned at the sound of the bell ringing over the front door.

The dressmaker, Madame Belinsky clasped her hands together and said, "Ah, very good. May I introduce Alexandria Crystal Foxz. She's opening a shop at the new resort. We will be working together."

Lulu could barely string together sentences, she was so excited. "You're the designer. A Crystal Foxz is you. What are you doing in Galveston? I love your lingerie!"

Annie asked. "Are you really Boris's cousin?"

"Yes. Why does everyone keep asking me that?" Crystal's forehead crinkled. "Do I look strange?"

Lona snickered. "No. It's just that the guys are so big and you're so petite."

"Well, they'll have to get used to it." She shrugged and took in the shop. "I love that mirror. Tiger will be all over it. I'll have to get one made for her or I'll never hear the end of it."

Somehow Lulu's eyes opened even wider. "Wow, Tiger Marz. She's so beautiful. Is she nice? I mean, to work with."

"Tiger likes to have fun." Crystal moved a few steps closer to

Sahara. "This is lovely. It fits you like a dream. Madame Belinsky's gowns are exceptional."

Lulu piped up. "The wedding is going to be beautiful. I can't wait to take the photos. I'm a photographer."

Crystal nodded. "I've seen your articles in magazines. Very impressive."

The bell over the door chimed again. Boris followed by Misha and Niko walked in and formed a perimeter at the front of the shop.

Lulu jumped to stand in front of Sahara. "Boris! You can't be here. You're not supposed to see the bride in her dress before the wedding. Niko, I told you he couldn't come into the shop if she was in the dress."

Niko bristled but didn't say anything.

Misha smiled apologetically. "We came to introduce you to our cousin."

Sahara moved to the edge of the platform but before she could step down, Boris scooped her off her feet.

Gazing into her eyes, he said, "You must be careful. You promised me, we would dance at our wedding."

Sahara giggled, "I remember. Now put me down so I can change."

Crystal addressed the room. "I'd like to take us all to dinner. I brought my great-grandmother's memory book. I thought you might like to see it. It has pictures of your great-grandfather in it and some stories from their time together."

Boris cleared his throat and glanced at Misha. "We would like to see it. Most of our family pictures were lost or destroyed during the revolution and later wars."

Sahara noticed Niko hadn't said a word or even blinked since he arrived. Something was off. Then she caught the faint upturn at the corners of Crystal's mouth. Their cousin was enjoying this meeting, especially the part that was rubbing Niko the wrong way. She'd have to get the background on that from Boris later. She slipped into the dressing room but kept her ears tuned to the showroom conversation. She didn't want to miss a word of it.

Crystal said, "I will make reservations and bring the book. Where would you like to eat?"

"*Nyet.*" Came out of Boris before anyone had time to take a breath. "I will make our dinner and you will be our guest. Niko will give your driver my address."

"I see you have inherited Vasili's commanding disposition. How interesting. I'm looking forward to this evening." She snickered at Niko's sullen expression. "I promise not to throw my shoe at you." She tipped her head in his direction and crinkled her nose.

Misha's brow wrinkled. "Is that an old custom?"

"Depends on how you look at it. There is an interesting story about the time Vasili first met Charlotte. She was having a very bad day and he apparently did something to upset her. She threw her shoe at him. He didn't take it well at all. They had an extremely serious discussion. After that, she never threw her shoes at him ever again."

"Is that story in her book? I would like to read it if you will allow it." Misha turned his hopeful, puppy-dog eyes on Crystal.

Boris grunted and grumbled, "I want to read this story also. My grandmother told me that Vasili was a ruthless man on a good day. On a bad day, people stayed out of his way."

"You can judge for yourself. There's that one and many more. I think you will like your great-grandfather. He was a brave and strong-willed man." She tilted her head a tiny bit to the side and eyed Boris. "He also liked to have things done his way."

Sahara returned wearing her usual cargo pants and a new Galveston Island t-shirt. She kissed Boris before he, Misha and Niko said their goodbyes and left the shop.

When they were safely out of sight, Sahara mumbled, "Well, that went well."

"Wow." Lulu shook her head. "If you ask me, that was intense."

"No kidding. And we have to sit through dinner with them. I feel a case of evening-sickness coming on." Sahara put her hand over her tummy.

Crystal softly snorted. "You might want to rethink that. Grammie wrote some pretty interesting things in her book. She had a bit of a temper. Vasili had met his match and they had some rather heated arguments. Just because she didn't throw anymore shoes at him doesn't mean she didn't throw other things." Crystal winked at the ladies. "One time, on her way to a ball, he mentioned her dress was hideous. A little while later, she threw it out the carriage window at him. It landed over his horse's head." Crystal leaned back laughing till tears leaked out from the corners of her eyes. "He was so mad." She wrapped her arms around her middle. "The horse panicked and almost threw him."

Annie grinned, her eyes full of mischief. "Oh, my God! Did she go to the ball in her underwear?"

Crystal wiped the tears from her cheeks. Still chuckling she caught her breath and said, "When she got out of the carriage she took one of her guard's coats, buttoned it up over her petticoats and marched into the ball. After that, military coats became a fashion." She pointedly looked at Lulu. "You might have liked being there for that."

Madame Belinsky interrupted, "I will bring some refreshments. Sit, and visit. Good stories from the old days are worth telling."

Lona leaned closer to Crystal. "Tell us more about Vasili."

Crystal settled on the couch getting comfortable. "Well, Grammie got tired of Vasili always doing the honorable thing, as she put it. She took matters into her own hands. While he was busy preparing the guards and carriages to take her mother to their winter home, Charlotte seized the perfect opportunity. She ordered the grooms to saddle her horse and told them she was going to her hunting lodge. She rode out alone."

"No! I bet that didn't go over well back then. I like her already. Go Grammie." Annie whooped.

Crystal raised an eyebrow before continuing. "She arrived at her lodge and started a fire to warm the place up. When Vasili stomped through the door that night, she was lounging on a nest of furs, all warm and cozy in front of the fireplace. Icicles hung off his beard and snow covered his greatcoat. She laughed at his appearance, which did nothing for his disposition. There was lots of yelling on both sides and then they spent their first night alone together."

Lona huffed, "Then what happened? You can't stop there."

Crystal grinned. "You'll have to come to dinner to hear the rest."

In a flash, Lulu offered, "I can show you around the island if you'd like. Annie can help Sahara get dinner ready." She turned a conspiratorial look at the ladies.

Boris concentrated on fixing a traditional meal of beef stroganoff complete with fresh, crusty bread from the Russian bakery. "I want to make our cousin feel welcome. Without her, we would still be in Russia."

Sahara arranged the table with placemats Annie had brought over and colorful paper napkins.

Sahara didn't look up. "I'm glad for whatever she did."

Annie stood by the counter, polishing her grandmother's silver flatware. "I never thought I'd get to use this stuff."

"It's beautiful. It'll make the table look lovely at the family celebrations we're going to have." Sahara took a handful of forks. "We never had anything like this at home."

"Great. You can help me wash it. Silver can't go in the dishwasher." Annie carried the knives and spoons over to the mat next to the one Sahara was working on. "It's a lot of bother but it does put a touch of sparkle on the table."

"I hope Crystal likes it." Sahara straightened the placemat in front of her.

Annie said, "I'm sure she will. This is so much better than some noisy restaurant. After dinner, we can relax and look at Charlotte's book." She turned her eyes toward Boris. "It's going to be wonderful to be able to see the pictures and read her stories."

Boris continued to stir the stroganoff. "I've never seen Misha talk and laugh with someone he's just met."

"Let's put him next to her at dinner." Sahara smiled at Annie. "You should sit next to me. The guys can look at the book first. When they're done, we can take our time looking at it."

"We'll have to get our hands on it before Lona. She's determined to find out what happened to Vasili." Annie snickered. "Your sister is crazy about all things Misha."

Boris nodded. "Crystal says Misha looks like Vasili. She told him he is perfect."

Annie smiled. "He is perfect and I like Crystal. Do you think she'll spend much time here at the new resort?"

"I don't know." He kept stirring. "She has a business to run."

Sahara arranged the last fork. "We could invite her to come for holidays and family celebrations."

"Lulu is taking her for a quick tour of the island. We can ask her." Annie gave the table one final look. "It's beautiful. Fit for a princess."

Sahara looked at Boris. "Why didn't you tell me, you're related to Russian royalty?"

Without looking up, Boris answered, "Vasili was a common man."

Sahara recalled the beginning of Crystal's story. "Look at me." Her eyes met and held his. "Charlotte didn't think so."

CHAPTER 26

Weddings were always stressful no matter how well planned. Books had been written about it to help nervous brides deal with the last-minute jitters. Sahara had read a half-dozen of those books but still wondered, *did they have one for impending doom?*

Lulu's decorations were perfect. The wedding chapel overflowed with candles and flowers. Their dresses resembled works of art, and after the wedding, they were headed to display windows at the resort. Nothing was wrong. That wasn't in Sahara's book of normal.

Try as she might, she couldn't shake the foreboding cloud hanging over her head. The locket was in the hands of Balboa's heir. No one had heard from North. Natasha was trying to behave.

She plopped onto the ornate boudoir chair and stared into the dressing table mirror. "I'm scared. What if this is some kind of terrible mistake? What if I ruin everything and make Boris miserable?"

Annie rubbed Sahara's shoulders. "The only way you'll make Boris miserable is by leaving him standing at the altar today. So, what's the real problem here?"

"Problem! What problem?" Lulu squealed, shut the door in Natasha's face and made a beeline to Annie and Sahara. "We're not having any problems today. I've got this wedding planned right down to the last toothpick."

Sahara trembled. "Trouble follows me everywhere I go. It isn't right to put my problems off onto Boris."

"The only trouble you've got is your brother, North. Boris can handle him. So, unless you've got some other doubt bothering you, we're good."

Lulu cocked her head to one side. "Uh-oh. Natasha was standing right behind me and she must have run to tell Boris. I hear trouble on the way."

Sahara didn't have time to brace herself before Boris and Niko barged into the room.

There wasn't enough room to turn her seat but Sahara twisted around just in time to see Niko move ungracefully to the side and Crystal duck under Boris's arm.

Niko grumbled, "You are worse than terrorist."

Crystal shot him a self-satisfied grin. "And don't you forget it." She wrapped Sahara in a hug. "What's the matter?"

"North could show up any minute and wreck everything. He likes doing that. He'll never give up. It's not fair to bring that down on all of you." Sahara's worried eyes fixed on Boris.

Annie patted Sahara's shoulder. "He's not getting in here. We've got that covered."

"Of course, we do." Crystal leaned closer and spoke softly. "I've got Rafael on it. Nobody is wrecking this wedding. The only thing you have to worry about is cutting the cake."

"I want to talk to *Kroshka*." Boris pushed his way to Sahara's side. "Alone, now."

Nobody needed to be told twice. They filed out and he closed the door behind them.

"Okay, you tell me what is wrong?" He marched the few steps it took to reach her. "I don't like seeing you frightened on our wedding day.

"Even after Alessia married Salvatore, Balboa chased them down and killed them. What if North comes back? He's sneaky and mean."

"That will not happen today. What is bothering you? You must tell me the truth." He eased her up to her feet and enfolded her in his arms. "If you do not love me enough to marry me, you must say it now."

"Oh, no. I do love you with all my heart. That's the problem. I don't want you to get hurt because of me."

"If you leave me, that will break my heart. What could be worse than that?" He stroked his hand down her back.

"Nothing." She sniffled. "No matter what I do, you end up getting hurt."

"*Nyet*. North cannot hurt me. He means nothing to me. You are everything I live for."

"We'll have to run away together." She sniffled again.

"Yes, okay, good. We can run away together on *Salvatore's Alessia* as soon as Misha builds it. We will go to Sea Wolf Bay and live happy together forever."

She looked into his deep blue eyes and saw love shining back at her. She gently caressed his cheek. "I need to change clothes. We don't want to keep our guests waiting. Especially not Crystal. She talks like this is the wedding of the century. I don't get it."

"She is very protective of her great-grandmother's side of the family. Vasili was Charlotte's hero." He put his hands on her shoulders. "I hope we do him proud today. Our two sides of the family are together now."

"You're right. It is a great day. I'm marrying my hero."

Boris smiled. "Okay, I will tell Lulu to come help you get dressed. Mason is waiting to walk you down the aisle." He kissed her thoroughly.

It was all Sahara could do to keep breathing. The man was deadly with his kisses. She didn't want to faint but lord-have-mercy, that was hottest kiss on the planet. It was the sort of thing one expected on the honeymoon. Well, with Boris it was no surprise that he was stepping up his game and leaving nothing to chance. If she'd had any doubts about marrying the man, he'd erased them with that kiss.

∽

Sahara stared in bewilderment at the cosmetics scattered on the dressing room table. When Lulu and Lona opened the door, she gestured at the table. "What is all this? I don't wear makeup."

Lulu squeezed Sahara's shoulder. "It's for bringing out the best in your photos. I promise I'll only accentuate what's already beautiful. Okay, we gotta get you dressed and ready to walk down the aisle." She unzipped the garment bag. "The groom saw the bride in the dress and then he saw the bride in the church before the wedding so this might be the unluckiest wedding in history but it's going to have the most amazing pictures." She snorted softly.

Sahara looked at Lona and with trepidation asked, "How is Crystal?"

"She's out there looking every bit her daddy's pride and joy. People aren't sure what to make of her. They have no idea about her Grammie. That would really make things interesting."

Sahara sat up straight for Lulu to apply foundation with an airbrush. "Boris will look out for her. Vasili loved Charlotte to his dying day. Crystal is her family and that means Boris will protect her as long as he lives."

Lulu picked a light shade of peach blush and a soft brush. "Crystal already has plenty of protection. She's married to an ex-Montana cop that runs his own security agency. Then there's Rafael and the security team for the fashion business. I'm not sure she can go to the toilet alone. Talk about no privacy, ever!"

"She gave me a beautiful gold hair comb to wear. It's got tanzanite and peridot to go with my dress." Despite Lulu's squawks of objections, Sahara turned to Lona. "I want to give her something from *El Anochecer*. We'll have to look through what's left and pick something really nice."

"Yeah, and something without a curse on it." Lona held the hair comb up to the light. "Beautiful, just beautiful. I wonder what would have happened if Vasili had come to America with Charlotte?"

"I wouldn't be sitting here getting my makeup done."

"What do you mean?" Lulu dusted a golden glow powder over Sahara's cheekbones.

"If he hadn't stayed in Russia and had children with the woman he married, there wouldn't be any Boris or Niko or Misha."

"I hadn't thought about it like that." Lulu shook herself as if to dismiss the idea. "But he did come over, I read that in the book."

"Years and years later after his wife died and their children were grown." Lona picked up an eyebrow pencil and held it toward Lulu. "It's all in the past now. You've already got Niko, and Boris is getting married today, if you can get the bride to the altar."

"Oh, she's going to get to the altar. Mason is giving the bride away. He's been practicing. We're good." Lulu put the brush down and took the pencil from Lona. "This is it. Next, we put on the dress and then the lipstick. I hope everyone is ready."

Lona took the dress off its hangar. "This is so beautiful." She held it up in front of herself. "I think I want something in pink and cream for my dress."

"Whatever Madame Belinsky makes will be beautiful. And Lulu's pictures will be amazing. Have you picked a place yet?" Sahara stood up and turned away from the dressing table.

"Uh, no. Misha hasn't asked. I don't know what's taking him so long."

Lulu picked up the white silk chemise from the settee. "Here, let's get the slip on without wrecking your hair and then Lona can help with the dress. We're running out of time. People will start getting nervous if we keep them waiting too long."

Lona asked, "Were you nervous when you married Niko?"

"I was too busy trying to breathe. I'd started showing just in time for my wedding. Charlene had to cinch me up tight to get me in my dress. I was afraid I was going to faint the whole time." Lulu giggled. "Niko was so mad. He undressed me in record time when we left the reception, he said it wasn't good for the baby."

"Maybe he was in a hurry to start the honeymoon." Lona chuckled. "Who knows what goes through a man's mind these days."

Lulu adjusted the slip. "The same thing that's always going through their minds." She snickered knowingly, took in a deep breath, and let it out dramatically. "I was supposed to keep it a secret but I don't want you messing things up this afternoon. Misha is going to propose during the reception and you'd better act surprised when he does."

"Oh, yes, hallelujah, finally!" Lona practically threw the dress over Sahara's head. "Hurry up. It's not nice to keep the groom waiting."

∾

Boris stood at the front of the room, his heart still stuck in his throat. Natasha had made him think he'd been a half-second away from losing his *Kroshka*. She was wrong, Sahara was his, the end. The only problem Sahara had was jitters thanks to her worthless brother, North. The bastard was still alive somewhere.

Niko leaned close to whisper, "I've been keeping track of North. He hasn't run up any new gambling debts. Nobody will give him any credit. He is broke, so it is only a matter of time till he surfaces again."

Boris grunted low and deep in his throat. "We'll deal with that problem when he shows his face. What I do not understand is why Natasha is so against my getting married."

His crew had already arrived and started celebrating. The people coming in now were from other Tugger's crews. Santos and Annie moved among the crowd and helped people get settled.

"Natasha is afraid you will get your heart broken."

"What do you think?"

Niko clapped Boris on the shoulder. "I think Sahara is perfect for you and you are perfect for her."

Boris studied his brother for any sign that he was joking and didn't see one. "When did you decide this?"

"The day she barricaded her door." He laughed. "I knew then, it was done. The only thing to do was wait and see how long it took the two of you to figure it out."

"I think the cursed treasure had something to do with it."

"Believe that if it makes you feel better. Lulu told me the tides brought your boats together for a reason and I believe her." Niko dipped his head. "Crystal is coming this way."

Boris chuckled. "You should run, brother."

Niko stood his ground. "I will not run from that tiny woman."

Crystal glided to a stop between them and looked up at Boris. "The judge is ready to begin. Mason is ready and so is Sahara." Crystal turned and looped her arms through theirs. "Come on. Let's get this man married."

Boris enjoyed the way Niko tried not to squirm. "I am grown man. I can walk."

"And I am Princess Alexandria and I am escorting you both to the front of the room. Let's go." She gripped his arm with surprising strength.

Boris grinned knowingly at Niko. "You are right. She is terrorist."

Niko glared at Crystal. "I think she is part Cossack."

"Exactly. Now you're catching on." Boris let out a short laugh. "She is family."

Once Boris and Niko were in place, Misha signaled for the music to begin. Lona walked ahead of Sahara and Mason. The sight of Sahara in a dress fit for a princess made Boris misty-eyed.

When Mason and Sahara came to the end of the aisle, the judge asked, "Who gives this woman in marriage to this man?"

"I do, Mason Dixon Staze, her brother." Mason squeezed Sahara's hand and took his seat.

The rest of the ceremony was a blur for Boris. He vaguely recalled muttering, "I do, and I will." When the judge pronounced them man and wife, Boris kissed Sahara to the sound of their guests cheering.

The reception started with lots of handshakes and congratulations. He needed a drink. Maybe more than one. Lots more than one.

Drink in hand he turned away from the bar and caught sight of Rafael looming over Crystal. She didn't look happy. He walked up in time to hear her tell Rafael, "It's nice to know you're taking care of me but I'm not ready to leave."

"Why does she have to leave?" Boris scowled.

"Some of your guests have figured out who she is. Someone at the hotel put it out online that Crystal Foxz is in Galveston attending a wedding." He turned his attention back to Crystal. "How do you want me to handle this?"

"I guess you'll have to be my date." She smiled up at him. "Would you care to dance with me?" She held out her hand to Rafael.

Boris grinned. "You stay as long as you want. You are surrounded by family. No one will bother you here."

He watched her dance away on Rafael's arm. She was his cousin and it showed in the way she held her head, the stubborn set of her chin, and the mischievous glint in her eye. He hoped she'd come back to visit often. He liked having her around, if for no other reason than to irritate Niko, and he wanted to meet her husband. *Heaven help that man.* That thought made him chuckle quietly to himself.

CHAPTER 27

When Crystal twirled across the dance floor with a very handsome man, Sahara asked Lona, "Who's Crystal dancing with?"

"That's her chief of security, Rafael. They're like childhood friends. He's married to the super-model, Tiger Marz."

Sahara squeezed Lona's hand. "Oh, this is going to be great! Lulu would change the tides to take pictures of Tiger."

"Uh, it's already started. Crystal is talking about doing something with a magical mermaids theme. Lulu pitched her ideas for advertising Crystal's resort boutique yesterday at lunch. I think there's going to be lots of wedding planning at the resort with photos and advertising by Lulu and clothes from Crystal's."

"What about Madame Belinsky?"

"The website will feature her wedding dresses. Brides can order in advance and have the dress ready and waiting when they get here."

"What about your wedding dress?" Sahara eyed Lona.

"Misha is on the shy side. I don't think we're going to have a big wedding. Get him up in front of a big crowd like this and he'd never be able to say two words. We'd have to choke 'I do,' out of him." That wouldn't be good. A small family gathering with a few close friends will be fine. I'm still going to get something nice from Madame Belinsky, so our wedding pictures look great." She snickered. "And I'm going to invite cousin Crystal."

"I'm glad you accepted his proposal."

"It's not like I had much of a choice. That damn curse is on us and working overtime."

"Yeah, I know. The *Desperado* brought us a lot of luck on that one."

"What are you going to do with it? Misha says it's not really seaworthy anymore."

"I'm going to clean it out and Misha is going to salvage all the usable hardwood and brass for *Salvatore's Alessia*."

Lona sighed dreamily. "Misha showed me the plans. It's going to be amazing. You're finally getting something that won't be in danger of sinking every time the sea gets rough."

"The *Lucky Desperado* has been good to me. I'm keeping the best of it for good luck." On a different note, Sahara lowered her voice and leaned close to Lona. "Have you heard anything about North?"

"No, why?"

"I'm afraid he's going to show up eventually and ruin everything."

"We left him on a boat in the Bahamas with the *Sundown's* treasure. He got what he wanted, which was way more than he deserved. I don't care what happens to him."

Sahara straightened up. "You're right. I just never thought it would turn out like this."

"We got lucky, desperado kind of lucky. North is going to end badly someday. I'm hoping he took the hint when that rust-bucket he was standing on ran out of luck."

"Luck is a relative term. Did you by any chance invite Sebastian de Balboa to my wedding?" Sahara quirked an eyebrow at Lona.

"No. What are you talking about?" Lona scanned the room.

"Look over there. He's here." Sahara pointed across the room. "He looks like he hasn't slept in a month. Something tells me Salvatore's Heart hasn't brought him his true love. Go see what's up with him."

"No problem." Lona sauntered away.

Before Lona reached Sebastian, Boris snaked an arm around Sahara's waist. "This is our dance."

She turned into his embrace. "Yes, it is. They all are."

He was an excellent dancer. He led effortlessly, allowing her to be carried along by the music. Funny, she'd never asked him if he could dance. She'd asked for candlelight and soft music but dancing had been left off her list. Well, now that she knew he was so light on his feet, she'd have to add a romantic waltz around the deck to her list.

He leaned close and asked, "What are you smiling about?"

"I think we should dance in the moonlight when we go to Sea Wolf Bay."

"Yes, we will go when it is a full moon." He spun her under his arm and pulled tight to his chest. "Dancing is good for thinking about making love. Until then, we can dance at home."

She giggled. "Uh, Mason will be living with us. Dancing in the living room in the dark might be embarrassing."

"*Nyet*. He will be working late with Misha some nights. We will be fine." He grinned and twirled them around twice.

Sahara laughed and searched the crowd for Lona. She spotted her next to Sebastian, shaking her head. Now what?

∼

Lona stared at Salvatore's Heart clutched in Sebastian's hand. "It works. The wedding you're attending is proof. You will find your true love."

"I have found her, but she is engaged to marry another man. He is rich and powerful. My family and his have been enemies for years. He will not let her go."

"Well, hell, there's got to be something you can do."

He tried to push the locket into her hands. "If I give this back to you, perhaps the curse will return and I will have no love at all. That would be better than being in love with a woman that can never be mine."

"I'll ask Sahara. There might be a clue or something in Alessia's book."

"What about Alessia's book?" Cami peeked around Lona and glanced down at the golden heart. "Wow, that's beautiful."

Sebastian held it out to her. "Here, take it."

Lona was too late to block him. "No. It's cursed!"

Cami held the locket up to get a closer look at it. "This is very old and very valuable. The engraving was done by a master jeweler. You can't get anything like this now at any price."

"How can you tell?" Lona studied Cami like she was some kind of unknown species. "You're a marine biologist. Antique jewelry is not exactly in your line of work."

Cami turned it over and studied it carefully. "My grandfather was a master jeweler. I liked hanging out with him. He would show me what he was working on and explain it as he went along. I loved the stories he would tell me. There's always a story to go with the jewelry." She looked up at Sebastian. "What's your story?" She fingered the seam of the locket. "This one has a trick to opening it. It'll take me awhile to figure it out. I don't want to damage the catch."

"Whoever has the locket will find their true love." He gazed sadly at the locket. "But it has brought me only heartache."

Lona quietly cleared her throat. "Look, it's not over yet. Your ladylove isn't married yet, right?"

"Not yet. Elena doesn't want to marry Phillip but her family is set on the match. They keep a close watch on her." He looked from Cami to Lona. "It's the same as what happened to Alessia."

"Right!" Lona perked up. "That's it!"

Cami asked, not looking away from the locket, "What?"

"Sebastian will have to run away with Elena. Here, you're gonna need this." She snatched the Heart from Cami and handed it to Sebastian.

He slipped the locket back into his pocket. "I can't kidnap Elena. That's against the law and her family will hunt us down."

"You're not going to kidnap her. We're going to get Zala to help us. She can find anybody and snatch them out from under the best security. She's an international bounty hunter." Lona shrugged one shoulder. "Among other things."

"It sounds like the bride is getting ready to throw the bouquet." Cami tapped Lona's arm. "Come on. We have to go stand there with other single women."

"Have a drink and some cake. You'll feel better and I'll give you Zala's number later." Lona let Cami tow her away, only to call over her shoulder, "I hope you have lots of money, 'cuz Zala's services are not cheap."

"I will pay whatever she asks, if she can bring me my Elena."

"Great."

Lona and Cami squeezed in among the other single women.

Lona stretched her fingers, getting ready to dive for the bouquet. "So, what do think about all that?"

"I think there's something inside that locket." Cami craned her neck to see Sahara waving her bouquet.

Sahara glanced over her shoulder and flung her bridal bouquet of pink and white roses into the crowd. Good hell! It hit Cami Fiero in flurry of rose petals and baby's breath.

Cami stared dumbfounded at the bouquet. "This can't be right. I don't even have a boyfriend."

CHAPTER 28

Sahara and Boris came back from taking a short honeymoon to Sea Wolf Bay. Boris had danced her around the deck more than once. Sahara hummed contentedly as she cleaned out the few things in the cabinets over the sink. The *Lucky Desperado II* was down to the last few loads before it went to Misha's.

On the one hand, it was sad to see the *Desperado* go. They'd been together so long and been through so much. On the other hand, it was getting a new and better life by being integrated into *Salvatore's Alessia*. There would be lots of wonderful trips to Sea Wolf Bay on the new boat. She wasn't alone anymore. She had Boris. She had the sea goddesses and Salvatore's Heart to thank, and she did, every day.

Thanks to Alessia's curse, they were all getting new and better lives. Alessia couldn't save herself but she'd saved them. She whispered, "Thank you Alessia."

From behind her an unwelcome, familiar voice said, "I wouldn't thank her just yet."

Sahara turned and sucked in a strangled breath. "North, what are you doing here?"

"I'll tell you once we're underway." He waved a thirty-six caliber, snub-nose revolver at her. "Don't get any bright ideas. Get back and keep your hands where I can see them."

She moved across the small space keeping an eye on the pistol. It would definitely do some damage if it went off.

"People will notice us leaving. The *Desperado* is supposed to be going to dry dock."

"You can tell them you're taking it out for a last sentimental sail." He hit her upside the head with the butt of the gun.

Sahara went down in a crumpled heap.

North muttered, "Have a nice nap."

~

Sahara regained consciousness with one hell of headache. They weren't tied to the dock anymore. She recognized the sound and the motion of the *Lucky Desperado* moving through the waves. North wasn't the world's best sailor but he knew enough to get a sailboat underway and out to sea. All her weapons were gone. She'd taken them to Boris's house first thing to keep them safe. She was definitely in trouble.

She sat up and braced herself against the cabinet. Her blood pounded an unholy rhythm in her head and her stomach rolled. Things were going from bad to worse. No weapons and the radio mic was gone. She looked over at her bunk. Hallelujah! Her backpack was still where she'd left it. She crawled slowly in that direction. With North at the wheel, it should be safe to use her phone.

She reached up and pulled her pack to the edge of the bunk and worked it over the edge careful not to make any noise that might alert North that she was awake and moving. She unzipped it and reached inside. Her phone was there and she still had a signal. Before anything else happened, she called Boris.

His voice came over the airwaves clearly. "*Da, Kroshka.* What you need?"

"Quiet!" she hissed. "It's North. He's got the *Desperado*. We're out at sea. I'm in the cabin."

"Put phone on silence and keep it on you. I am coming for you."

"Okay. And in case things don't go well, remember I love you."

"I love you. Now, hide the phone, hurry."

She clicked it to silent mode and shoved her pack into the cabinet under the sink next to the box of rat poison. The phone went in the support band of her maternity underpants. Her maternity clothes were coming in handy. Hiding a phone in a thong would have been displeasing to say the least.

She crawled to the other side of the counter toward the door to the deck. The farther she got from the bunk and kitchen the better her chances were that North wouldn't pay any attention to her missing backpack.

She barely got settled near the door when it opened and North said, "Glad you're awake. Get up."

"Why?" She didn't move.

"I said, get up." He yanked her to her feet. "You always did like to argue."

He pulled her out on deck. She didn't know how long she'd been unconscious but it was getting to be late afternoon, judging by the position of the sun.

She unsuccessfully tried to shake off his hold. "Where are we going?"

"I'm going to New Orleans." He twisted his lips into a sneer. "You are going wherever the current takes you."

"What are you talking about?" A cold trickle started in the pit of her stomach and fanned out.

He shoved her up against the rope safety railing. "I'm getting rid of you once and for all. Now, start climbing down. You have a nice life raft to sit in while you drift out of my life, never to be seen or heard from again."

"You're crazy. You can't do this."

"Sure, I can." He grinned. "We went out for a sail, hit some rough seas, you washed overboard, and I couldn't save you. It was terrible since we'd finally mended our differences."

Sahara gripped the safety railing with her free hand. "Nobody is going to believe that story." She needed to keep him talking to buy time for Boris. He'd find her. He'd done it before.

"They don't have to believe it. As long as they can't prove differently, I'll collect the life insurance policy I took out on you two years ago."

"You took out a policy two years ago, what for?" She scanned the horizon. There was a storm blowing in. Not a good time to be on the water.

"You were bound to have a diving accident eventually. I thought for sure the sharks would get you with a little help from the chum bucket last year, but you got away."

"That was you? Are you kidding me?" She jerked her arm from his grasp and punched him in the nose. "You bastard!"

He grabbed his nose. "Bitch! No. That would be Mason. You raised Daddy's little bastard and talked our old man into giving him a fair share of everything like the rest of us."

Sahara drew back her arm to hit North again but this time he caught her and jerked her off balance.

"Quit stalling and get in the raft or I'll throw you overboard."

"There's a storm coming and you're headed for rough seas. Do you really want to sail through it on your own?"

"You think I need you? Please. Once you're gone, the rest of us can get on with our lives."

"You're making a mistake. If you turn around now, we can all walk away from this."

"I'm sailing away and you..." He shrugged, "Well, there's no telling how far you'll drift before you die of exposure or drown. Either way, I'm free of you and back in the money."

He shoved her shoulder over the safety netting support causing her feet to leave the deck. Sahara scrambled for footing to keep from diving head-first into the Gulf.

It was a slow climb down the ladder. She had to time stepping off into the raft just right to keep from ending up in the water. The waves had been getting choppier while they'd been arguing on the deck.

North cut the rope that secured the raft. "Goodbye, Sahara Starze."

She flipped him the bird. "Bilge rat!"

She sat in the raft and watched the *Lucky Desperado II* shrink on the horizon. Looking around the interior edges of the raft, she discovered he hadn't left her the paddles or the first-aid kit. That was less than ideal but she and little B were going to be okay. She only had to hang on long enough for Boris to find them.

She whispered into the gathering gloom, "I need some help here Alessia. It's going to be a stormy night, so the sea goddesses will be too busy to worry about this miserable rubber raft."

She rubbed the phone plastered to her abdomen. Talking on it would only use up the battery faster. She needed it to keep sending out the locator signal as long as possible. "It's going to be okay little B. Your daddy is coming for us."

∽

Three tugboats plowed through the water at full-throttle. The *Connie, Lulu's Song,* and *Mi Vato Santos* powered eastward, leaving the setting sun in their wake.

Boris shouted over the din from the *Connie's* engine, "Captain Winters, the signal has stopped moving."

"I read you, Captain Boris. How much farther? It's getting dark."

"Maybe another hour. We will need lights."

"No problem. I have full batteries, we'll find her." Annie radioed, "Captain Rustov, how are your lights?"

Niko barked, "I have full charges on all batteries. The *Desperado* is still moving, heading northeast toward Louisiana."

"Let it go. We need you with us. We will have to sweep wide in these waves. It's getting rougher by the minute." Annie's voice trailed off.

They pushed on through the ferocious waves as darkness closed in around them. When the sun sank below the horizon, their lights blinked on. If there was a yellow life raft to be seen, they'd find it.

Standing at the wheel, Boris searched the rolling waves. The sea had given him Sahara and the sea could take her away. Tonight, in the inky darkness and churning waves, his heart could be dragged to the cold depths of the Gulf. He would fight with his last breath to save his *Kroshka.*

Boris searched the illuminated water with a desperation he'd never known before. Several long minutes later, he yelled into the mic, "There! Off to my starboard."

Annie shouted, "I see it! Change course. Coming over to starboard."

Niko's voice growled out of the speakers. "*Da*, coming over to port. I see her."

Boris's heart beat faster when the figure in the raft waved both arms over their head. "*Da*, that's my *Kroshka*."

She was alive. He could finally admit to himself that he'd never been so scared. And he was never letting her out of his sight again, ever.

As he drew nearer, he cut the engines so he could pull alongside and take her aboard. "Ivan, take the wheel."

Boris dropped a rope ladder over the side. Water sloshed in the bottom of the raft and the sight of Sahara, soaking wet, clumsily slipping and sliding as she maneuvered toward the ladder had him rooted to the spot. His arms reached out to grab her as she climbed aboard.

She wrapped her shaking arms around him and held on. Through shattering teeth, she said, "I knew you'd find us."

"Always. You are safe now." He scooped her up and marched toward the cabin. "I have good hot coffee for you."

She shivered uncontrollably. "I'm so damn cold. I may never get warm again."

He put her down on the padded top of the equipment locker. "Take off clothes. I have warm blanket for you."

"I need a towel."

"Okay. I get for you." He pulled two large dish towels out of the cabinet under the counter and grabbed one of his spare t-shirts so she'd have something dry to wear under the blanket.

She peeled off her wet clothes and patted herself dry while he fixed her a cup of steaming coffee.

"Your hands are shaking. Here, let me help. I will hold cup so you can drink."

Even wrapped in a blanket, Sahara continued to shiver nonstop. "I've never been so scared." She rubbed her runny nose. "North took out a life insurance policy on me and cut me adrift to die in that raft."

"It's over, you're safe. You are very cold and I need you to drink this to get warm."

"I don't want coffee." She hiccupped. "I want you." She slid off the end of the bench and put her arms around his waist.

He put the cup on the table and pulled her tight against himself; her skin was like ice. "It's okay. I will keep you warm. I promise."

He readjusted her blanket and sat down with her on his lap. He picked up the cup. "You must drink this. It will help. I put sugar and creamer for you, the way you like it."

She took a couple sips while he held the cup. He kept coaxing her to drink. When the shivering stopped, she fell asleep on his lap.

This was how they had started. Him holding an exhausted Sahara while the *Connie*'s strong engine propelled them toward shore. He stroked her damp hair and quietly said, "It's okay. I will take care of you and little B. We are going home."

∼

Annie had to raise her voice to be heard over the *Santos*'s growling engines, howling wind and crashing waves. "Captain Rustov, come in."

"Captain Winters, Captain Rustov here. What you need?"

"This weather is getting worse."

"The storm is going toward Louisiana."

"I'll call Zala on *CaliGirl* and have her keep an eye out for the *Desperado*."

Niko's snarled. "We have family meeting tomorrow."

The static didn't do anything to hide his angry, menacing tone from Annie's ears.

"Got it. Captain Winters out."

"Captain Rustov out."

A huge wave rose in front of the *Santos*.

Annie gripped the wheel. "Come on you bastard. Let's dance."

CHAPTER 29

Boris made sandwiches and iced tea. A family meeting wouldn't be complete without plenty of food. Once lunch was over and they had the house to themselves, he'd do his best to help her get warm. That thought made him smile.

Annie and Santos were the first through the door followed by Niko and Lulu. Misha and Lona showed up with a large container of potato salad. Natasha and Ivan were the last to arrive. Lulu put her cake down on the counter next to Natasha's apple pie.

Mason said, I'll go tell Sahara that everyone's here," and headed down the hall.

Annie pulled out her buzzing phone and studied the screen. "Oh shit."

Santos leaned over her shoulder. "I'll be damned."

"What is it?" Lulu looked over at them, her brow creased.

"It's Zala. The *Lucky Desperado* was found by the Coast Guard this morning." Annie made a face. "The main mast must have broken off in the storm and North got tangled in the rigging." She looked around the kitchen at everyone and murmured, "He's dead."

The only sound in the room was Lona's butt hitting the chair Misha shoved under her.

In a small voice, Lona said, "Finally, we're free. It's over."

Mason stood in the doorway looking from one face to the next. "What's over? What did I miss?"

Sahara squeezed past Mason and went to Boris.

He wrapped his arms around her. "North won't bother you anymore."

Lona quietly said, "The *Desperado* took out North. We're going to be okay."

Sahara and Mason shared a disbelieving look.

Sahara asked. "How do you know?"

"Annie's friend texted the news just now. The Coast Guard found him."

"Oh my god, he sailed straight into the storm last night. I warned him not to. He didn't listen."

Boris put the plate of sandwiches on the table. "We should eat. We have much to talk about."

Natasha put a bowl full of chips next to the pile of sandwiches. "We need to celebrate our new family."

Annie clutched her phone. "Zala says she can tow the *Desperado* to Misha's if we want her to. She'll be coming this way on her next project for the university."

"That'd be great. I definitely want to keep the best of my *Desperado* with me." Sahara sighed. "Thank the sea goddesses he didn't sink."

Boris grumbled, "I'm looking forward to meeting this Zala."

"Zala is one-of-a-kind. And I hear she's going to help Sebastian de Balboa save his true love from an unwanted engagement." Annie cast an accusing glance in Lona's direction. "I wonder how he got her number."

"What? It's not a state secret. The man needs help." Lona shrugged. "You know, Cami thinks there's something inside the locket. Maybe she'll get it open by the time Zala gets here. Maybe it's a clue to another treasure."

Boris muttered, "Or another curse."

Sahara kissed him on the cheek. "It'll be fun, like 'baby's first treasure hunt.' What better way to christen *Salvatore's Alessia*?"

"*Kroshka,* if our baby inherits your love for adventure, I will never know peace again." He pulled her into a kiss. "And I wouldn't have it any other way."

The End

ABOUT THE AUTHOR

Nellie Krauss is a Pro member of Romance Writers of America and San Antonio Romance Authors. She writes contemporary Romances with sassy heroines. Her cross-cultural stories are inspired by her time spent living with Native Americans on the Pine Ridge Reservation in South Dakota. The Renaissance Fair is her favorite place to be when she's not in the Black Hills or at the beach. Her biggest thrill is hearing the roar and rumble of her Harley's engine on the open road. She has travelled the Caribbean, the Bahamas and Western Europe in search of adventure. Her next destinations are the romantic Greek Islands. Opa!

Previous titles include:

Queen of the Black Roses Ball

The Moon Over Sea Wolf Bay